Twice Raped

Audrey Savage

Book Weaver Publishing Co.
Indianapolis

TWICE RAPED
by
Audrey Savage

Published by:

Book Weaver Publishing Co.
Post Office Box 30072
Indianapolis, Indiana 46230

Copyright (c) 1990 by Audrey Savage
Cover art copyright (c) 1990 by Paula Frantz

Library of Congress Catalogue Card Number 89-091663

Printed in the United States of America

printing number
1 2 3 4 5 6 7 8 9 10

ISBN 0-929698-01-0 Softcover

This book is dedicated to
Sheryle Geen,

the woman who saved my sanity more than once
as I suffered through this ordeal of being twice raped.

Acknowledgments

First and foremost I must acknowledge the two men who provoked the writing of this book: David Forshile, the man who illegally raped my body, and Trevor Halbert, the Barrister for the defense, who legally raped my mind, emotions and soul. Because of their actions I did two things. I searched deeply into my being for the emotions buried there and I launched on a search for every piece of information I could find on the subject of rape. The more I learned the more outraged I became, not only at the act of rape but by its extent, the belief of the men who perpetrate it in all its forms and the victims who believe what the rapists want them to believe; that they are to blame. I would have preferred that these two men had not come into my life, but since they did I must acknowledge that the power of the experience became the drive to write this book. If it inspires only one woman to do what she needs to do to make men accountable for their beliefs and behavior, David Forshile and Trevor Halbert's actions against me will be vindicated.

On the other side of the coin I am profoundly grateful to my therapist, Lee Verner, for the loving and sensitive way in which she brought me into the full meaning of this rape experience at my deepest psychological level. I credit her for bringing me back to my sanity and to some semblance of a normal functioning human being. I am especially grateful for her suggestion that I write this book as a personal experience, rather than as a novel, since fiction would defuse its power.

This incredible cover was painted by Paula Frantz. Her vision of the damage done to the perfection of the rose by the rape of man says more than my thousands of words. I feel as though I enter the picture every time I look at it. I thank another artist, Nancy Jaussaud, for her redrawing of the pictures of women as objects taken from a pamphlet on rape published by Caroline Sparks of the Feminist Institute, Inc.

Next, I am grateful to Susan Brownmiller (*Against Our Will*, 1975) and Susan Griffin (*Rape, the Politics of Consciousness*, 1986) for their precedent setting books about rape. Both have served as my basic education in the subject. Also, Anne Wilson Schaef's work, *Woman's Reality* (1981), has never been far from my desk as I write. Her ground breaking work in naming "The White Male System" and "The Reactive Female System" has had a profound effect on my thinking and writing.

I also want to express my appreciation to my many clients, both male and female, who have given me such a solid grounding in the dynamics of rape, an education I could have gotten nowhere else.

Charlotte Wright and Pat Sexton, again, suffered through my misspellings, ridiculous punctuation, and independent style of wording to edit this book. Their perceptive eyes, red pencils and patience with my mistakes were invaluable. I trusted them completely to tell me exactly what they thought; a quality more valuable than any amount of empty praise. Even more important was their friendship and support as I dealt with my own intensity around this most difficult subject.

Gay Reese, Ruth Purcell, and Jan Kreuscher are especially appreciated for their legal opinions and suggestions on the question of libel.

Without Mary Jeanne Pies I would not have lived through the production aspects of this book. She, along with doing my marketing and publicizing, also did the hard work of locating, letter writing, and calling the owners of the many copyrights used in this book. Her excitement about my writing has sustained me during many a long night at my keyboard.

I thank Linda Alis, a therapist who specializes in working with rape, for her powerful belief in my book to the point of saying she wanted **all** of her clients to own a copy. Also to Michael Bowman, Julie Joy and Debbie McClure for their sensitive readings.

And lastly, I thank all of the strong women I have known who have modeled and given me the courage to be irreverent, to be totally honest and to use my considerable perceptive abilities to write about my rape with the amount of intensity it took to complete this project.

What Readers are Saying

This is not a book to be read over bon bons. It is a book to make you think - to make you be aware . . . and to make you change your way of thinking. Paula Frantz: Artist and Psychic

Twice Raped burned itself into me. I recognized its tremendous rage and anguish. Those are my own screams and the screams of all the women I have ever worked with, of all the women I may never meet. I weep for the war being waged between male and female on this earth and I pray for healing. Linda Alis: Rape and Incest Therapist

Twice Raped is a very powerful book that exposes every woman's deepest fear. You have spoken from a depth where only women would be able to comprehend the full intensity of feeling. I admire and appreciate your risking to say those things that come from so deep within your own pained womanhood, your own violated being, your own determination to heal. Your words touched me in my own innate fear. Reading *Twice Raped* was a very uncomfortable expeience -- one that I, several times, wanted to run from. Staying with it was a powerful and cathartic experience. Mary Jeanne Pies: Visitor Representative

From the man's point of view *Twice Raped* was very enlightening. It made me look at how the men around me look at rape and their attitudes. I like to think that I would be caring and understanding under those circumstance. I will, now, always think twice. Michael Bowman: Computer Programer

Table of Contents

The Rape

"All pain is shattering; but when it's shared, at least it is no
longer a banishment. It is not out of morose delectation, nor out
of exhibitionism, nor out of provocation that writers often tell of
hideous or deeply saddening experiences: through the medium of
words they render these experiences universal and allow their
readers, deep in their private unhappiness, to know the
consolation of sisterhood. In my opinion one of the essential
functions of literature, a function which means that nothing else
can take its place, is the overcoming of that isolation
which is common to us all and which nevertheless
makes us strangers to each other."
Simone deBeauvoir

The Therapy

I was shredding Kleenexes into bits . . . tinier and tinier bits. Kleenexes, soaked with my tears and my snot. I was standing, not because I wanted to stand, but because my therapist told me to stand. She sat in front of me, looking worried. I didn't know what was happening except that I couldn't stop shredding. Tears were streaming down my cheeks. I was shredding . . . shredding . . . then suddenly I was ripping. Ripping them . . . tearing them . . . not knowing what I was doing. The soggy Kleenexes were dropping onto the floor, making a mess.

"What are you doing?" my therapist said.

I couldn't answer. All words had disappeared. I just looked at her out of vacant eyes.

"Is there a sound?" she said.

It was then that I heard it. The sound that had been waiting in my chest for more than a year. At first it was like a cry. Then it turned into a scream, a raw scream . . . the scream I hadn't screamed at the time. The scream that might have ended my life had I screamed it then.

And it repeated itself. The scream. Again and again I heard it resounding in my own ears.

It was the scream of fear. It was the scream of the fear I had felt at the time. No! It was more than fear. It was panic that I felt. It was panic. Knowing there was nothing I could do; that I was like a cub cornered in a cave, about to be killed by its would-be captors. The scream resounded throughout the room, repeating itself in my ear. Was the sound in my ear an echo or was it my own voice? All I knew was that it kept coming . . . the scream. Again and again . . . the scream.

I vaguely knew that I was still ripping Kleenexes.

My therapist pulled a very large pillow from the corner of the room and placed it at my feet. She gently pushed me to the floor. Now I was screaming at the pillow. I saw him. Yes, I saw him. There he was with his fetid breath and filthy body. He was there hitting me . . . then hitting me again. I was falling to the ground, covering my face, feeling the blood, feeling my swollen jaw . . . . I knew what he was going to do . . . . I knew I had no choice.

My screams changed to the only word I knew. "No, no, no, no, no, no, no, no, Noooooo." I ran out of breath. I sucked in enough air to keep going. "No! No! No! Noooooooo! No, no, no, no, no, no noooooo. Nooo. Nooo. Nooo. No, no, no, no, no."

Then there were sobs, deep sobs . . . as he violated me. Sobs that came up from some unknown source, from someplace deep within my torn insides. Again and again the sob wrenched its way out of my tortured self as I saw him above me . . . as I felt him inside my body . . . inside **my** sacred body. My body twisted as the violations multiplied themselves in my day-to-day life. He violated my relation-ships. He forced his way between me and my lover. He stood between me and any other man who wanted to be my friend. He stole a part of me. He killed that loving, open place in me. He killed it! He killed that place in me. That part of me I thought would live forever.

Then the hatred started. A rage rushed over me like white heat. I could feel my face change. I heard a different sound. I felt my lips turn down in a snarl. I heard the sound that came out of my mouth. It was that deep, bottomless sound; that sub-terranean sound that belongs to all women who have been violated by men. My chest was heaving . . . my breath was finding its way to the bottom of my belly; and the sound that emerged welled up out of the garbage of the violations; all the violations I had allowed . . . and this violation. This violation I had not allowed. The growl was the sound of an animal . . . ready to make its kill. I knew it. I could feel it. I was possessed by rage.

I fell upon the pillow. I twisted it. I beat it with my fist, with my arms, with my total body. I snarled. I growled. I raged. The sounds that came out of me were pure animal. I was a panther protecting her young. I was a lion ready for the kill. I was a woman . . . defending herself against the most horrible of violations . . . Rape! !

My breath was coming from someplace . . . deep inside myself . . . deep . . . and rapid . . . like a giant pant. The snarl . . . and the growl. They protected me . . . from my attacker. I threw myself at him and took my hands and twisted . . . and twisted . . . and twisted . . . until he moved no more. Until he was dead. Dead on my therapist's floor in the middle of Indiana, in the United States of America. He was dead. He would rape no more. He would not destroy another woman, as he had destroyed me. Never! Never again. He was dead.

I dropped into the pillow, sobbing. I had killed. I had killed the man who had taken my self-respect . . . who had destroyed my trust . . . my sexuality . . . my humanness with men. I had killed a man . . . because of what he killed in me. What he killed in me was beautiful: a zest for life without fear . . . an acceptance of all people for who they were . . . a naivete that I was safe . . . and a sure knowledge that I would never kill. Now I knew that no more. I knew I could kill. I had. He lay at my feet on the floor in that room. I killed. I killed.

Exhaustion filled my body. I was spent. All my strength was gone. I lay on the floor crying. The dead body was pushed as far away from me as possible. Tears were running, more gently now, down my cheeks, and forming pools of water on the floor. Then I felt her touch. It was the first thing I knew . . . my therapist's touch. She touched my back. I felt her hand, cool, on the heat of my body. She had witnessed my rage . . . my pain . . . the rape . . . my killing . . . and she was still there. She was touching me . . . with her cool hand. She had not run from the room. She had not condemned me. She was touching me with gentleness and love.

As I pulled myself to a sitting position she wrapped her arms around me. She wrapped her arms around me as I had so often wished my mother would when I cried . . . when I felt afraid . . . when I felt alone. She had seen the depths of my rage . . . she had even seen me kill . . . and she was putting her arms around me. She was saying to me . . . without words: "It's okay. I still love you."

For the first time I heard myself speak . Out of a gravelly and very hoarse voice, I said, "What happened?"

She said, "I just witnessed a murder. The kill was clean. Clean and beautiful. He's dead. He can't hurt you or anyone, ever again."

I said, incredulously, "He's dead?"

"He's dead."

"He won't ever hurt anyone again?"

"Never again. He's destroyed."

Tears continued to stream down my face dropping onto her blouse.

"You were like a lion after its prey," she said. "I have never seen a piece of work so clean. You were strong and straight, and I'm awfully glad you're on my team. I'd hate to have you against me."

We both laughed.

But I knew that I had done something that was no laughing matter. I had killed. I knew I was capable of killing. I had never known that before. The man who violated my body and my very soul lay dead on her office floor. He was not going to bother me any more . . . but I had had to kill to retrieve my soul.

And the horror of it is that now I know that if any man ever tries it again . . . he will not be dead on any therapist's floor. I will not wait that long. He will never know what hit him. Now I know what I am capable of. I will not wait for the justice system. I will not wait for anything. I will never be raped again. Never.

And I grieve for my lost innocence.

The Rape

He was talking to me from above, standing behind the wall - his form hardly visible in the sunset. He was saying words I could barely hear and couldn't understand. Out of the jumble of words I could make out, he seemed to be telling me that I shouldn't be here. That I was not allowed to camp here. That I was in trouble.

I closed my book knowing that, for the moment, my peace was broken. I had been sitting with my back against a rock reading in the waning sunlight. I had been camping here for three out of the last four days, on these rocky cliffs over-looking the sea near the resort town of Llandudno, Wales on a peninsula they called the Great Orme.

It was toward the end of my visit to the British Isles. I had been there for almost three months, absorbing the English wisdom, finding myself perplexed by the English culture, doing what tourists do: seeing Westminster Abbey, the Tower of London, the British Museum, Covent Garden and Picadilly Circus. I also did things tourists did not normally do. I rented a tiny room in a basement flat in a transient area of London. From there I traveled all over the city getting to know its people in ways few tourists do. I engaged in difficult conversations with its cockney speaking residents, listened to unknown musicians in tiny out of the way pubs, went to concerts attended by some of the city's punks, shopped at its tiny markets and with its street corner vendors, ate its Cornish pies daily, and talked politics with its most fervid labor enthusiasts. I even talked to the British about what it was like to be inundated by Americans every summer . . . and with great regularity I got lost.

What kept me in London far beyond my planned departure was the London theatre. I discovered it, or it discovered me. I'm not sure which. I frequented the abundance of London theatres seeing everything from the classics to British pop. Some weeks I saw a play a day. Shakespeare's work got into my blood. I saw every Shakespearean play produced that summer, finding them in diverse locations from local parks all the way to Stratford Upon Avon. I discovered the glories of sitting in the back row or of standing behind the barriers. Wherever was cheapest, that's the way I did it. I was determined to do the most with what little money I had, because I **had** very little money.

In the last three weeks of my stay, I spent some time away from London, traveling the English countryside. I had just a little over a week left when I boarded a bus and traveled to Llandudno, Wales - a town that will, now, never leave my consciousness. It was just a town, a part of Wales that I thought would be nice to see. The bus deposited me in Llandudno with about fifty pounds in cash and all my camping equipment. I spent my first day exploring the town, the beach, the areas near the sea, and finally I walked out on a peninsula called "The Great Orme." It was perfect. It was quiet, grassy, full of sheep and mountain goats, and right on top of the English sea. It was perfect.

I pitched my tent and settled in to commune with the sheep, to watch the sea below, and to read. The road was about fifty yards above me, close enough that I could hear conversations of people as they walked by and the movement of a few cars. A five foot wall separated the road from the grassy knoll on which I sat. The terrain was steep; steep and rough . . . and abounding with rocks in a variety of sizes. I had to work hard to avoid sitting on the thorns in the grass; but the sheep and the sea made it all worthwhile. It was the quietness I was always searching for. I felt safe and secure.

I stayed there for three out of the four nights I was in Llandudno. It was my last night there when **he** intruded on me. I had been especially enjoying the last few minutes of light, and the beauty of the sun disappearing below the sea. I knew I would be leaving in the morning to go back to London, and from there to Romsey - a small town in the south of England. There was a class in Romsey, my last chance to participate in some English wisdom and I was going to take it. I already had my bus ticket.

When I heard his voice I closed my book and looked up to see who was talking. I couldn't believe anybody would be talking to me; but there was no one else he could be talking to. Yes, he was talking to me all right. He was saying over and over again that I shouldn't be there, that I couldn't camp there. He was wearing something dark, and in the dusk he looked like a British Bobby.

"Maybe it's against the law to camp here," I thought. "Maybe I'm going to have to move. But, that can't be. I saw other pitched tents down the road a bit."

"What did you say?" I said to the shadowy form.

"You can't camp there. You have to leave," said the form.

"Am I doing something wrong?"

"It's dangerous to camp there," he said.

"Dangerous?"

"Fourteen Welshmen . . . down from the hills . . . kill you . . . in the pubs . . . crazy men . . . ."

"He doesn't sound like a policeman," I thought. "He sounds more like a nutter." I waited, still wanting an answer to my legal status.

He was quiet. I was getting angry. I hated the thought of packing up all my gear, trudging the three miles back to town, finding another camp-sight and repitching my tent. It was almost dark, and finding another sight would be difficult. Staying at a bed-and-breakfast was out of the question. I just simply didn't have the money. Nutter or policeman, I was aggravated.

"Have you got a cigarette?" he said after a pause.

"He's not a policeman," I thought. "No policeman would ask for a cigarette." I felt relieved. I didn't have to move. I didn't have to walk the three miles back to town.

"No, I don't smoke," I said to the silhouette, now clearly labeled as a nutter. "Go away. I'll be just fine," I said, sitting back down with my back against the rock. There were a few more minutes of daylight left and a few more pages to finish in the chapter. I looked out at the sun just setting over the sea. It was a beautiful sight: the red of the sun and a bit of the red on the low-lying clouds.

How he did it with no sound, I don't know; but suddenly he was standing there beside my rock, obviously also agitated. Now I could see him clearly. He was wearing a black sweater with holes in both sleeves, had sandy unkempt hair and a stubbly beard. Small. Wiry. Agitated.

No policeman, this one.

But I still wasn't wise enough to be afraid. Not yet.

"I'd appreciate it if you would go," I said. "I would like to read."

"You can't stay here," he said, dancing from one foot to the other. "People are crazy here. They'll come and beat you up. Welshmen . . . all the Welshmen . . . forty-four of them, from the hills. They're drinking up there . . . they'll be down here by 11 o'clock and they'll beat you up. They'll kill you."

Now I knew I was dealing with a nutter. "Just go away," I said. "There are no Welshmen going to bother me."

He was becoming more agitated. "Yes . . . yes . . . yes they will. They're going to kill you. You've got to go."

Now I was beginning to worry. "Just go away. I'll be fine."

"If you won't go, I'll get my bed and set up right here next to you so you'll be safe."

Fear stabbed at me. "I'm **not** in danger from any forty-four Welshmen," I said, " but I sure might be in danger from you. Now get out of here!"

He didn't seem to hear me. He continued to agitate. "Do you have any water?" he asked.

"Just a little," I said, thinking about my half-empty canteen I'd been rationing since I set up camp the night before. It was barely enough to see me through the morning.

"I want some," he said.

"I want some," I repeated in my mind. Not, "Can I have some-I want some."

"Let me have some water," he said. "I'm thirsty."

"If I give you some water, will you go away?" I said, with all the strength I could muster.

"I'll go," he said. "But you shouldn't be here. They'll hurt you."

If only he had changed "they'll" to "I'll", he would have been telling the truth. But I was not smart enough . . . or afraid enough . . . yet . . . to really hear him.

He drank. I watched what little water I had go down his throat.

He started to leave; and I breathed a little easier. When he was halfway up the hill, he turned around. "What's your name?" he said.

"Mary," I yelled at him. "Now go."

"Mine's David," he said.

I held my breath. Was he going to turn around and come back? No. He continued on up the hill. I watched him until he was back on top of the hill, through the opening in the wall and down the road.

Now, I didn't know what to do. It was getting darker by the minute. Fear told me to get away. My rational mind told me to stay. I was afraid he'd come back. I wanted to believe he wouldn't.

I kept checking the road. There was no sign of him. I looked over the terrain. The only easy way out was through the same open space in the wall where he'd disappeared. The rest of the terrain was covered with rocks and full of jagged crevices. **And** it was incredibly steep. By this time there was very little light left. If I packed up and walked out the same way he did, he might be waiting for me. If I walked the other way I could kill myself falling into a crevice. I could leave my gear and find a place to hide. Then he might steal my gear. I needed my gear. Everything I owned was right here on this cliff in Llandudno, Wales. What should I do? What should I do?

Then I remembered I had a cartridge of mace in my backpack. Ah! Now I knew what I was going to do. I could stay and protect myself. But was the mace working? I had been carrying it with me for the two years I had been traveling. I had never had to use it. Was it still all right? "Check it, dummy," I said to myself. "Damn! It isn't working. Now what should I do?"

Fifteen minutes had passed. There had been no sign of him. Perhaps I was safe. Perhaps he wasn't coming back. Perhaps he meant me no harm anyway. I needed to feel safe. I was convincing myself.

I waited a little longer. I saw nothing on the road.

I made a decision. I would stay.

I justified my decision. I had waited just a little too long to run. It was too dark by now.

I crawled inside my tent, fully clothed, hoping beyond hope that I really was safe.

I hadn't been inside the tent for more than five minutes when I heard his footsteps. They were coming towards me from above. My heart sank. It seemed to stop beating and at that moment of death, he made it to my tent door. He was calling to me from outside. His voice was right against my ear. He was right there. "Mary. Mary," he said. "Unzip this door."

I did nothing. I didn't move. I probably didn't even breathe.

"Open the door," he said again, louder this time. "Mary. Open the door."

I laid perfectly still. Maybe he would think I wasn't there.

Then I heard the sound that signaled my doom. He was beginning to unzip my tent door. "Go away," I said.

"Open the door," he said, ripping at the zipper.

The thought of him inside my little tent horrified me. I made another decision. "Stop that," I said. "I'll open it."

I unzipped the tent and crawled out, my heart pounding. This was happening. This really was happening. There was no longer any doubt in my mind. This was happening.

I stood up facing him. I could see his face, his ugly face. He looked strange standing there leering at me. He was carrying two huge plastic bags on one of his shoulders, both bags with straw sticking out of the top. He threw the bags onto the ground.

"I'm going to stay here and protect you," he said. "They'll be here soon, and they're going to break your ribs."

Now I was into full blown panic. Break my ribs? Break my ribs! I knew a paranoic when I heard one. **They** were not going to break my ribs. **He** was going to break my ribs.

"Go away," I said, still acting brave. " Nobody's coming to get me."

"I'm staying," he said, moving toward me.

My fear took over. I lost control. I don't remember what happened next. I must have kept fighting with him verbally because the next thing I knew, my head was spinning - - first to the right and then to the left. He had hit me. He was quick. I hadn't seen it coming. I'd had no time to dodge, no time to fend him off, no time to retaliate. Blood dripped from my mouth and I could feel it swelling.

He lunged at me and started tearing at my jeans.

Now I knew what I was in for. Suddenly my head cleared. I knew that I had in front of me a very violent man. I knew that my diagnosis of a nutter was absolutely accurate. I knew I **could** be killed if I didn't cooperate. His words "break your ribs" were prophetic.

I decided to save my life.

"Are you going to rape me?" I said, with whatever courage I had left.

He didn't answer, just kept on tearing at my clothes.

"Wait," I said. "I'll take them off." I'd decided I would rather do it myself than have this insane man crawling all over me.

I struggled out of my jeans.

He lunged at me again. "Get your knickers off," he ordered.

"I'll do it. I'll do it," I said.

I took my panties off.

"Get down," he said, and began to take off his own dirty pants.

The ground was covered with thistles that tore at my bare hips. I reached inside the tent and tried to pull out my sleeping pad.

"What are you doing?" he said.

"I want to put something under me," I said, getting a hold of it, pulling it out and rolling onto it, before he could stop me.

He was standing over me. I could see his outline in the dark. I knew this was it . . . every woman's nightmare. Every woman's greatest fear. The thing she was warned about, directly or indirectly from babyhood on. The thing she protected herself against with all manner of self-imprisonment.

I know what they would say. They would say something like this: What woman who wasn't asking for exactly this would have been out there camping alone in the first place? Why wasn't I home, under the protective care of my husband? Why wasn't I in my woman's place, taking care of my house and children, or my garden and dog if I had no house and children? What right had I to travel alone to another country to camp alone on the Welsh countryside, this Great Orme? Since I had refused to stay in my proper prison, I was getting only what I deserved.

And get it I did. He dropped down on top of me, pushed my legs apart and stuck his ugly organ into me.

I covered my face with my hands, as if not seeing would keep me from feeling.

But I felt. I felt every ugly thrust. I felt every horror a woman could feel in that moment. There are no words in the dictionary to describe what I felt. Inflicted . . . infested . . . invaded . . . seized . . . trampled . . . infested by creepy, crawly things . . . ravaged . . . infested with the plague. Nothing. No. Nothing could describe what happened to me in that moment. Nothing could describe my very self that was being destroyed in that moment. His one moment of pleasure . . . of inflicting his power over me . . . of proving his right to take what he wanted . . . of proving that he was a man and had the right to dominate . . . to subjugate . . . to make me submit to his superior physical power.

He was mercifully fast. He finished in only two or three thrusts, shooting his offensive liquid into my insides. He finished . . . breathing hard and contorting his face into even more ugliness. He finished his little task of proving his manhood by destroying my womanhood . . . and pulled out.

I quickly grabbed my jeans, put them on, and sat shivering in the cold sea air. I wrapped my arms around my knees and sat, like a lost waif . . . all wasted and unable to move.

It wasn't long before he was at me again. I don't know what I expected him to do when he got through. Did I expect him to go off into the wilderness? But here he was, at me again. "Get into the tent," he ordered.

My tent was small. Room enough for one person to be comfortable, and sometimes uncomfortable at that. The thought of being in that tiny space with this monster was more than I could bear.

"Let's just sit out here and talk," I said, aware of what he had already stolen from me, but not knowing what he would try to do to my body in that tiny space where I had absolutely **no** way to escape. Mercy of all mercies, he stopped insisting.

I cannot remember all that we talked about in that hour that I managed to keep him out of my tent, but I do remember that I had learned my lesson. I remember that I was totally cooperative and passive. I did not argue with him. I did not threaten him in any way. I was the picture of quiescence. When he asked a question, I answered it. When he expounded, I listened. No matter how crazy he was, I listened. I knew where my survival was. I wasn't out of the woods yet.

I remember some of his conversation. My daughter is in England having a baby. My son-in-law is trying to kill me. There is a man in the moon . . . didn't I see him . . . who is a communist, who is going to swoop down and get us. Welshmen were trying to put him in jail, and he knew just how to get out. His plastic bags were full of steak and kidney pies that he'd stolen from the store, and did I want one? He slept in the streets every night and the straw was what he slept on. He was from Liverpool and he didn't know his family. He had destroyed them a long time ago.

He was twenty-five. Did I have a cigarette? Just a minute, he'd go up to the road and find one. I'd better not move from where I was. There were men watching us from the road, and we'd better get inside the tent. Where was my water? He wanted some. And, "Get in the tent."

He was becoming agitated again. He was getting threatening and agitated. He was talking about broken arms and crushed feet. I was not stupid. He was talking about **my** broken arm, and **my** crushed feet. He wanted in my tent.

I crawled inside, and he crawled in after me. He zipped up the door. I was trapped in my tiny tent with this smelly, dirty, animal. And I knew he was going to do it all over again. He was all over me, tearing at my clothes. What difference did it make now? Once. Twice. What difference did it make? I took off my clothes.

He was flaccid. His pleasure was eluding him. He sneered that I was uncooperative. I asked him how I could be cooperative while I was being raped. From the look on his face I thought I was going to be beaten again. In his demented mind, it was my fault. I was uncooperative. You bet I was!

Mercifully, he gave up.

He prepared to go to sleep. He wrestled around, removed some of his clothes, put on others and unzipped the tent to get something from his plastic bags. When he finally settled down I was on the inside of this tiny tent with him closest to the door. He had a vice-like grip around my body and there was no way I could move. He went to sleep while I was left to wonder how I was going to get away.

I stared into the top of the tent obsessing. How was I going to do it? This monster had moved in and had made a nest. He'd found a receptacle for his sickness and he wasn't going to let it go. How could I get away? I had to get to London the next day. I had my ticket. How could I do it?

At first light in the morning I woke him and told him I had to get out, that I had to go to the bathroom. I had to go to town to catch a bus. I had to get to London.

"It's too dangerous for you to walk into town. They'll be waiting for you," he said.

"If you think I will be in any danger, you can walk with me," I said, in my most cooperative tone. I didn't care how I did it. I just wanted to get to that bus. By this time I was obsessed with the bus. It was my escape.

As I was taking the tent down and packing my things he said something that I took careful note of. Very lucidly, he said, "I'm glad you stopped fighting me last night. You saw how I was." He didn't say he would have brutally beaten me if I hadn't cooperated, but I knew he would have. He didn't say he would have done whatever he needed to do to have his way if I hadn't cooperated, but I knew he would have. He didn't say he would have killed me if I hadn't cooperated, but I knew he would have.

I knew my cooperation had saved my life. Yes, I had seen how he was. **And** I had enough sense of self-preservation to stop fighting with him. I had lost much; but I **had** saved my life. At that moment, my life wasn't worth much, but I had saved it. He told me so.

The walk into Llandudno was a delirium. He talked incessantly. He was unintelligible. I nodded and agreed and kept my opinions to myself. The bus, I kept thinking. Only the bus is important.

We passed a public toilet. I had to go in. He told me to wash my face. It was dirty. I used the toilet. I didn't wash my face.

When I came out, he told me again to wash my face. I gave my face a spit wash. He continued to harass me about washing my face.

We passed two Bobbies on the street. I thought about screaming. I thought about rushing up to them and telling them I was imprisoned by a monster . . . a monster rapist . . . but I didn't. All I wanted to do was get away. All I wanted to do was get to that bus and get on it. He was busy picking up cigarettes from the street and smoking them. I was hurrying to the bus.

When we got to the bus station, it was abandoned. No buses, no people, no activity. I panicked. I was sure I'd missed that bus. There wasn't another one until late afternoon. I was wishing I'd screamed at the Bobbies. I saw myself imprisoned forever. I forced myself to calm down a bit. I realized that he couldn't keep me imprisoned if there were people around. Then I **would** scream. We were no longer isolated on the Great Orme. People would be around soon. If he didn't let me go, I would scream and scream and scream. People would come and help me.

I thought about the bus again.

A young woman walked into the area and sat down. "Are you getting on the bus to London?" I said, knowing that the answer to that question meant my survival.

"Yes," she said. "It should be here any moment."

I was going to live.

"Do you have anything to write on?" he said to me.

I handed him the tour schedule I had in my backpack.

In a childlike scrawl he wrote, "David Forsythe". "That's my name," he said. "I'll be famous some day. You'll know about me." In my befuddled mind, I knew he had given me something valuable, and it was not the knowledge that he would be famous some day. What he had given me was the knowledge of who he was. I quickly tucked the schedule into my pack for safe keeping.

I spent the rest of the time until the bus arrived memorizing his appearance, right down to his shoe laces. I had a name, I had a description and the bus was on its way. I was going to live. I was going to get away.

"Do you have any money?" he asked.

"I have six pounds."

"Give it to me," he demanded.

I wasn't going to mess up this close to my escape. "I'll give you five," I said. "I'd like to keep one pound just in case I need it."

He didn't argue.

Five pounds was cheap enough for my escape.

The bus rounded the corner.

We stood up.

When it came to a stop, I was the first in line. I climbed on board and found a seat. I sat near the front in the no-smoking section. I was numb. I didn't know anything, except that I escaped. I was no longer trapped by this monster. The bus seemed to take an interminable time -- maybe a minute or two -- before it started to move. I think I died then. I knew nothing except that I was free. I was ravaged and dirty, and my self-respect was destroyed . . . but I was free. I sat there staring at the seat in front of me . . . paralyzed. Knowing nothing.

The First Twenty-four Hours

I was a basket case.

I slumped into my seat and stared.

I sat alone. There was an older woman in the seat in front of me. I dumbly thought about moving into the seat next to her, dissolving into tears and asking her to hold me.

I stayed in my seat. I stayed numb.

The bus finally left the depot and I could think about only one thing: how glad I was to be on that bus . . . how glad I was to be alive . . . and . . . somewhere deep inside of myself, wishing I weren't.

The bus traveled a long way before I knew anything but numbness. I finally noticed a road sign that I knew to be at least sixty miles out of Llandudno. Vaguely I began to look around. I looked at my rumpled and dirty clothes. I felt my dirty, matted hair. I smelled ugly. I could smell him.

I slipped back into numbness.

The bus stopped to take on new passengers. They poured on in droves. Most of them were young. Oh, God! Most of them were men. I shrank against the window knowing that one of them would surely sit next to me. I came out of my numbness into full panic.

I wasn't much for praying then; but at that moment I prayed: "Give me a seat-mate that is a woman . . . if you must give me a seat-mate. Please don't give me a seat- mate at all . . . .but if you must . . . give me a woman."

A man sat down.

I cringed and tried to push myself into the side of the bus. Out the window if possible. The side of the bus didn't give way; and I was stuck with a man blocking my way into the restroom where I could throw up.

My sensations were returning. I began to feel everything. Anger. Hatred. Rage. I couldn't stand having that man next to me. I had all I could do to contain my body . . . to keep it from screaming . . . and beating the shit out of that man.

I was not yet so crazy that I could give into that urge. I compromised. I took out my journal and started to write. I did not know what I was writing. When I looked at it later, I still didn't know what I wrote. It looked more like the scribbling of a mad woman than the journal writing of a Ph.D. psychotherapist.

But write I did. My words tumbled out of me at a furious pace. I wrote everything I could think of . . . all my feelings. I wrote for almost two hours . . . until we were half way to London . . . until I had written it all . . . until I had written all I had in me.

After I put my journal away, I spent the rest of the trip staring out of the window, seeing nothing - both hating and fearing the male energy that was next to me.

Arriving in London, there was only one thing I knew. I knew I had to find a way to get clean, to wash off the filth, to wash off the smell, to wash off the monster, to take off and burn the clothes I had been wearing.

I looked at my bus ticket to Romsey and realized I had a little over an hour to wait. I could do it. I could get rid of the filth. Victoria Station and a public shower were only three blocks away. I put my pack on my roller and headed down the street. There were people everywhere. People coming and going. People whose lives were exactly the same as they had been yesterday and the day before yesterday and the day before that. People who had no idea that I would never be the same as yesterday. I would never be the same again.

The sunlight hurt my eyes. The people confused me. I felt lost in a sea of other people's purpose. It was only the sheer determination to wash that kept my feet walking and my arms hauling my pack behind me.

Finally Victoria Station loomed in front of me. There I faced more people, bunches of shops, announcements on the loudspeakers, vendors, moneychangers, tourists with backpacks, tourists in pinstriped suits with seventeen suitcases. Finally, the stairs to the women's room.

"Oh, God! There's a line. How long will it take to get to the head of the line? How long will it take to get to the top of these stairs? I don't have much time." I was panicking.

I maintained control. I waited and moved toward those showers, one step at a time. It seemed as though I waited forever. It was ten minutes.

When I got to the head of the line, I deposited my five pence to go through the turnstile. I ran toward the showers. Then I saw it. The sign. The sign that said, "Showers Closed until 3 P.M." It couldn't be. I could not wait until 3 P.M. I couldn't wait one minute longer. I had already waited five interminable hours on the bus and thousands of interminable minutes climbing those stairs. The showers couldn't be closed.

Frantically, I hunted for the attendant. Certainly she would understand my state and open the showers.

"The showers can't be opened until three," she rigidly told me.

I pleaded.

"There's no way I can open the showers until three. You'll have to come back."

"I can't come back," I shouted at her. "I have a bus to catch. I have to get to Romsey."

She stood resolutely between me and getting rid of the horror that was on me.

I lost control.

I rushed past her to a jury of my peers. "She won't open the showers," I yelled at anyone in my path. "I have to have a shower. Help me get her to open the showers," I shouted.

Staid English women stared at me in disbelief. They stopped moving in and out of their stalls to stare. Mouths hung open. Only one woman tried to understand. "There are wash rooms toward the back," she said.

Unable to thank her, I tore off in the direction she indicated. There it was. It was an open washroom with a sink. I rushed toward the wash basin and I looked in horror at the mirror above. My lower lip was twice its normal size. My right eye was black. I still had dirty smudges all over my face. No wonder my attacker had told me to wash my face. He could not stand to see his night's handiwork all over my face.

I tore off all my clothes. I took soap and a washcloth out of my pack and ran water into the sink. There was no drain stopper so I kept the water running, wet the cloth and washed myself all over. I splashed water all over the floor. I didn't care. I really didn't care. All I knew was that I had to get clean.

I lathered my naked body with soap and water. Puddles gathered at my feet. Suddenly the door to my room filled with the form of the attendant.

"You cann't do that in here," she said, looking aghast at my behavior.

I still had no self-control. She became my enemy. This was all her fault because she wouldn't open the shower. She was trying to make me keep his filth on my body and clothes. I screamed, "You wouldn't open the showers. You wouldn't open the damn showers until three o'clock so I **can't** take a shower. All I wanted to do was take a shower. You wouldn't let me. I have to get clean. This is the only way to get clean. If you had opened the showers, I wouldn't have to do this."

With all my screaming I forgot my nakedness.

She quickly changed the subject. "Well, I'm not going to mop up this room," she said.

"I don't care who mops it up," I yelled loudly enough for every other woman in that big room to hear.

She **knew** it was no use. She backed away and bumped hard into another woman headed for a stall across from **my** wash room. She excused herself, but still backed away, then turned and scurried down the hall. She is probably still telling anyone who will listen about her encounter with a crazy American in her restroom, a naked crazy American.

I finished washing, took clean clothes out of my pack and dressed. I left the messy washroom and dragged myself back down the stairs, then threaded my way through the busy London crowd back to the bus depot. I had one more task to finish before I could rest - get to Romsey. I was cleaner. I was better. I was far from well.

In Romsey I was to be picked up by my teacher at the train depot. I knew I would have to find my way from the bus depot to the train station. When I got off the bus everything was a haze. I sat down on a bench for a few mintues to try to collect myself. Then I asked for directions to the train station. I tried to follow them but the first thing I knew I was lost. I was lost going around the block. I asked someone else, and got lost again. After asking seven or eight people for directions to a station that was only two blocks from where I had left the bus, I found it. I gratefully sat down on one of the benches outside the station to wait. Through my haze I realized that it would still be an hour before I would be picked up. Even in that state I knew what I had to do. I tore a page out of my notebook and wrote a letter to the Llandudno police.

People walked by me and glanced at me, probably just seeing a woman writing something in a notebook. They didn't see a woman who had been destroyed by one man's act. They didn't suspect the sickness that was taking me over or the swelling rage inside me. After an hour of forever, a woman stood in front of me, and told me to follow her to her car. She was introducing me to three other women who were coming to the class. I tried to act like a perfectly normal woman. I doubt that I pulled that off.

When we arrived at the cottage where we were to have our class, I was shown around an interesting English cottage, then taken to my room. During my tour I had seen the only thing that mattered to me - the shower. I was not through with water yet. I was **not** clean. I needed to spend two or three hours under hot water. Maybe . . . just maybe, then, I would be clean. As soon as I was free from social obligations I dove into it. I came out physically clean, but psychologically still filthy.

Class began that night without my feeling any less crazy. I could not hear what the teacher was saying. I could not interact with the other students. I felt as if I were not even there. I was crazy in my head - reliving the horror of the past twenty-four hours. I had regained enough restraint not to do what I wanted to do. I wanted to stand up and shout to the group, "Please help me. I was just raped!" Maybe I should have. I certainly would have felt better. Instead I just sat and felt crazy.

When I tried to sleep, the night was full of more insanity. Monsters chased me and cornered me in tiny tents. I woke in the morning with my head throbbing and my body aching. I had gone a second night with no restful sleep. I showered again but still could not wash off his ugliness.

I went to the morning's class still in a haze, still unable to tell anyone what had happened to me. People weren't at this workshop to hear from me. They didn't want to listen to a crazy American who had just been raped. They were here to learn. These were stolid, staid English people. Reserved, that's what they were. All English people were reserved. I knew that. I couldn't tell anyone.

I told someone. About half way through the morning, I told someone. We were given an exercise to do in pairs. For my partner I deliberately picked the woman who looked the most understanding. Whatever the exercise was, we didn't do it. I talked instead. I poured out my story to my partner. I was totally incoherent, I'm sure. She saw the black eye. She'd been raped, too, many years ago. She not only understood, but she was outraged. She said I should talk to the instructor.

During lunch, I made an appointment with the woman who was teaching the class. She did something that surprised me. She gave me a bottle with a strange formula in it and told me it was a homeopathic shock treatment. She told me to take two drops in a glass of water every half hour. I scoffed at the possibility that two drops of anything would do me any good; but I agreed to try it because it was the only hope I had.

It worked. By nighttime, I was able to be part of the class. I was able to make friends with my roommate, a friendship that has lasted since that time. I began to communicate with the other members of the class and I felt relatively safe. My pain was not over. Life would never be the same again, but for the moment, I was safe.

What About the Man Who Loves Me?

When a woman is raped, she is blamed and becomes the victim . . . again. The victim becomes the victimized. **She** is the guilty one . . . not the man who did the raping. She is the one who did it. She is the wrong one. It's common knowledge that that is the way it works. Everybody knows that.

Women have been divorced by their husbands for being raped. They have been turned away as unclean . . . as no longer worthy because they were raped. Coldness has descended between them as a result of her being raped. Men have first gone after the rapist and then after their wife, because she was raped. Whatever happens, the relationship is never the same. Sometimes she changes it. More often he changes it.

Back home in America, I had to confront my lover, but first I had to see a gynecologist. I had to find out whether this filthy vermin had given me a disease. The exam and tests took three days.

When he finally came through the door it was wonderful to see him. "When did you get back," he asked.

"Three days ago," I said.

"Why didn't you call when you got in?" he logically wanted to know.

"I had to go to a doctor first," I said.

"Why? Is something wrong?"

"Yes," I said, noncommittally. I was trying not to say the words I knew I had to say.

"What's wrong, baby?" he said.

Would he call me "baby" after I told him?

The words started to tumble out, one after another, the whole story. As I talked I could see the shock on his face . . . followed by the anger. Was it at me?

I wasn't halfway through my story before the tears were beginning to trickle down my cheeks.

He wiped them away with his finger.

I kept talking. The tears kept coming.

When I was through, he said, "I'd give my life to have been with you to protect you from this. I'm so sorry."

It was going to be all right, I told myself.

Or was it?

We hadn't seen each other for the three months I'd been in London. Would he still want to make love to me, as we always did when we hadn't seen each other for a while? If we made love would he feel the same about me? Would I be able to make love with him? Would I feel the same about him? What was going to happen?

Once in the bedroom, as he began to touch me, I found my body recoiling. I found myself pulling away. I didn't want him to touch me. My body was still dirty. I was still dirty. "Don't touch me."

But he was a patient and gentle lover, and my love for him, won out. His touch started to feel good. It began to be all right. I knew who was touching me. It wasn't brutal and horrid. It was loving and caring. It was the love I had known for so many years. It was beautiful, as it always had been. It was all right. No it wasn't!

It wasn't all right. Nothing was all right. I began to see another body above me. I felt pain in my face. I felt thistles underneath me. I felt revulsion. This was not the man who loved me. This was the man who hated me. **And** I hated him. I hated him and his penis. I hated it. It was a weapon. It was not going to give me pleasure. It was going to give me pain. It was going to give him power over me. It was going to make me heel, it would take away everything that was me and subject it to him. It was a part of him I hated. I hated him. I hated all men.

I started to cry. I pushed him away.

"What's wrong, baby?" he said.

Of course, he couldn't know. What's wrong? What's wrong? Yes. WHAT'S WRONG?

Now there were sobs. Great gushing sobs from the very bottom of my feelings, from the very bottom of my gut, from the very bottom of the pain of every woman who had ever had this kind of horror perpetrated on her. They were my sobs. They were every woman's sobs. I thought they would never stop. They kept coming, coming and coming and coming.

He rolled over and cradled me in his arms. He held me while my whole body vibrated with the bottomlessness of my sobs. I buried my head in his shoulder and cried out the ugliness, the filth, my fear, my aloneness and, worst of all, my shame. Yes, that was part of what I was feeling. Shame. I felt shame for what had happened. As if it **was** my fault. As if the truth really was as people had been saying for years. It **was** my fault. I couldn't believe it. I felt shame. A man had forced me. He had beaten me to subjugation. He had taken my most precious possession against my will. And **I** felt shame.

I cried out my shame against my lover's shoulder.

While he held me.

And made me feel whole again.

Until he could come back into me; and I could know who was there. That the man who was loving me was a man who honestly did love me. Me! He did love me. He didn't want to take from me what was mine. He didn't need to force his power on me. He didn't want me submissive to his bullying. He wanted me because he loved me.

And when I finally knew that, I could love him again. I could be with him as we had been so many other times before. I could know my body as clean. I could finally wash off the filth. I was not all right. But I was a whole lot better. My improved health was a tribute to a man who did not make me more of a victim. What ever made me think he would? He loved me and I loved him. And that was the way it was. No matter what crime had been perpetrated against me, it was not his crime. He loved me.

Yes. That was the way it was. He loved me.

The First Year

I spent the next year not talking about it.

I spent the year talking about it - only when I was forced to.

I spent the year insulating myself from the pain of the truth - from the pain of letting anyone else know my truth.

I spent the year hating men and fearing women. I ran away from everything and everyone.

In that year, I learned to understand a great deal about the wheels of justice: those wheels that had already been set in motion even before my plane landed in the Indianapolis airport. The Llandudno police had done their job. They had informed Interpole (International Police) of my letter; and this organization's giant tentacles had immediately gone into action. Interpole had arranged for a detective to interview me in Indianapolis. By the time I had settled in, he had left several messages with my secretary in my Indianapolis office. I explained the messages, disclaiming any notion of what **any** detective would want from me. I couldn't say to my secretary, "Oh, yes. I was raped back in England and a detective wants to interview me to get the story." I just could not say that. I was much too raw.

Raw or not, I did have to talk to the detective. I had no choice in that. If I were going to prosecute - and I knew I was going to prosecute - I had to talk to the detective. I made an appointment, assuming I would be interviewed in a "Hill Street Blues" atmosphere - in the middle of police hubbub, at the station.

Instead the detective came to me. He made me comfortable on the couch in a friend's living room. Since I was still in the middle of my traveling, I had no home of my own to sit in. He faced me with his tape recorder. He warned me about what I could say and what I couldn't. He asked good questions; and he listened. He was as understanding as a man could be, but he was still a man. He was still part of that dreaded group - men: that dreaded group who wanted to do me in. I told my story as factually as I could. Factually, because that is all the law wants to know. "Just the facts, Ma'am. Just the facts." On the outside I appreciated him for the gentle way he treated me and for the understanding he gave me. Inside I was scared to death!

Then came the phone call that made me feel as though it had all been worthwhile - the phone call from Interpole. The Llandudno police had obviously been doing their work. They had him. The police in Llandudno had caught him; and they had him in custody. They wanted me to know. David Forshile, the man who had beaten and raped me, was in custody in the town where it all happened. My belief in the justice system, which had been systematically eroded over years, took on new hope. They had him. He would rape no one else. He would demean no more women, at least for now. They had him.

Now it was inevitable. There would be a trial. I would testify. He would have to be convicted and put away for as long as rapists are put away. For a long time, I was sure.

I welcomed returning to England for the trial. I was adamant! I would do anything I had to do to put my rapist behind bars, to keep him from doing to any other woman what he had done to me. I knew a lot about rape. I had worked with innumerable rape victims in my practice as a psychotherapist. I knew their pain. I knew their shame. I knew what it had done to their lives. I knew it had ruined, forever, more than one. I was willing to go through anything to see that David Forshile, my rapist, got what was due him.

I didn't, then, know what I was to go through. Had I known, I might have thought differently.

For the time being, I was once again on American soil. I was once again among my friends, but I still couldn't talk about it. It did not help that I was a respected therapist in Indianapolis, a person who drew people to her to talk about their problems. I still couldn't do what I needed to do to purge myself of what had happened to me. I had been working on myself for years. I was an expert at it. When something troublesome came up, I worked on it. That meant talking about anything in my history that caused me to be unhealthy, any part of me that was keeping me from being all that I wanted to be. An even more important reason was to clear myself of any conflicts I might project onto a client. For years, I had been insisting that colleagues (therapists, and students alike) do the same thing. "Get rid of your own garbage so you can be clear when you're working with other people," I had said, insisting to the point of being a bore. Now, here I was, unable to talk about my own problem, unable to do the very thing I had relentlessly harangued others to do.

I could not trust anyone, including my lover. His understanding had been wonderful; but he was still a man. I knew that men were all one species, that they all had the same violent disdain for women. I just had to look at history to know the truth of that. There has been rape and possession through the centuries. I simply had to look in the newspaper to know that this violent disdain continued. There I read about wife beatings, incest, murder, child beatings, kidnapping, mutilation, rape etc., etc., etc. I finally paid attention to the prime time television shows and again I knew the truth. The majority of what I saw was cop show after cop show complete with one guy out-toughing the other. This truth was exhibited even in my own office where my male clients tried to take power from me; to show me who was in charge. Either that or they tried to seduce me and get me in their bed. My female clients told tales of male abuse that I was now accepting as absolute truth.

I had clearly lost my ability to see the individual differences in men. I saw them as all alike. All violent, power-hungry and selfish to the core. There was no logic that could sway me from that belief.

I could not trust my women friends, either. I did not know why. I just could not - not even my women therapist friends who knew every despicable part of me. I couldn't. I just couldn't. For some strange reason, this rape was worse than every other trauma I had ever experienced and told them about. The rape was worse than my hatred of my mother, my estrangement from my husband, my oedipal love for my father, my feelings of unworthiness, my confused and painful sadnesses that I had gradually permitted to be seen through the years. It was worse than my anger at myself and the world, that had finally erupted against numerous pillows, my lonely, inadequate self who could never be loved or respected, the self who had to keep running away because she couldn't stand love when it came her way; that manipulative, designing woman I had been. I had exposed it all. Some of it I had even laughed about. But not this. Not the fact that I'd been raped. This was unspeakable!

My therapist self knew I had to speak about it. My therapist self knew I was pretending. My therapist self knew that I was lying to myself when I said everything was all right; that the experience was behind me; that if I didn't talk about it, nothing was wrong. My therapist self knew that nothing was right; and everything was wrong.

But the part of me that was not a therapist, that didn't know anything about therapy, had developed a hard, distant edge to her exterior. Nobody could reach down into my insides, not any more. The pain that lived there was too great. I was hiding.

But what was I hiding? I didn't know. It would have to wait.

I began travelling again. I was already committed to a little time in India and six months in Africa. But it was different now. I was afraid to travel alone. I had to be with people, even those people I didn't like or enjoy. I had always been able to be alone rather than with people I did not enjoy. Not anymore. Now I found myself smiling sickly and acting interested in people I clearly didn't enjoy.

Since I was making London my base for further travels I was in and out of that city. While there I stayed with my friend, the friend who had been my roommate during that fateful weekend. I hadn't even told her.

I kept in touch with the Llandudno police, as I tried to find out when the trial would be held. I found myself feeling complacent about the fact that my rapist was still in custody.

Finally, one day one of the arms of the justice system called me at my friend's home. She took the message. I could no longer get away with not talking about it. She deserved some kind of explanation about the contents of that message.

For two hours I talked to her. I cried. My body shook. I alternately raged and wept. For two hours she listened, asked questions, raged, and wept. When I was through, I was spent; but I had talked about it. When I was through, I knew I had been heard, understood, and met at the very deepest primitive level of being a woman - at the level that only women know, at the level of my very soul. She knew. I didn't have to tell her. She knew. And I knew she knew. It is something women know.

All women know. We can't help but know. We are steeped in it from childhood on. But we pretend. We pretend to be all right, just as I pretended that I was no different with men than I had been before. Just as I pretended I still trusted women. Just as I pretended not to know what I knew I knew.

Now I could quit pretending. I had spoken the unspeakable, and my friend had heard me. But now there was no place to hide my rage and my pain. I had spoken and been heard. My rage and pain were now my woman's legacy. I could no longer pretend it was not. This was the gift my friend had given me. She had listened to me speak the truth and understood. She spoke the truth back to me in a way I could understand. I will be forever grateful for the way she touched me in my soul, the way she held me, the way she took care of me, the way she helped me to speak. I was not yet ready to tell the world; but now I knew my woman's legacy.

My life continued to be eventful. I traveled in India, my raw self barely able to tolerate the pain of what I saw. I traveled in Africa, raging at the status of women imprisoned behind their shrouds or imprisoned within purchased marriages, doing 95% of the work and gaining the privilege of raising all of the stair-step children. But at least I could feel again. Little by little I was learning to feel again. I was not quite ready to trust, but at least I was feeling again. I did not stay as far behind my edge of hardness as before.

When I was finished with my travels I returned home to the turmoil of financial disaster, and the need to bend my mind to feeding, clothing and sheltering myself in something other than a tent. Once home I found the hand of the justice system was still interfering with my determination not to talk. Messages left at my numerous temporary homes caused questions that I needed to explain. I trusted a few more people with my story. Some understood what was in my soul - some did not. I must have been getting stronger, because when I encountered those who did not understand I was not destroyed as I had feared.

It was almost fourteen months from the date of the rape when the case was brought to trial in the Welsh city of Chester. The Crown flew me back to England, then transported me to Chester to testify. By spending all of those hours in the plane, I had plenty of time to think. I had plenty of time to realize that this was going to be a difficult time for me, but the one thing I was absolutely clear about was that I was doing the right thing. What I learned from going through the trial was that I knew nothing about the destruction of one's soul until I had experienced my devastation at the hands of the defense barrister.

When the trial was over, I picked up the pieces of what I had left of myself and came home once more. Now I knew what I had to do. My silence was over. Now two men had raped me, the second worse than the first. I had to speak. I had to let people know. I had to give up my safety. My determination was different now. Before, I had been determined to do whatever I needed to do to put David Forshile behind bars. Now, I was determined to do whatever I needed to do to save other women from what I had been through. My shell had to crumble. I had to let go of my fear. I had to say what I knew.

I began by doing what I should have done a year earlier. I made an appointment for a therapy session. I wasn't in that room more than a few minutes when "I was shredding Kleenexes into bits; tinier and tinier bits. Kleenexes, soaked with my tears and my snot. I was standing . . . ."

Now I know what I am capable of. Now I know what is in my soul. And now I must speak what I know.

The Trial

The following pages are an exact transcript of the trial of Regina vs. David Forshile held in the Crown Court of Mold, Wales before His Honor Judge David, Q.C. on September 22nd and 23rd, 1986. The transcript was taken from public records and transcribed by Lee and Nightingale Ltd. of Liverpool, England. I have added a description of the "Cast of Characters" along with observational comments.

The Trial of David Forshile

Cast of Characters

COMPLAINANT - Audrey Savage Ph.D.: At the time of the trial I was fifty-four years old, and on sabbatical leave from my private practice as a Gestalt Psychotherapist in Indianapolis, Indiana, U.S.A. I had left my practice two years prior to this incident to travel and to write. During the first year of my sabbatical I traveled the United States; the second year I spent writing a novel in my lake cabin in Wisconsin; and I started my third year by living for three months in London and traveling around the British Isles.

I would describe myself as energetic, excited about life, easy going, likable, and with a strong sense of myself. I had never had a problem being alone and had traveled much of the United States, and parts of Mexico and Canada with only my dog for a companion. I was a respected Psychotherapist in the Indianapolis area and had a flourishing practice. I had the skills of a good psychotherapist -- knowing myself very well, knowing another person quickly and of being able to use those two pieces of knowledge to work well with another person's psychological issues. I am 5' 7'' tall, weighed about 150 pounds at that time, have short, curly brown hair and blue eyes. People told me I neither looked nor acted my fifty-four years. Most people guessed that I was in my early forties.

As a child I was extremely quiet, shy actually. I was shy to the point of it being painful. My mother taught me to be a good girl, not to express any feelings, to respect the authority of men and to be generally inadequate in my social skills. She also taught me to be independent, to work hard and to know how to handle money. Those skills of independence and hard work took me a long way in both my education and in facing up to my own psychological issues and inadequacies -- plentiful as they were, especially in my earlier years.

Since as a child I hadn't been allowed to express my feelings, I grew up sexually repressed. It wasn't until my early forties that I learned to experience the beauty of a loving and sexual union between a man and a woman. I had never known harshness or force in my sexual relationships; but I also didn't realize the joy of the tenderness, the sensual delight in both the giving and the receiving and the wonder of the total freedom of my body. By the time of this incident I knew what sexual "intercourse" was all about.

SOLICITOR FOR THE PROSECUTION - Cheryl Davies: A young woman, about twenty-seven or twenty-eight with short, sandy-colored hair worn close to her head. She had pleasant features and smiled frequently. She was slim, about 5' 6" tall. She had pleasant, friendly energy, talked easily, and moved in and out of conversations with facility. She was chosen by the police to represent them in the trial and she picked the barrister who would represent me. I liked her. She related with me easily, appearing in the witness room off and on to see if I was all right and to keep me informed of how things were proceeding in the court room. I had had no prior contact with her up to the day of the trial and on that day she asked me no questions.

BARRISTER FOR THE PROSECUTION - Richard Fairley: A tall, slim, man in his mid- or late - thirties with dark hair cut square to his face and flat on the sides. He had a long nose, dark hollow eyes and thick lips. His eyes tended to penetrate wherever he looked, and his eyebrows remained upraised most of the time. His voice was slightly nasal and very deep. When he spoke, he spoke with great authority and intelligence, but no warmth. It was as if everything he said was of utmost importance and there were to be no wasted words, neither by him nor by any of the witnesses. I felt virtually no connection with him at any time. I got the sense that he was just doing his job, was very interested in the adversarial aspect of the trial, but could have cared less about me or my well-being.

During the trial I tried to imagine him as a child. What I imagined was a child who was allowed to play very little, learned early from a very imposing father that the intellectual course was the only one, and never developed a sense of humor. The rule in his house would have been that laughing would be a waste of time, and probably beneath him.

During the trial he wore the black robe common to barristers in England, and the white curly wig. He was inclined to push the robe aside as he spoke, putting both thumbs in his pants pockets and rocking back and forth.

DEFENSE SOLICITOR - Meirion Jones: A young man, probably in his late twenties, with a lot of unruly dark hair and a pleasant heart-shaped face. His face seemed untainted, as yet, by the tribulations of his work in the law. He seemed to be very busy during the trial, moving from place to place with great determination and goal orientation. I had the feeling that he was trying very hard to please his barrister **and** was very dedicated to his work. I learned that his work as a solicitor earned him in the area of 9,000 pounds per year, much less than he would earn if working in a firm. He had to be dedicated . . . or angling for barrister himself.

DEFENSE BARRISTER - Trevor Halbert: This man turned out to be more my enemy than the man who raped me, the defendant at this trial. In describing him I will try to be fair, but it will be difficult. He was tall, probably around six feet, and slim. His hair was straight, very blond and about ear-length. I would say that his face was beautiful , but hardening around the edges as though his work, and especially this kind of trial, was taking its toll on him. As I looked at him I kept thinking about a book by Oscar Wilde titled *The Portrait of Dorian Grey*. In this story a prominent and rich Englishman makes a pact with a beautiful picture of himself painted during the prime and magnificence of his youth. The young man implores the picture to take on the physical aspects of his aging and depravity while his own body will remain as youthful and as beautiful as the picture is now. Thus, he can live as corrupt and depraved a life as he chooses without it ever showing.

I kept having this wicked thought as I watched Mr. Halbert during the trial. I kept thinking that he had his own beautiful and youthful picture sitting in his living room. He, however, had not yet made his pact with the picture that would keep his behavior and intentions from showing on his face and in his body. It seemed to me that he had better hurry lest the kind of cruelty he was showing to me, and probably to other women in my position, began to be evident on his face.

Mr. Halbert wore glasses while questioning his witnesses; and also wore the black robe and white wig common for the English barrister. When I faced him from the witness stand in full formal legal attire, he looked like quite a large man. Later, when I saw him in the lunch room without his robe and wig, I discovered that he was actually quite small.

He had an incredible ability in his use of his voice. He was especially good at modifying his tone to produce his desired effect. For instance, his voice was soft and deferential while talking to the judge, but it changed to strained and harsh when he was questioning witnesses. He was absolutely frightening in his ability to destroy the evidence presented by my barrister. His voice would take on a superior tone. Then he would make statements diametrically opposed to those brought out by the prosecution. His superior tone served the purpose of giving the impression that anybody who would believe anything other than the statement **he** had just made was absolutely stupid at best or out of their minds at worst. He used this tone of voice to attempt to destroy the credibility of my testimony. With it he attempted to diminish me to a woman who would want and ask for sex with a crazy, brutal vagrant who appeared in my life while I was trying to camp peacefully by the sea. He made statement after statement indicting me not only as a woman who consented to sex, but who was actually the aggressor. As I denied statement after statement, he simply went on with another absurd and incorrect statement, using his superior tone to indicate to all listeners the untruth of my version.

All of this made me feel diminished, confused, defensive, and especially angry. It was very difficult to keep my head clear in the face of this onslaught. My emotions, already high after telling my ugly story, were thrown into disarray. It wouldn't have taken much more to cause my emotions to get out of control. If I had slipped even slightly he would have taken that as an opportunity to pounce on my words. If there had been **anything** in my earlier testimony where I was unsure, where I was not totally connected to myself, where I had in the slightest stretched the truth, he would have used that like a knife to open up a gaping wound in my truth. Then he would have twisted the knife in the wound until I was really unsure of myself or stopped knowing what the truth really was. He would use his superior tone to say to the jury, "See, she was a liar all along."

He was **very** good at what he did to me. He was a very clever man. He was a destroyer, using the process of diminishing to win. And I suspect he wins . . . a lot.

In my imagination I see him as a child who learned to win at most anything he tried. I see him early in his life developing that superior tone and that diminishing way . . . insuring his ability to win. I see his father diminishing him . . . teaching him that diminishing way.

But Dorian Grey may get him yet . . . .

JUDGE - His Honor Judge Robin David: An older man, perhaps in his mid- to late - fifties, about 5' 10'' tall with a face that could quickly alternate between stern and kind. I often felt warmth from him and periodically was able to laugh at his humor. In spite of his warmth and humor the police said that he had a reputation for being stern. My impression of this sternness was more along the line of "competent." He spoke several times during the trial about being fair. Fair he was.

He also wore the white curly wig and the black robe of the English legal profession; but his robe was decorated with red and purple bands running across his shoulders and tied at the waist. He listened attentively to everything that was said and took copious notes. When he was unsure of some of the testimony, he stopped the proceedings to question the witness. I had a sense of his ability to pick out the absolute essence of anyone's testimony, even making sense out of the confusion and craziness of the words of the defendant. With great skill he used all of this information in his charge to the jury.

His skill was clear to me when I heard that charge to the jury. During that part of the trial I was an absolute basket-case. I had just finished listening to the summation by the defense barrister where he completely destroyed my integrity, my self-esteem, and anything else he could get at. Even in this state of my emotions, I heard Judge David's fairness and knew that he believed the truth that I had been raped.

As I imagined Judge David as a child I saw him with a very stern father and a wonderful kind mother. I saw both of them loving him and treating him with as much fairness as parents can possibly treat a child. Either that or he was born under the sign of Libra.

DEFENDANT - David Forshile: When I met the defendant (if met is the proper word) he was thin, approximately 100 pounds, with muscular shoulders, unkempt, short sandy hair and a stubble of a beard. He was wearing a black sweater with holes in the sleeves, greenish, gray heavy broadcloth pants, baggy and shabby, canvas shoes with heavy strings used as laces, and was carrying two plastic bags over his shoulders. He was agitated, violent, and talked in a way that I could only describe as "bizarre." As a therapist I listened to his crazy conversation and recognized that his words did not connect with much of anything, a process I would call disassociation. His imaginings were of a very violent nature, a process I would call projection. In other words his psychological process was to attribute his angry and violent inner thoughts to someone or something else, i.e., "Seventeen Welshmen were coming out of the hills to hurt me." As a projection it was **his** thought to hurt me. If frustrated (as I so sadly learned) he projected those violent feelings and thoughts out onto whomever was in his immediate environment.

He told me he was from Liverpool, where his family had turned him out. He was living as a street scavenger and had been living this way for at least six years. He picked up cigarette butts from the street and smoked them, and ate stolen kidney pies that he stowed in his plastic bags.

He talked constantly, mostly about how violent he could be. Specifically, he talked about how he could be more violent than anyone else, and in that way he would always win. In the process of his ramblings he told me that he had ridden out to the park with a woman "whom he thought he might have been able to get some money off of," but got out of the car near my camping spot instead, "got lucky and met me." **He** was certainly the only lucky one in that meeting.

When David appeared at the trial he was clean, his hair was cut neatly, parted and combed, and he was wearing a suit. He had put on weight and looked healthy. He was sitting in the defendant's box at the rear of the court room, under guard. It was easy for me to see him during the whole of the trial. There was almost no facial expression at any time during the various testimony. He looked as though he were simply "out of it." I felt very little for him during that time; little hatred, and certainly no compassion. My attention was riveted to the proceedings in the front of the room.

In thinking about David as a child, I could imagine him living in a poor family, perhaps rather large, where violence was a way of life. In my more compassionate moments I could see him as a sensitive child, unable to comprehend or tolerate the family violence. On the other hand I could also see him as a totally unmanageable child whom neither of his parents could handle. In either case, his response was to become more and more frustrated, violent, and crazy.

The Policemen who handled the arrest and testimony at the trial

POLICEMAN NO.1 - Collin Edwards, Head of the Criminal Investigating Department in Llandudno: Tall, with thinning dark hair and firm-looking, clear eyes. My impression was of a very orderly man. His consideration of my welfare was obvious during the whole procedure. He consistently kept my friend from London informed of events as they progressed. He also picked us up at our motel and brought us to and from the trial.

POLICEMAN NO. 2 - Eifion Jones: He was about 5' 11'' with short, slightly greying hair, a heart-shaped face and warm eyes. He was very friendly, talked with me whenever he had a chance and asked a lot of interested questions. He seemed concerned about how I felt throughout the trial. He did seem a bit uncomfortable on the witness stand.

POLICEMAN NO. 3 - Warwick Gabbetis: Tall, muscular and well-built with balding curly hair. He was what I would call handsome. His eyes were a little red and tired, and he looked as though he worked hard. He was very straightforward in his conversation, but reserved. He talked to me about America, of which he knew a little, but he didn't seem to know quite what to make of me. I had a sense that he felt pride in himself for having caught the defendant so quickly.

SOCIAL WORKER - Terrence James: A rather thin, small man with disheveled brown hair. One of his legs was stiff which made it hard for him to get around. While the prosecution witnesses sat in the waiting room, he sat in the corner, very quietly, listening intently to our conversation. When he talked with us, he talked with energy and interest, but when he got on the witness stand he seemed to lose much of his energy as though **he** were insignificant in comparison to the giants of the court.

WITNESS - Anna Marie Garden: A tall, slim, dark-haired woman in her late twenties. Very pretty and full of energy. She was well educated and professionally competent. Originally from New Zealand, she had been living in the United Kingdom for approximately seven years. During that time she had spent a year or so studying in the United States. Following the rape, she was the first person to hear my story. We were paired for an exercise during the workshop I attended. I poured the whole story out to her, and she was wonderful. She understood what I was going through because she had been raped several years earlier.

WITNESS - Caroline Navarro: Well-known Tarot card reader, teacher, and healer. She was the leader of the workshop I attended in Romsey. Small, slim, with light-brown hair and blue eyes. She was a quiet, reserved woman, slightly over thirty, sensitive and knowledgeable, but not overly-assertive in her demeanor. I told her my story at the suggestion of Anna Marie. It was Caroline who gave me the "Rescue Remedy," the natural product for people in shock, that felt as if it saved my life the afternoon after the rape.

WITNESS - Chandra Ghosh: Psychiatrist who worked in the maximum-security hospital where the defendant had been taken in March in preparation for his trial in September. She was a native of India and wore the silk sari worn by women of that country. She was very small, perhaps not even five feet, with long black hair worn in a bun at the back of her head. She seemed young for having achieved so much. She spoke softly, very clearly, and with great authority. She was very knowledgeable in her field.

REPORTER - Mr. Dee: He seemed to be everywhere. When I learned that he was a reporter I understood the reason for all of the activity. He had a round face, an abundance of curly hair, a reddish beard and large eyes. He was about 5' 10'' tall -- certainly not a large man, but large in his activities. My impression was that he was interested in all of the goings-on, but not devious.

One of his interests was how I felt about the trial. After my testimony on the first day, while making an appointment to interview me, he asked how it felt to come all the way from America to testify. This question gave me the opportunity to talk about how important the trial was to me, essentially to expound on my beliefs to the press. I told him that, as a therapist, I worked with many women who had been raped. I knew the effect on them, the often life-long effect, and I was not about to allow anybody to rape **me** without taking the consequences. At least **I** was not going to be the reason justice was not rendered.

FRIEND - Sheryle Geen: She was, for me, the most important person at the trial. She became my friend at the workshop in Romsey and has remained so ever since, to the point of offering me her home when I was visiting London. At various times from my arrival in London for the trial until I left again for America she was a bit of everything to me. She played adversary in preparing me for the trial; she supported me in all of my emotions ranging from total chaos to abject rage; she was my crying towel; and she took me out and got me drunk when that was the only thing that would ease my pain. She is approximately forty, a large and very powerful woman with a wonderful energy and sense of humor. She has dark, short-cropped hair and a face that is full of expression and honesty. Without her I'm afraid they would have been taking **me** to the maximum security hospital along with the defendant.

JURY - As they sat from left to right in the front row and left to right in the back row.
1. Man somewhere between forty-eight and fifty-three with a good bit of grey-ing hair, which would have been a naturally light color had it not been grey. He had a reddish complexion and freckles. He looked like a moderately successful business man, but did not seem particularly confident.

2. Young man between twenty-five and twenty-eight, very clean-cut looking with a pointed face, mustache and dark hair. He looked like the nice type.

3. Woman in her early thirties, with dark, well- coiffed hair, dark eyes and an intense look. She followed the case with great interest, seemed to have some sense of humor and would laugh at the judge's funnier statements. I remember being drawn to her as I told the story of my rape. She was the only member of the jury from whom I felt compassion. However, later in my testimony, I felt this compassion withdrawn. She was a very neat woman, and my sense of her was that she would not want anything dirty to touch her.

4. A large man with receding dark hair, probably around forty. He had a round, impassive-looking face, with a weak, receding chin. He was wearing heavy brown

sports clothes and a tie. He struck me as a brawling hollow man, who might believe that there were seventeen Welshmen coming down from the hills to get me.

5. This man had a rounder face than the man next to him and more of a receding hairline. He had lots of hair at the back and was totally bald in the front. I did not note his age, but from the state of his hair I would say late thirties. He struck me as having a good bit of confidence in himself. I envisioned him as a man who might like to booze it up a bit with the boys at the bar.

6. This man was tall, thin and fair-haired and wore glasses. He had a long face. He seemed to be in his forties. He struck me as the type of man who was probably well-looked after by someone, someplace. I had a sense of him as a weak man in his own right, a man who usually went along with the crowd.

7. A tall man, 6' 1'' or so, with short dark hair which fell into his eyes with impunity, and an especially long nose. He wore a blue suit and dark tie. His eyes had a vacant look as though he were out of his element in these proceedings.

8. Young woman in her early twenties. Round face, short brown bobbed hair, a little chubby, with clear eyes and a small amount of becoming makeup. My impression of her was that she was very immature and had little experience which would prepare her for the seriousness of a case such as this.

9. Another young woman in her early twenties. She had permed curly hair, a little longer than the woman who sat next to her. It was obvious to me that she was bored with the proceedings. I observed her yawn periodically. My impression was that she wanted to be out having fun, not sitting in this boring courtroom.

10. A woman with dark hair, around twenty-five or twenty-six. I had a sense of her intelligence as she followed the case. She seemed as though she were more than a homemaker, most likely a very efficient secretary. She was elected foreman, and my sense was that she was a good choice. In giving the verdict she spoke clearly, although not loudly; loud enough that I could hear across the room.

11. A man somewhere between twenty-eight and thirty-two with dark hair. He was big as well as tall. His body was strong and bony. My sense of him was that he played sports very well, but now was locked into a clerk type job and felt harried.

12. A man in his mid-forties, impeccably dressed, down to the cuff links in his shirt. He had fair, greying hair and was thin. He appeared to be the office type.

As I looked at the jury during the trial I had the sense that they were bland. They appeared to follow the case well, listening attentively, but I suspected they had little compassion for me. The only time I experienced their compassion was during my description of the rape itself. Even then their compassion was fleeting. With a sinking heart I realized that a conviction of rape in this trial would probably rest on the women, and the women seemed singularly naive, without the maturity it would take to understand what rape was all about. Sheryle worried about their capacity, I hoped beyond reason, and Anna Marie said she didn't see much maturity or depth in them.

Description of the Courtroom

The court was in a rather new and modern building in the town of Mold, just outside of Chester, England. Mold, itself, is in Wales. Sheryle and I were driven from our motel to the court and back each day by one of the policemen. When we entered the building we were shown to a small room off a corridor to the right. This was the room for witnesses for the prosecution. I was nervous, to say the least, knowing I would be the first witness. When I walked into the room I was surprised to see Anna Marie and Caroline, not knowing that they had been subpoenaed to testify. I'm sure they would have been happier spending the day somewhere else, but I was grateful to see two friendly faces. There were the four of us in the room plus an unknown man whom, we later learned, was Mr. James, the social worker. He seemed very interested in our conversation, but didn't participate. A woman, whom I later learned was the solicitor for the prosecution, dropped in and out of the room and kept us informed of what was happening in the courtroom. She told us that our case would be delayed for a short time because the defendant was going to be tried on another case before ours began. She thought this case would take no longer than fifteen minutes. As it turned out a decision was made to try this case after mine was finished. Therefore we proceeded.

I was led into the courtroom and given a seat on a hard, wooden, brown bench on the right-hand side facing the center. Where I sat, there were two rows of these tiered benches, apparently for seating witnesses. I looked carefully around the room and found that it was different from what I knew of American courts.

Each member of the court had a specific position in the downstairs area, while all visitors were in a small gallery upstairs. There was no center aisle, but instead there were two aisles, one on each side of the central area. In the front was the judge's bench, flanked on both sides by a brown wooden table, one for each clerk. The witness stand, also of brown wood, was next to the clerk's table on the right. There was a microphone attatched to the witness stand. In front of the judge's bench were three sets of long brown tables. At the first set of tables were the two barristers, both dressed in black robes and grey wigs. At the table behind were the two solicitors. At the table behind that were the police dressed in street clothing. Behind the police was an area within a short wall where the defendant sat surrounded by three guards. To the right of the defendant's area was a table for the psychiatrist, and further to the right, a table for the press.

My position was almost opposite the area where the defendant stood and behind the three tables containing the barristers, etc. Directly across from me and on the left side of the courtroom were two more sets of benches. These were separated by a door. These also faced the center of the court. The jurors were seated in those benches and toward the front of the room closest to the judge. Exactly opposite me was the other set of benches, and these were used for the original eighteen members of the possible jury. Prior to the trial, twelve of these eighteen were chosen by lot to make up the final jury. There was a Bailiff at each door and one near the witness stand.

The court was remarkably quiet considering the number of people in attendance. All participants seemed to be following some formal set of rules regarding their courtroom conduct. There was little of the hustle and bustle I had expected.

The Case for the Prosecution
(Here begins the authentic transcript)

Mr. Fairley: I call Mrs. Savage.

Audrey Savage is sworn

Examination by Mr. Fairley

Fairley: Is your full name Audrey Savage?

Savage: That is correct.

Fairley: I believe you are, in fact, a married lady, a Doctor of Philosophy and you are by qualification a Psycho-therapist?

Savage: Yes.

Fairley: And your address is Guilford Avenue, Indianapolis, Indiana?

Savage: Yes.

Fairley: You came on holiday to the United Kingdom last year, and in July, I believe you were in the South of England where you met up with other persons at a course in Astrology, is that so?

Savage: (This question confused me. I was not in a course for Astrology, but was learning about reading the Tarot. I did not take this course until after the incident.) Are you talking about the weekend I spent in Romsey?

Fairley: Before coming to North Wales did you meet some people?

Judge David: Does it matter?

Fairley: No, it may not matter. Is it right that you came up to North Wales in the week that ended on the 26th of July, 1985?

Savage: I think it was the 26th. It was a Friday.

Fairley: Were you on your own when you came up to North Wales?

Savage: Yes I was.

Fairley: Did you have with you a tent, and were you going to camp?

Savage: Yes.

Fairley: By the evening of Thursday, is it right, that you had got to the Great Orme at Llandudno (pronounced Clan-did-no)?

Savage: Yes.

Fairley: That is Thursday, the 25th of July.

Savage: Yes.

Fairley: And had you by that evening set up your tent, and in fact were outside it at about 9:30 p.m. reading, overlooking the sea?

Savage: That is correct.

Fairley: Would you just look at the photographs, and would you indicate on Photograph 6, and the others, where it was that you had your tent pitched?

Savage: Do you want me to look at all the photographs?

Fairley: Yes.

Savage: That looks like where I walked down.

Fairley: You went through that wall?

Savage: Yes, I walked down toward the sea.

Fairley: We can see in Photograph 6 the lighthouse station in the far distance about three hundred yards away?

Savage: Yes, I recognize that.

Fairley: Those rocks there, do they ring any bells with you?

Savage: Yes, I believe it was the close rock on which I was sitting. I remember the smaller rock next to it.

Fairley: At that time, 9:30 p.m. when you were reading there, did you hear a voice coming from above you?

Savage: Yes, I did.

Fairley: What did the voice say?

Savage: He was telling me that I shouldn't camp there, that it was dangerous. I don't know what he said was the reason why I shouldn't camp there, he was just telling me I shouldn't camp there.

Fairley: Did he come down to you?

Savage: Not immediately, but he did later. I probably wouldn't have responded to a man talking to me in that manner, but it had occurred to me that it might be against the law to camp in that area. I didn't know the laws. When I looked up to see who was talking I noticed that he was wearing something dark. I thought he might be a policeman telling me I couldn't camp in that area.

Fairley: And he came down.

Savage: Yes.

Fairley: First of all let us deal with his appearance. Was his face bearded or not?

Savage: As I remember he had a stubble. It was getting dark and I couldn't see him very clearly at that point. I saw him in the morning but not that evening.

Fairley: Was he carrying anything?

Savage: Yes, he had two bags. I thought they were plastic. They were rather large, and he carried them over his shoulders. There was some straw sticking out of them.

Fairley: Did he tell you what he was going to do?

Savage: He said he was warning me about some Welshmen who had been drinking and who would come down from the hills and hurt me, and he said that he would stay near my tent to protect me. I told him I didn't want him to stay near my tent. I didn't feel I was in any danger from any Welshmen that would come down from the hills, and I didn't want him to stay.

Fairley: Was this repeated or was it just the once?

Savage: I repeated it several times.

Fairley: After he had said he was going to stay, what did you say?

Savage: I said if he didn't leave me alone I was going to pack up. I started toward my tent to put my things together. I had every intention of leaving unless he left. Then he asked me if I had any water. I said I did, then I said, "If I give you some water will you go away?" and he said he would. I gave him some of my water and he drank it. I didn't have very much. He drank some of it and gave it back to me and then he left.

Fairley: At that stage had anything been said about names?

Savage: It was just as he was leaving. I believe he asked me my name , and I was angry with him and I was very irritated, and I said, "My name is Mary."

Fairley: But in fact your name is Audrey?

Savage: Yes.

Fairley: Did he tell you his name?

Savage: Yes, he said his name was David.

Fairley: And he left?

Savage: Yes, I saw him go away. I watched him as he walked back up to the road, and he went out of my sight.

Fairley: What did you decide to do then?

Savage: I was very frightened. I was wondering whether I was really in any danger from him or whether I wasn't. I went to my tent. I hid the money I had in the end of my sleeping bag, and I sort of waited to see if he would come back. I waited quite a while and debated whether to pack up at that point and leave.

Fairley: But you didn't?

Savage: No. I thought I might be able to get my backpack packed and get away without him seeing me, but I didn't think I would be able to get my tent down. I was worried about loosing my gear. I didn't have very much with me.

Fairley: And so you went into your tent and closed it?

Savage: Yes.

Fairley: In that tent a little later, you became aware of what?

Savage: Footsteps.

Fairley: What happened?

Savage: The footsteps were walking around outside the tent, and I heard him, and I had a horrid feeling - I knew he was back.

Fairley: And the next thing that happened?

Savage: He was calling "Mary". As I remember I didn't say anything right away. I didn't respond at all, hoping maybe that he would think I wasn't in the tent. He came up to the door of the tent and tried to open it. It was a very small tent, a tent for one person. I didn't want him to come into the tent because there was nowhere to get out, no freedom.

Fairley: So you didn't open it?

Savage: He started to open it, and then I finally opened it myself. I felt I would be safer outside.

Fairley: Was it light or dusk at this time?

Savage: It was dark by then. It had been getting dark when I **first** saw him. It was about ten o'clock by then and it was dark.

Fairley: Before he returned, did you check anything, in the sense of having anything to protect yourself?

Savage: Yes, I did. I had a spray can. I am not sure what is in it, but we use it in America to protect ourselves. I realize now that it is illegal here, but I did have it with me, and for many years before I had been around the States and had carried it with me and never used it, so before I went into the tent I checked it to see if it was working and it didn't work.

Fairley: You had gotten into your tent prior to his return?

Savage: Yes.

Fairley: Had you undressed?

Savage: No, I didn't undress.

Fairley: Having gotten out of the tent, what then happened?

Savage: Some of the early part is a little vague, but I remember being very frightened. I came out of the tent, and I was standing here, and he was standing opposite me. I was facing the sea and he was facing the road. I remember that. How much conversation passed between us I don't know, but I remember I was telling him not to do it. "Please don't do this," I said. I don't remember whether he had threatened me or told me to take off my clothes. I don't remember specifically, later I did, but at that time I didn't, but I remember trying to stop him, telling him not to do whatever it was he was planning to do, because I was pretty sure I was going to be raped, and he hit me. He was very rapid, very quick. I didn't see it coming. I couldn't get out of the way.

Fairley: Where did he hit you?

Savage: He hit me on the face. It was three times he hit me, like that.

Fairley: You have indicated slaps?

Savage: I think that is what it was. I know I felt my lip was swollen after that, and the next day I realized I had a tremendous black eye. The left eye was black, and at that point I realized I was dealing with somebody who could be very brutal. And I just said inside myself that there was no way I could fight this man any more. I had better give in or I was going to be perhaps brutalized even worse, so I did what I had to do. I gave in.

And after he hit me he was tearing at my clothes, trying to get them off. I said "Are you going to rape me?" I think I said it then. I may have said it before he hit me. I don't remember for sure. I said "I'll take them off." Then I removed them myself. I didn't want him to be tearing at my clothes or to be that physically close to me. I had a pair of jeans and underpants on, and I did take them off. He told me to lay down, and I did. And if you look at the photographs you can see there is a lot of thistles and I was being scratched. I asked him if I could get a pad which I usually sleep on, and I pulled it out of the tent. He pushed my legs open and I was lying on the ground.

Fairley: Was he undressed?

Savage: Yes. He took off his pants. He had a shirt on, as I did. I had a sweater on and a shirt, and he had his shirt on. I guess it was still the black sweater he had been wearing before.

Fairley: He pushed your legs apart?

Savage: Yes. He stood over me. I remember seeing him standing there. He pushed my legs apart and came on top of me and . . . and then . . . and then he entered me. *I stopped talking here, because I couldn't any more. I had been close to tears off and on, and at this point I didn't think I could contain them any longer. I stopped talking until I could bring myself back under control.*

Judge David: Would you like a drink of water? Someone bring Dr. Savage a drink of water.

Savage: *After a short drink...because that was **not exactly** what I needed at the time.* I just lay there, I didn't do anything, and he thrust, he . . .he . . . moved into me . . . about . . . about three or four times. It was mercifully quick. He ejaculated, and then he . . . he rolled away.

Fairley: Did he then say anything about staying or leaving?

Savage: He wanted to get into the tent with me, so I knew he was intending to stay. He wasn't going to let me go. I didn't want him to be in the tent with me because it was so small, just a tiny tent, and I decided that the best thing to do would be to talk to him so that he would stay outside the tent. I said "Let's just sit here and talk." I didn't know what would happen to me if I got inside the tent with him. *At this point the worst had already happened, but what I didn't want was any more of it. I rationally decided to use my therapeutic skills to keep myself out of any more danger. I decided to try to talk to him, to keep him calm, to try to be a human being with him in order to keep myself safe.*

So we sat outside for quite a long time, at least an hour I'm sure, and by this time he was calmer. He had been very agitated before that. As long as he stayed calm I was less afraid of him.

Eventually he insisted I go into the tent. He was getting agitated again, and I was very frightened he would hit me again. The time we had been sitting outside he had been talking about my ribs being broken. He wasn't talking about him breaking my ribs, but I had the sense that if I didn't do exactly what he wanted he would break them, and I knew he would break them because I could feel my lip was swollen. *As a therapist I was sure I was listening to a projection, a process I knew plenty about. Projections put outside what goes on inside. He was talking about broken ribs but my sense was that he was talking about breaking mine if I didn't do exactly what he wanted.* So I got into the tent. As I started to get in he pushed me the rest of the way.

Judge David: And you were afraid if you didn't do what he said your ribs would be broken.

Savage: Yes. He didn't make it as a threat, but it felt like one to me.

Fairley: And in the tent there was a further act of intercourse.

Savage: Yes. He tried it a second time, he entered me and thrust quite a bit, but I don't think he was able to accomplish anything, and he accused me of not being co-operative, and I said, "It is very hard to be co-operative when you are being raped."

Fairley: What happened to your right arm?

Savage: I was laying on the left side of the tent, and he was towards the door, and he was on top of me, sort of half on top of me, I was laying on top of my sleeping bag, and he took my right arm and put it around him, so in a sense I was holding him, and he put his arms around my back and clasped me to him so that we were locked together there for the rest of the night.

Fairley: And that is what happened, you were there for the rest of the night?

Savage: Yes, I was, and I didn't sleep.

Fairley: What about him?

Savage: He slept. I was unable to. I had a bus ticket to go to London the next day, I was really afraid he wasn't going to let me go so I could catch my bus.

Fairley: Had you got some bus schedule with you?

Savage: Yes, I had my ticket and I had a schedule with me.

Fairley: Was there anything written on that schedule at some stage?

Savage: Yes, he wrote on it.

Fairley: When?

Savage: After I got to the bus depot. When we got to the bus depot he wrote his name on the schedule.

Fairley: At about five o'clock in the morning you got up, you asked if you could get out of the tent?

Savage: Yes, I had to go to the bathroom very badly. Up to that point I was afraid to move, I was afraid he might hurt me again, and I had to go to the bathroom. It was getting light then so I thought it was time to start towards town if I was going to get my bus, and I knew I had a job to do to get him to let me go.

Fairley: At that stage did you tell him what you were intending to do?

Savage: Yes, I had told him even earlier that I had a bus to catch. I told him I had to catch a bus to London, and I was going back to America. My daughter was getting married, and I very much needed to catch that bus.

Fairley: What did he say to you?

Savage: He told me I was going to be in great danger if I walked to the bus from where I was. I knew he was trying to talk me out of it. He had been telling me I was in danger before. I figured the only way to get to that bus was to take him with me, so I said, "If you want to protect me between here and the bus why don't you walk with me?"

Fairley: You told him you were going back to America?

Savage: Yes, I told him I was an American. There was a lot of crazy conversation at that time.

Fairley: You packed up the tent, and by close on six o'clock you were walking back to Llandudno?

Savage: Yes.

Fairley: Which took you about three-quarters of an hour?

Savage: Yes, into the town.

Fairley: As you went into the town did you see any police officers or anybody whom you could have sought help from?

Savage: Yes. Can I tell you about something that happened before that? We passed a bathroom on the way in and again I had to go to the toilet. I asked him if it would be all right if I went to the toilet, and he said, "Yes, and while you are there wash your face." I didn't think about having been struck the night before and about there being dirt on my face, but I didn't wash. I just went in and did my business and came out. And he said, "You didn't wash your face, get a cloth and wipe it off." I did that. *He was totally in charge at this point. I was doing whatever he wanted, and asking permission all the way. He had taken all power away from me and I was willing to let him have it. I wasn't going to risk getting him agitated again and not getting on that bus. Nothing was going to keep me from getting on that bus. I was obsessed with getting on that bus.*

When I was back in London I looked at my face and I had dirt all over and I realized I had a black eye. He apparently saw that and was trying to get me to wash it off. He wanted me to wash off evidence of the beating.

Fairley: Did you see a police officer in the town?

Savage: When we were walking through the town we did pass two bobbies, and at the time I passed them I thought, "Should I yell out and tell them I was being kept by this man"? And I made a decision not to do that. All I wanted to do was to get away from him. I felt so awful. My feeling was I had to get free of him. So I made a conscious decision not to say anything, and I was conscious we were far enough away for him to hurt me again, and I was very afraid of that.

Fairley: You get to the bus station. You had to wait for your bus. During that interval of time did he make some demand of you?

Savage: Yes, he asked me for money.

Fairley: Did you give him some money?

Savage: Yes, I gave him five pounds.

Fairley: Now, about his writing something on your bus schedule, was that done then?

Savage: Yes. We were sitting waiting for the bus, and he wrote his name on the schedule.

Fairley: That is exhibit 1. Is that the document to which you refer?

Savage: Yes.

Fairley: What is written there?

Savage: I think it says D. Forsythe. And there was some scribbling on the other side. He started to write it there and then moved it down.

Fairley: There are copies for the jury, but they can see the original in due course. And with that you mounted the bus and went by bus to London?

Savage: Yes. *The understatement of the trial. I got on the bus and felt crazy all the way to London.*

Judge David: So he let you go?

Savage: Yes.

Judge David: What time did your bus leave, do you remember?

Savage: I think it was supposed to be a quarter after seven. I think it left shortly thereafter.

Judge David: About twenty past seven?

Savage: Yes, it was fairly close to that time, for which I was very grateful.

Fairley: At London you went to 44 Parliament Hill, which is the address of Caroline Novarra?

Savage: No, I took another bus to Romsey. There was a workshop that was going on in Romsey which she was running, and I had to be there that evening. Before that I went to Victoria Station, took a shower, and got some of the dirt off me. *Not exactly the truth, given the drama I experienced there.*

Fairley: Do you mean Victoria Railway Station?

Savage: Yes. I came into the bus station and then walked down to the railway station where I knew there were showers, and that was when I realized I had the black eye and the dirt on my face.

Fairley: So you took the bus to Romsey?

Savage: Yes. I didn't have much money so I was travelling as cheaply as possible.

Fairley: Did you at that time, at Romsey, write a written letter of complaint?
Savage: Yes, I did. I got to Romsey early. I was going to be picked up there.

Fairley: What time was it that you wrote that letter of complaint?

Savage: About five o'clock in the afternoon. I was going to be picked up at 6:15 p.m. so I wrote to the Llandudno Police. I wrote it on pages from a notebook.

Fairley: You sent these pages in an envelope to the North Wales Police at Llandudno?

Savage: Yes, that is right.

Fairley: Just identify that envelope. That is written by you, is it?

Savage: Yes.

Fairley: You were in fact to see two ladies, that is Anna Maria Garden, and the lady I have referred to Caroline Novarra, and I think they saw you on the Saturday as well?

Savage: Yes. I arrived there on Friday, and Saturday morning I talked to Anna Maria.

Fairley: And you were to return to America on which day?

Savage: I believe I was leaving on Tuesday following that weekend. It might have been Wednesday, but I think it was the Tuesday.

Fairley: The 29th or 30th.

Savage: Yes.

Hindsight is 20 - 20. Everybody knows that. If I had been a little more willing to follow my intuition I would have packed up and left that camp sight as soon as I had any hint of trouble from an unknown male. But I made the crucial mistake of staying. Admitting this one crucial mistake, I admit no others. Once events began to unfold, I did all the right things. I did all I could to take care of myself under these traumatic circumstances. When I realized this man was going to rape me I remembered something I already knew; that rape is an act of violence and has little to do with sex per se. Somewhere inside of me I was smart enough to save myself by letting him have the power - all the power. I knew he was willing to beat me to a bloody pulp in order to prove his power. I realized I couldn't save myself from this horrible invasion of my rights, nor could I save myself from the psychological after affects, but I could save my physical self from further brutality. Therefore, I let him have the power he demanded. I cooperated in every way I knew. I believed then and I believe now, that cooperation was my salvation. He was a brutal man. I knew it. I knew it by his conversation and by his behavior. The defense, however, maximized this decision and used it against me.

After my testimony there was a break. I spent the time outside on the steps of the courthouse, trying to compose myself after that ordeal. The solicitor for the prosecution stopped to chat. She complimented me on what a fine job I had done in my testimony. She said that I was clear and had come across as telling the truth. I said I felt good about it {although, inside, I was worried about how little emotion had been elicited by the prosecuting barrister, and by a lack of response on the faces of the jury. Then she said, "The worst is yet to come." I said I thought I was ready. Now I realize that there was no way I could have been ready for what the defense barrister did to me.

Cross Examination by Mr. Halbert

Halbert: You said in a reply to my learned friend earlier that you had travelled for some considerable time in the States before this?

Savage: Yes.

Halbert: Have you travelled outside the States?

Savage: I have been to Canada and Mexico. I came to England at the end of April, and I had been in London and around England since.

Halbert: I think you have been in Africa since?

Savage: Yes. Since then I have been to India and Africa.

Halbert: On the evening in question, was this the first night you had spent in Wales?

Savage: I had been there for four days.

Halbert: Where had you stayed prior to that night on the Great Orme?

Savage: I had been on the Orme one night before that and then I had gone back into town and stayed in a field, and then I had come back to the Orme.

Halbert: In the same area, Llandudno?

Savage: Yes, the same place.

Halbert: What was the first you knew of the defendant being there that night?

Savage: When I heard somebody talking to me. I heard somebody shouting that I shouldn't be in that place, I shouldn't be camping there. I had been sitting reading with my back against a rock looking away from the road, and that is when I turned around.

Halbert: Was there much activity on the road, do you remember?

Savage: There was some. It was late in the evening so it was just about time the gates closed, so there wasn't much about at that time. During the day there had been some.

Halbert: Do you remember noticing a woman in a wheel-chair at all?

Savage: No.

Halbert: And you say that the first thing he said, or you remember hearing, was something about you shouldn't be there?

Savage: I shouldn't be there, yes.

Halbert: And you said you thought he was someone telling you that you were breaking the law by being there?

Savage: Yes. I thought he might be a policeman. He was wearing something dark, and it was getting dusk, and that was my quick impression.

Halbert: How far from the road were you? Was it as far as the width of this Court?

Savage: I would say it was further than that, and I was down and he was up, and it was getting dark.

And now he begins his relentless pursuit of my emotions by diminishing me and trying to destroy my truth.

Halbert: What I must put to you is this. In fact the opening gambit, if you like, the introduction to the meeting between you, was not him saying you shouldn't be there, but it was he asking you for a drink of water?

Savage: No.

Halbert: That was initially what he wanted, wasn't it?

Savage: No.

Halbert: And he came down to where you were and you sat and talked for a few minutes?

Savage: *Indicating to the jury that we had just had a nice pleasant chat.* He was telling me how dangerous it was to be there.

Halbert: What was the nature of the danger?

Savage: He told me there were some Welshmen who were going to come down from the hills and that it was dangerous for me. Then he asked me for a cigarette, and then I knew he wasn't a policeman because I knew no policeman would ask me for a cigarette. Then I turned back to my reading, and it was at that point that he came down. He didn't ask me for water at that point, but he did ask me for a cigarette.

Halbert: And he came down?

Savage: Yes.

Halbert: Did he sit down?

Savage: No.

Halbert: Isn't it a fact that he came down and sat down and you talked for a few minutes.

Savage: As I remember he was standing all the time. I was sitting and he was standing. I *refute the idea that we were having a pleasant chat.*

Halbert: And it wasn't a question of him asking you your name, you volunteered it, didn't you? Didn't you tell him that your name was Mary?

Savage: No. He said later, "What is your name?"

Halbert: Why did you give him a wrong name?

Savage: I was irritated and angry. I didn't want him to know my real name.

Halbert: Were you frightened at that stage?

Savage: Not as frightened as I was irritated at that point. I didn't become frightened until later. I **was** frightened enough to try to take care of myself.

Halbert: What happened to the spray?

Savage: I don't know. It didn't work.

Halbert: Did you throw it away?

Savage: Yes. I got another one and the English Police took it away from me when I was leaving the country. They said it was illegal here. I didn't realize that.

Halbert: By the time he had left were you really thinking you were in danger or not?

Savage: I thought seriously enough about being in danger that I hid my money and I checked my aerosol spray, and I thought seriously about packing up and leaving.

Halbert: Why didn't you?

Here begins the strategy of making the jury believe that the reason I didn't leave was because I wanted him there. Not only wanted him, but called him back.

Savage: I believe it was because I didn't want to leave my things, and it was hard to get up to the top of the hill without going directly to where he was, or where I had last seen him. The only other way out would have had to go down, and it was a very difficult area to walk in. I was also concerned about packing up my things. It would take a long time and I didn't want to leave them there.

Halbert: You said he walked away from you?

Savage: Yes.

Halbert: You watched him walk back onto the road?

Savage: Yes.

Halbert: And he walked out of your sight?

Savage: Yes.

Halbert: Had he walked any distance, or did he go out of your sight straightaway?

Savage: He walked up to the road and down twenty to twenty- five feet before I lost sight of him. It wasn't very far before he disappeared behind the stone wall.

Halbert: Did you think to go up and see that he had gone?

Savage: No.

Halbert: Was there any reason why you didn't?

Savage: I didn't think of it. I wanted to believe he was gone.

Halbert: You were not contemplating going because you are saying you would have to go out through the same gap in the wall that you saw him go through?

Savage: I contemplated going but decided not to, and I felt the only way out was to go through the same area, and I was afraid he might still be there.

Halbert: But you didn't think of going and checking?

Savage: No. I didn't want anything more to do with him.

Halbert: Isn't it right that after he had gone back up to the road and turned out of the gateway, the hole in the wall, and had walked some little way down the road, you called him back?

Savage: I did not.

Halbert: You knew his name was David, didn't you, by that time, he had told you?

Savage: He told me.

Halbert: And you called him. "David!" And he came back?

Savage: Are you suggesting that I called him back?

Halbert: Yes, I am.

Savage: That is ridiculous! I did nothing of the sort!

Halbert: And hadn't you seen in one of the bags he was carrying that he had a sheet of plastic?

Savage: Inside?

Halbert: Yes, inside.

Savage: No, I didn't see it.

Halbert: And in the other one was some food?

Savage: I didn't see that either, but I found out later.

Halbert: When?

Savage: In the morning when he gave me some of the food, but all I saw that night was some straw sticking out of one of the bags.

Halbert: I put it to you that you called him back.

Persistent fellow

Savage: I didn't call him back.

Halbert: And the reason that you called him back was because you knew at that stage that all he had to sleep in for the night was a sheet of plastic?

Obviously the defendant, or the defendant's barrister, was playing on my compassion. How could I let a poor fellow sleep in only a sheet of plastic when I had this comfortable one person tent?

Savage: I didn't know that, I didn't know anything about that, and I didn't call him back. He irritated me and I wanted him gone.

Halbert: Didn't you say, "Wouldn't you like to stay the night, you can't sleep in a plastic sheet?"

Savage: Nothing of the sort.

Halbert: And he at that stage in the evening offered you food?

Still trying to convince the jury that we settled in for a cozy chat.

Savage: No. He offered me food in the morning. I knew nothing about what was in the bag.

Halbert: And far from being the one who was annoyed, it was he if anything who was annoyed at your attitude, because you were pressing yourself on him?

Savage: *I couldn't believe this statement.* Absolutely not. I didn't want him there. I told him repeatedly to go. I told him I wasn't in danger from Welshmen coming down from the hills. I told him I thought I might be in danger from him. I told him I would give him water if he would leave, and he left. *I remember feeling a little hysterical here.*

Halbert: I put it to you that you called him back.

Savage: No.

Halbert: And you allowed him to stay the night.

Savage: No, I did not.

Halbert: And when he came back to the tent it was you who opened it and climbed out?

Savage: No. It was him that was opening it. If I hadn't opened it when I did he would have gotten it open and climbed in there with me. I would have had no chance then. *I was barely maintaining my rationality here. Luckily Halbert changed the focus of his cross examination and gave me a little relief, but not for long.*

Halbert: You say you got out of the tent and you were standing facing him?

Savage: Yes.
Halbert: And he was standing with his back to the sea?
Savage: Yes.
Halbert: And you say he hit you?
Savage: Yes.

Here he goes again.

Halbert: That is not true at all, is it? He never struck you. I am putting it to you that you were not struck by this man?
Savage: Yes I was. I was struck very hard. I didn't see it coming.
Halbert: How many times?
Savage: At least three times.
Halbert: You described it as a slap. It wasn't a punch?
Savage: *A slap is not nearly as violent as a punch. Everybody knows that.* No, I don't think it was a punch. It was so fast I couldn't stop it. All I know is that my head was reeling, and my lip was cut open, and I could feel that it was swollen. *Even a slap can be violent, you see.*
Halbert: You said you decided to give in to him?
Savage: Yes.
Halbert: You didn't decide to run for it?
Savage: No. It was very difficult to run anywhere in that area. *I'm also a fifty-four year old woman and he was a twenty-eight year old man bent on rape. I wouldn't have had a chance.*
Halbert: We have seen the photographs. There are one or two rocks and thistles, but there isn't a lot between you and the gate in the wall?
Savage: No. There was a kind of a crevice very close to where we were standing which I would have had to cross going in the other direction. I wasn't thinking of running away toward the road, but in the direction where I would have had to cross the crevice, and I thought the terrain was impossible.
Halbert: He wasn't between you and the road?
Savage: No. That's right. He had already hit me. He was very fast, I knew that. I didn't have any notion he was going to hit me when he did, it was so quick. *I think I'm losing it here. I'm not even answering the question. What I was trying to say was that I was too afraid to run, in whatever direction.*
Halbert: You say that he was clawing at your clothes?
Savage: Yes.

Halbert: That is not true, is it, you took your own clothes off. He never touched you?

Savage: How do you know? You weren't there. *The best statement I made all day.*

Halbert: I must put my client's instructions to you, and I must put these questions to you. I apologize if the manner of my questions annoys you, but it is necessary.   I put it to you that you quite voluntarily took off your own clothes?

Savage: *What he seems to be saying is that it's all right for him to ask questions in an annoying manner, but not all right for me to get annoyed.* No, I didn't.

Halbert: You got your sleeping mat out of the tent.

Savage: *Now he's about to use my getting my sleeping mat as his next gambit to prove that I wanted this most delightful and interesting young man to have sex with me.* Yes.

Halbert: Are you saying that a man who had already been brutally violent to you, was intent upon raping you, stood back while you got your sleeping mat out of the tent?

Savage: I was on the ground at the time. I could feel the thistles underneath me. *By this time in his process of rape, I was being nothing but rational. I was taking care of myself in the best way possible. I knew rape was inevitable from the moment he hit me. But I was losing my rationality with this defense barrister. I was not answering the question. There was now some danger of his winning this battle.*

Halbert: Where was he then?

Savage: Standing over me.

Halbert: And you asked him, "Can I get my sleeping mat?"

Savage: *As though that proved I wanted to be raped.* Yes. "Can I get the mat out of my tent?"

Halbert: And this is the man you said was violent and was about to rape you?

Savage: *For some reason I'm rational again.* At that time he knew he had won, he was in charge, I was just too scared to do anything else.

Halbert: It is not going to be disputed at all that you did have intercourse with the defendant that night?

Savage: He had intercourse with me. I had no intercourse. *Intercourse is a matter of definition in this instance.*

Halbert: You gave him the impression you were consenting.

Savage: I gave him **no** impression I was consenting. When I was beaten up I felt I had no choice.

Halbert: Where did you put your clothes when you took them off?

Savage: I just threw them to the side.

Halbert: Outside the tent?

Savage: Yes.

Halbert: Did they remain there?

Savage: I put them on after it was over.

Halbert: When?

Savage: After he raped me.

Halbert: But you also had intercourse in the tent?

Savage: Yes.

Halbert: Were you wearing clothes again?

Savage: No, he took them back off again.

Halbert: You had intercourse outside the tent, put your clothes back on again, got back into the tent and your clothes were taken off?

Savage: Yes.

Halbert: By whom?

Savage: I think I took them off again. I can't remember exactly. *One way I took care of myself during this whole ordeal was to keep him from pawing all over me. I had seen him frustrated and I knew what could happen, and removing jeans can be a frustrating experience. I think I took them off to keep him from pawing. But Halbert got me again. He confused me. First I said he took them off, then that I did. I'm not even sure today which is true.*

With his best superior tone.

Halbert: It must have been an incredibly difficult exercise?

Savage: *All sweetness and light.* Yes, it was.

Halbert: You were in a tiny tent barely big enough for you to lie in?

Savage: Barely big enough for one.

Halbert: A small one person tent you could scarcely sit up in?

Savage: Yes, barely.

Halbert: Yet you managed to undress with him there?

Savage: Yes.

Halbert: There is no dispute that you had sex inside the tent, but I put it to you that intercourse took place with your consent?

Savage: It did not. None of it took place with my consent. I didn't want him there. I did everything I could to get him to leave and stay gone. But he wouldn't.

Halbert: You say he dressed inside the tent when you were inside the tent.

Savage: He had his sweater on when he raped me the first time. He took his pants off there and then. I don't remember whether he put them back on again. I think he did.

Halbert: You were sitting outside the tent for an hour?

Savage: Yes. It was cold, so I think we both had our clothes on.

Halbert: What about inside?

Savage: As I remember he took most of his clothes off. He was rummaging around a lot, I remember. I kept mine on until he made me take them off. He had a t-shirt on or something.

Halbert: But nothing from the waist down?

Savage: I don't remember exactly. *Halbert is still pursuing the idea that I wanted this monster close to me with no clothes on.*

Halbert: When you got out to go and relieve yourself what were you wearing?

Savage: I was dressed.

Now he's going back to why I didn't run away. This was in his best superior tone.

Halbert: You got out of the tent, relieved yourself and went back to the tent?

Savage: I didn't get in.

Halbert: Why did you go back at all?

Savage: I had things there I wanted to take with me. *If I hadn't been concerned about that, I would have run the night before, when this rapist first gave me the chance by walking away. Halbert conveniently forgets that.*

Halbert: You had been brutally raped. Why did you go back to the tent?

Savage: So I wouldn't lose what I owned. It was all I had. I had been traveling a long time.

Halbert: Are you saying you were more worried about losing your possessions than about the fact that a very unusual gentleman had twice brutally raped you?

Savage: I told you, it was too hard to get away in that terrain.

Halbert: He is inside and probably semi-naked, and you are outside and clothed.

Savage: He was outside too.

Halbert: When did he come out?

Savage: Just after I did.

Halbert: In the tent, you say he slept and you couldn't sleep.

Savage: *Could you, in that situation?* Yes.

Halbert: And you gave us the reason, the fact that you were afraid of missing the bus?

Savage: I was afraid of everything. My whole body was agitated.

Halbert: You said you were afraid he wasn't going to let you go to catch the bus. Is that seriously why you couldn't sleep?

Savage: *You're not hearing me, Halbert.* I said I was afraid of everything. Missing the bus was part of it, but I was just afraid. I'm sure you wouldn't have been able to sleep in those circumstances either.

Halbert: He let you go to the bathroom, and you came back from where you relieved yourself, and you say by that time you came back he had got out of the tent?

Savage: *Where are you going now, Halbert?* Yes, he was out of the tent.

Halbert: But you didn't think of making a run for it?

Savage: *By pursuing that question, he allows me to make a pretty important* **point.** No, not at that point. He was fairly calm then, and I felt he wasn't going to hurt me again. He wasn't going to rape me again.

Halbert: You wanted to catch the bus to London, and you said to him he should walk down to the bus with you?

Savage: He told me I was in danger if I walked to the bus alone, *(one of his convenient paranoic fantasies)* and all I cared about was getting on that bus.

Halbert: You suggested he should walk to the bus with you?

Savage: Yes. I said, "If you think I am in danger, you walk with me."

Halbert: I put it to you that he said, "Do you mind me walking to the bus with you?" and you said, "No."

Savage: That is not true. I minded very much. All I wanted to do was get on that bus, and if he wanted to walk with me, I let him.

Halbert: And you passed the toilet, and you asked if you could use the toilet, and he said, "Yes, and also wash your face?"

Savage: Yes.

Halbert: Were you carrying your gear when you went into the toilet?

Savage: No.

Halbert: You didn't think of staying in there? *He persists in pursuing the running away theme, one that he uses with great devastation in his summing up, while I am pursuing my physical safety and the only chance I think I have to get away.*

Savage: I had a bus to catch, and he was outside.

Halbert: Where were the two Bobbies?

Savage: *Ah, now a new running away theme.* Standing in the street.

Halbert: How far from you?

Savage: A little further than the distance of this Courtroom.

Halbert: What was between you?

Savage: Nothing.

Halbert: By this time, you told us, he was calmer?

Savage: Yes.

Halbert: And you didn't think you were in any danger from him?

Savage: *This time I got the jump on him.* I wasn't about to run to those bobbies and tell them.

Halbert: Why not?

Savage: Because he might have turned on me. *I persist in saving my skin against a man who has already shown me his brutality in both speech and action.*

Halbert: If you had run to the Bobbies and yelled, "This man has raped me," what would he have done to you?

Savage: *I wisely refused to answer that question.* All I wanted to do was to get away from him. I knew I'd be safe on the bus.

Halbert: Why was that? He could have gotten on the bus with you. There were two policemen standing some thirty or forty yards away from you, with nothing in between, and yet you don't seek to complain to them.

Savage: I didn't.

Now we get into a shouting match or at least I was shouting. He, of course, kept his superior cool.

Halbert: Is that because at that stage you had second thoughts about what had happened the night before?

Savage: What do you mean?

Halbert: Because you had had sex by consent the night before?

Savage: No, I had not.

Halbert: If you had been raped . . . .

Savage: I was **raped**. *There is something important here, about the diminishing process of not being heard. It has been my experience that women are often not heard by men, and no matter how clearly we say it, we are not heard. Men try to prove a different point than the one we want heard. This was what was happening* *here, and by not hearing me, he was working hard at the diminishing process. Now Halbert and I begin to get ridiculous.*

Halbert: If you genuinely had been raped you would have been in such a state that nothing would have stopped you from going to those policemen?

Savage: I wanted to get to the bus. That is **all** I wanted to do, to get to that bus.

Halbert: Yet you passed up a prime opportunity to get away from him - Why?

Savage: *He persists - I persist.* I **was** getting away from him. To the bus.

Halbert: Why couldn't he get on the bus with you?

Savage: He couldn't. He didn't have a ticket *(and I was not about to buy him one)* And by then there would have been a lot of people around, and then I could have yelled.

Halbert: At 7:20 in the morning?

Savage: Yes! There were a lot of people on the bus. *Well, at least there was a big burly bus driver and a few more.*

Halbert: Did you think you were better able to get away because he did not have a bus ticket, than because there were two policemen standing opposite?

Savage: I wasn't thinking like that. All I wanted to do was to get on that bus.

Halbert: He asked to borrow some money from you, didn't he? *Ah, a new tack.*

Savage: No.

Halbert: Isn't that why you wrote his name on the bus schedule? *Now you're getting ridiculous, Halbert. Handwriting can be checked. And do you really believe that illiterate scribble was written by a Ph.D.?*

Savage: No, he wrote it on there, because he said some day he would be very famous and I should get to know his name.

Halbert: And he wrote, "David Forsythe"?

Savage: Yes.

Halbert: He asked if he could borrow some money from you, didn't he?

Savage: No.

Halbert: And I put it to you *(always dangerous words)* that he wrote his name because he borrowed money from you and it was a way of staying in touch so that he could repay you?

Savage: No.

Judge David: There is no address.

Halbert: No.

Judge David: *(Addressed to me.)* You are saying the name was written quite independent of the money?

Savage: Yes.

Judge David: And before you gave him the money?

Savage: Yes. There was quite a bit of time between his writing his name and my giving him the money.

Halbert: How long were you at the bus station?

Savage: I'd say about twenty minutes.

Halbert: What time did you arrive? Just before seven?

Savage: I think so, but there was nobody around when I first got there. I was afraid I would miss the bus, and then I worried that the bus might have gone before I got there.

Halbert: So you stayed alone with this man in the bus station?

Savage: Outside. Llandudno Bus Depot has a little building but it wasn't open at that time of the morning and we were outside. Another woman came shortly after me and I said, "Are you going to London?", and she said she was. I felt very relieved because I hadn't missed the bus.

Halbert: What is your profession?

Savage: I am a therapist.

Halbert: What kind of therapist?

Savage: A psychotherapist.

Halbert: The man you spent the night with, was he normal?

Savage: I didn't think so.

Halbert: I think paranoid schizophrenia is the phrase which is used?

Savage: That is what it felt like to me.

Re-examined by Mr. Fairley

Fairley: It has been put to you in a positive way, without going into details, that you gave him the impression that you were consenting. Was there anything that you did that you can think of that would give him that impression?

Savage: No.

*And that was the end of my testimony. At that point I would have liked to have shouted from the rooftops, "When did telling a man to **leave**, constitute consent. When did telling him I would pack up and leave if he didn't leave me alone, constitute consent? When did giving a man what little water I had left under the conditions that he leave me alone, constitute consent? When did submitting to sex after having been hit hard enough to blacken my eye and split my lip, constitute con-*

sent? From that point on I took care of myself in the best way I knew. I made one mistake, and one mistake only. I didn't leave when I had the chance and before I was subjected to more of this madman. After he split my lip I was his prisoner. I used all of my feminine wiles to keep from being further brutalized, something I knew he was fully capable of doing. I saved my own skin. Because I chose to save my skin in the way I did, I had to suffer my second rape (albeit, an emotional one) - at the hands of Halbert - as much a master of rape as was my original rapist. The only difference was that he was part of an institution while the madman that raped me first . . . was not.

The prosecution and police told me I had done a good job under cross examination. I didn't feel good, believe me. I felt that Halbert had undercut me at every corner. I felt like a child that had been naughty and was being questioned by the big bad parent who had only the intent of punishing, never understanding. Halbert would lead me to believe that I was the criminal here, that I had consented, and then tried to prosecute for rape. As I have heard from so many other women who have tried to prosecute for rape, the victim becomes the victimized. Now I understand why so few cases of rape are ever reported [statistics say only 10% of actual rapes are reported]. What woman in her right mind would want to go through what I had just been through? I am a very strong woman and as I read the testimony, I think they were right. I did do a good job. But even for me, it was without a doubt, the worst experience of my life. Worse than the rape itself. At least, there, I was only invaded, humiliated, beaten and disregarded in front of one person. Here, it was done in front of the whole court.

Yes, I held up well. I may have even won a point or two against Halbert's superior tone. But the psychological effect on me was incredible. But not as bad as his next foray into my well-being that took place the next day.

Witnesses for the Prosecution

(TWO witnesses, Anna Maria Garden and Caroline Novarra, were present to testify in my behalf. They had both witnessed my black eye and my state of mind while I was at the workshop in Romsey. The courts subpoenaed them, and when they resisted, insisted that they come anyway. For some reason, unknown to me, my prosecuting barrister chose not to put them on the stand. Earlier they had both written letters stating that they had seen my black eye, and Caroline made the observation that I was not the same energetic person she had met approximately a month prior to the workshop. I was disappointed that these two women were not put on the stand. I thought their personal appearance would have made a much more powerful impression on the jury than a cold reading of the letters. Anna Marie would have made an especially powerful impression. She is an energetic woman who is very articulate and exudes power simply by her presence. Her anger at her own rape a number of years earlier would have given her even more power. Her testimony would have been invaluable, but then nobody asked what to do.)

Fairley: I call Detective Sergeant Gabbetis.

Warwick Rayner Gabbetis, Sworn

Fairley: What is your full name, rank and station, officer?

Gabbetis: Warwick Rayner Gabbetis, Detective Sergeant 701 of the North Wales Police, stationed at Prestatyn.

Fairley: On the 1st of August 1985, you were on duty with Detective Constable Jones at 10:25 a.m. when you went to Holyrood House, West Shore, Llandudno, and there spoke to the defendant?

Gabbetis: Yes.

Judge David: Members of the jury, on Thursday, 25th July, Dr. Savage was on the Great Orme. On Friday, 26th she went from Llandudno and arrived in Romsey in the evening of that day. And while she was waiting to be picked up there she wrote the letter to the police at Llandudno which was received on the 31st July, and this witness is now giving evidence about a conversation he had with the defendant on the following day, Thursday 1st August.

Fairley: And in respect of that conversation you made notes, officer, did you?

Gabbetis: Yes.

Fairley: How long after the event did you make your notes?

Gabbetis: A matter of a few hours. I imagine it was about lunchtime, around one o'clock to half past one.

Judge David: The interview is at 10:25 and the officer is making his notes at lunchtime, so you would not expect them to be word for word, but it is fairly soon after the interview, and you may think the officer was able to record certainly the effect of it.

Fairley: Perhaps referring to your notes, would you tell us what was said during that conversation, having introduced yourself to the defendant?

Gabbetis: The conversation went as follows:

Q. We just want to have a word with you about general matters really. Have you been in Llandudno before?

A. No, I don't want to answer questions because of Civil Rights. You can't charge and detain me for anything.

Q. We don't want to. We just want a word with you, that's all.

A. I'm not going anywhere with you. What are you charging me for?

Q. We are not charging you with anything We just want a chat, that's all. Is your name David Forsythe?

A. David Forshile. We all have identities, but we lose them, my identity is complete, David Forshile.

Q. Have you been in Llandudno before, David?

A.. No.

Q. Are you sure? Weren't you here on Friday night last?

A. No, I wasn't. I haven't been here before.

Q. Well last Friday night an American woman who was on the Great Orme was attacked by a person answering your description and who gave his name as David Forsythe. Was that you?

A. David Forshile. I'm David Forshile. There was no attack. She wasn't

American - Swedish - European - Swedish - not American. Sexually different and not compatible.

Judge David: This was plainly an odd conversation?

Gabbetis: Yes Plainly.

Q. Have you had sexual experiences with non-European women then?

A. You can tell a woman who is sexually on. You pass them and you stop and you smell them and you turn around and you know.

Q. Did you have sex with a woman, an American, on the Great Orme last Friday night?.

The defendant evaded the question and started to go into a lengthy speech about women and sexual matters which I thought was of no consequence to the enquiry, and he was then asked to accompany us to the police station. He refused to do so, and the conversation then continued as follows:

Q. Did you meet the American woman?

Gabbetis: At this stage he was cautioned.

A. She wasn't American, she was Swedish. I haven't raped anyone.

Q. Who mentioned anything about rape?

A. She did. I didn't see anything until I heard a small voice, like a moaning over the wall. He ran off then.

Q. Who ran off?

A. The man with the beard. He'd raped her in the tent and then he ran off.

Q. Had you seen the man before?

A. Just his face. He ran away.

Q. Was the woman hurt?

A. She had a few broken ribs and her jaw was broken. She had blood on her face.

Q. Will you come with us to the police station then?

A. No. It's harassment. You are going to charge me. I'm not coming.

Q. Will you look through some photographs to see if you can identify the man?

A. Yes.

Q. The photographs are at the police station, so if this gentleman comes with

you will you come down?
A. O.K.

(The truth will out, even from a madman. The defendant's projections told the truth. Even when he was talking about a bearded man, he was talking about himself. For instance, his statement ,"He'd raped her in the tent," was exactly what he did, and the defendant was unshaven on the night of the rape. The defendant also made a series of statements beginning with, "I haven't raped anyone." Mr. Gabbetis then asked, "Who said anything about rape?" and he responded, "She did." He also told the truth in those statements. I did say, "Are you going to rape me?" and "It is hard to be cooperative when you are being raped." I did, indeed, mention rape. Even in this garbled conversation, he told, although projected out onto this bearded man, the truth.)

Judge David: Who was, "this gentleman"?
Gabbetis: I only knew him as Manuel, he was in the employ of Holyrood House.
Judge David: Is that a hostel?
Gabbetis: Yes.
Judge David: And you then took him to the Llandudno Police Station?
Gabbetis: Yes.
Judge David: How long did it take you to get to the police station?
Gabbetis: Five or ten minutes at the most.
Judge David: And then the interview continued?
Gabbetis: Yes. The interview continued as follows:

Q. Let's get back to this woman you met on the Orme. Had you met her before?
A. She was German. It was late and she was crying. I had to get her to safety. They were after her. She wouldn't lie still. She would have given our position away. I had to hit her. She was going to walk towards them.
Q. How many times did you hit her?
A. Across the face so she'd come down. You've got to persuade people some how.
Q. Where on the Orme was it?
A. Behind a wall. I could see them from behind the wall.
Q. Who?
A. They were after her.

Q. Can you show us later where all this happened?
A. Yes. Come on then, you can see.
Q. Have you had sex with any woman at all?
A. When they smell like it, it's all right.

*(No matter what a woman says, no matter how hard she says no, **he** could make an independent decision based on smell.)*

Q. Let's be honest Did this woman offer sex to you that night?
A. She was pushing. She smelled right.

(Smelling right meant I was pushing. Rigth?)

Q. So did you have sex with her? The defendant smiled and said:
A. She took her tights off.
Q. What happened next?
A. I told her, "Get your knickers off", like that.
Q. Did you force her to have sex?
A. Not me. She wanted it. I could tell.

(By smell again, I suppose.)

Q. So you did have intercourse with her?
A. Yes. It wasn't very good though. She had a broken pelvis.

(Which I would have had if I hadn't cooperated. In one lucid moment in the morning he said to me, "I'm glad you stopped fighting with me last night. You saw how I was.")

Q. What did she say to you?
A. You're trying to catch me out now. I'm not going to be charged.

Gabbetis: At this point the defendant became very agitated and threatening and the interview was concluded. Some time later the interview was resumed as follows:

Q. Okay, David, to summarize, you met this woman who was camping in a tent on the Orme and you had intercourse with her?

A. It's not rape. I didn't come in her.

Q. Did you ejaculate?

A. Yes and no. Possibly, but it didn't show on me.

Q. Did you stay with her the rest of the night?

A. Yes, and I helped her to the bus. This woman was aggressive on the bus. She was Swedish.

(I don't remember being aggressive on the bus, but I was certainly as aggressive as I knew how to be about getting to the bus.)

I then showed the defendant a Royal Red brochure and said to him, "Was it you or her who wrote this on this piece of paper?" And he replied, It's a name, but I'm Forshile." The interview was then concluded.

Fairley: I think later on that same day you got into contact with Mr. Terry James of the Social Services, and he came along at your request and was present at a subsequent interview?

Gabbetis: Yes, that is correct.

Judge David: Was that because you were a little bit worried about the defendant?

Gabbetis: Yes, Sir. I have to be careful what I say.

Judge David: His answers were very odd.

Gabbetis: Yes, his behavior was strange. We related to Mr. James what had transpired previously.

Judge David: Is this in the afternoon now?

Gabbetis: Yes.

Judge David: When did you make those notes to which you are going to refer now?

Gabbetis: They were made at the conclusion of the interview, and are subsequent to the trip around the Orme.

Judge David: Which would be about when?

Gabbetis: I would hazard a guess, within about two to two and a half hours afterwards.

Judge David: You may refer to your notes.

Gabbetis: In the presence of Mr. Terry James the following conversation ensued:

Q. David, Mr. James has come down to see you and I'm going to ask you some questions, just so that Mr. James knows all about it. Were you with an American woman on the Orme last Friday? Is that correct?

A. She was up there and she had a carbine rifle. She was ready to shoot me, so what could I do. I hit her - smack.

Q. Why hit her then?

A. To restrain her, that's all.

Q. Where was she at this time?

A. Talking. We were talking in the tent when they came down from the mountains.

Q. Who?

A. I don't know. They looked like terrorists to me. There were fifteen or thirteen of them coming down on us. Bang! Killed one and pushed him over into the sea. I killed another six on the road with my automatic and she got her head up, so I hit her like that - smack - smack - Get down! I had to hit her. She wouldn't stay down.

Q. Where did you hit her?

A. Her head and face. Had to or she'd be killed. They know what they're doing, you know.

Q. Did you sleep with this woman?

A. She was injured. She was badly injured, so I took her knickers and jeans off and kept her warm.

Q. How?

A. I pressed against her or she would have died of exposure.

Q. Did you have sex with her?

A. I had to keep her alive. That's how they train you.

The defendant then started mumbling and muttering about combat training and other matters which we considered irrelevant, and the decision was then taken to ask him to show us exactly where he had been with the woman. At approximately 4:30 p.m. the same day, together with Detective Constable Jones and Mr. Terry James, we went in the C.I.D. car up towards the Orme, and acting upon the directions of the defendant we arrived at Marine Drive.

As we were approaching the lighthouse he requested us to stop near a gap in the wall, and we left the car. He took us through the gap and down a slope for a further twenty yards and said, "Here." He saw a large paper sack and said, "There, that's mine." As we walked over to it, Detective Constable Jones asked, "What's inside it, David?" And he replied, "Pies." The sack was opened and we saw it contained approximately twenty to thirty pie trays, and small domestic aluminum ones with pastry on them. They were in a stale and decomposing state and had been attacked by hundreds of insects, and it was in view of that that we decided against seizing them. We thought it would be a health hazard. We then returned to the police station.

At 5:20 P.M. we again continued the interview in the presence of Mr. Terry James, and at this interview I made contemporaneous notes.

Fairley: I have copies for the jury. This will be exhibit 3. Were you the writer of the notes?

Gabbetis: To a large extent I was the writer, although I posed the odd question. I confirm that these are the original notes.

Judge David: Who was asking the questions?

Gabbetis: Detective Constable Eifion Jones.

Judge David: Is the question written down first and then asked out loud, or the other way round?

Gabbetis: Sometimes the question was asked and I made a note of the question and the defendant is asked to pause until my pen is finished writing and then his reply is taken down contemporaneously.

Fairley: Would you read the notes?

Gabbetis: The defendant was reminded of the caution.

Judge David: He does not have to say anything unless he wants to?

Gabbetis: That is correct. The interview went as follows:

Q. Do you understand?

A. Yes.

Q. We want a word about a certain incident that happened on the Orme on the 25th July 1985 when a woman alleges she had been raped. Did you on that date meet a woman on the Orme?

A. I never was on the Orme that day.

Q. When were you on the Orme?

A. On the 27th or thereabouts.

Q. Whatever date, can you remember meeting a woman, an American?

A. It could be anyone.

Q. You mentioned earlier that you saw a woman. What was she wearing?

A. A blue windcheater.

Q. I understand she was in a tent camping. Was she alone?
A. Yes.
Q. How did you first meet her?
A. I first seen her on the Orme crying her eyes out. I saw her late at night crying her eyes out.
Q. Why was she crying?
A. I don't know. I just wanted to be alone.
Q. Did you help her out at all?
A. Yes, she was starving and I gave her food.
Q. Did she tell you that something had happened?
A. No.
Q. Did she mention she had been raped?
A. I knew she had. I could see in the torch light the bruises on her face. She had been crying her eyes out.
Q. What injuries?
A. Black eye, maybe broken cheekbone, broken jaw, bruised lip, broken teeth, fractured ribs.

(All of that really could have been mine if I hadn't stopped fighting.)

Q. Did she say she had been raped?
A. No, she came out with it in the toilet. I heard the truth come out the following morning.

*(It was the following morning when he saw the bruises **he** made.)*

Q. Did you try and help her at all?
A. I tried to cradle her off during the night. I was lying there during the night.
Q. Did you get her to a bus the following morning?
A. Yes, I made her walk. Her pelvis was broken.
Q. Did she say where she was going?
A. To London and then to Germany.
Q. You gave her your name which you wrote on a Royal Red pamphlet?
A. Yes.
Q. Why?
A. Simple. So she would know who I was.

Q. Which one did you write?
A. I only put my signature and name.
Q. Did you have sex with her at all?
A. No, because her pelvis was broken.
Q. Did she invite you to have sex with her?
A. No. I've never seen her before.
Q. Earlier on you showed us where her tent was pitched?
A. That's not the one.
Q. Near the tent was a bag with pies in it. Did you find them?
A. I was given them.
Q. Where were you given them?
A. I found them in a layby when I was looking for cigarettes.
Q. How far from here?
A. About a hundred miles away. The last time I had them - I had them as I came
into Wales, past Queensferry.
Q. When you took her to the bus you looked after her?
A. Yes.
Q. Was she alright on the bus?
A. Yes, but I never spoke to her on the bus. I got on a bus myself.
Q.Did you have to hit this woman at all?
A. She came out of the tent and I manhandled her.

(Now, there is the truth, simple and without craziness.)

Q. Did you have to hit her hard?
A. I just made sure she went down arm up her back. She had something in her
hand.
Q. Did you have to hit her on the face?
A. I hit her on the side of the cheek with a slap. She had a gun - her head was
up, I had to slap her.
Q. What were you doing there?
A. I was trying to get clear of the town. I didn't even know who she was.
Q. Were you sleeping rough?
A. Yes, before I went to Denbigh 21 - 22 - 23.
Q. How big is she?
A. I'd say she was six foot.

Q. Heavy built?

A. Solid. Well trained.

Q. Pretty?

A. To some men. To most men.

Q. Did she give a name?

A. She didn't give me a name.

Q. Earlier today you mentioned that you had intercourse with a woman in a tent on the Orme?

A. Yes, I'm saying that - to make sure she was out of the country.

Q. You told me she removed her own tights and then you told her to remove her knickers.

A. Yes, there were bandages underneath supporting her pelvis. It's different to a man's.

Q. You told me that she invited you to make love to her, that she didn't resist you at all.

A. You won't find any sexual mark on me.

Q. You said that it wasn't particularly good and that you didn't ejaculate inside her. You weren't even sure if you ejaculated at all.

A. What would you do if someone was freezing to death on the mountain - warm them up - she was starving, hadn't been fed for weeks.

Q. After you had intercourse with her, what happened then?

A. I can't help you.

Q. What were you wearing that night, a black pullover?

A. I haven't got a clue. Some of my clothing has gone missing.

Q. Where is your black pullover now?

A. I told you, I buried it somewhere. I know where it is, I can pick it up any time. It's a safeguard.

Q. Against what?

A. Simple. Someone had been picking on me.

Gabbetis: That was the conclusion of the interview, and then I left Mr. Forshile's presence.

Judge David: You signed the notes?

Gabbetis: Yes.

Judge David: And Constable Jones did?

Gabbetis: Yes.

Judge David: And what about the defendant?
Gabbetis: The defendant didn't sign.
Judge David: Did he read them through?
Gabbetis: From memory it was read to him, but I seem to remember he got rather agitated again at this stage, so I couldn't honestly say whether he had the opportunity of understanding what was written there.

(Although it was garbled and mixed with many irrelevant statements, the defendant did tell a story similar to mine. These are his corroborating statements.)

"I was on the Orme on the 27th or thereabouts.

I asked the lady in the tent if she was all right.

She was a nutter on a mountainside. She was acting strangely.

She was from Indianapolis. Her name was Mary, Audrey, different names.

I asked for some water, and I told her to be careful.

You can tell a woman who is sexually on. You pass them and you stop and you smell them and you turn around and you know.

I haven't raped anyone. The man with the beard raped her in the tent and then he ran off.

I knew she had been raped. I could see in the torch light the bruises on her face. Black eye, bruised lip. She had blood on her face.

She came out of the tent and I manhandled her.

I had to hit her. She wouldn't lie still. I hit her across the face so she'd come down. You've got to persuade people somehow.

I had to be sure she went down.

So what could I do. I hit her - smack.

I hit her in the head and face.

I hit her on the side of the cheek with a slap.

Someone had been picking on me.

Have you been sexually provoked? I got annoyed.

You won't get me on a rape charge.

When they smell like it, it's all right.

She was pushing. She smelled right.

She took her tights off.

I told her, "Get your knickers off", like that.

(This is true. He did say "get your knickers off". I had not remembered that statement when I talked with the detective in Indianapolis, or in my testimon.y

It's not rape, I didn't come in her.

I took her knickers and jeans off.

I'm a man of the world.

(To the question Did you ejaculate?) Yes and no. Possibly, but it didn't show on me.

She was in an abrupt mood the next morning. Let's put it this way; I didn't smell it next morning.

I stayed with her the rest of the night and I helped her to the bus.

I carried her bag and trolley, a tartan trolley. She went in the toilet and I borrowed five or six pounds off her. I wrote my name on a paper."

(Quote from policeman) He was talking as if he was an S.A.S. trained killer.

(Quote from the social worker) Mr. Forshile became quite incensed and leapt out of his chair, put his fingers before the officer's eyes and said, "I could blind you."

(He didn't say it in the same words as I did, nor did he say it in an organized form, but he did say it. He said it all.)

Cross Examination by Mr. Halbert

Halbert: It was obvious really from the outset that the conversation you were having with this man was very peculiar indeed, wasn't it?

Gabbetis: Yes, it was peculiar.

Halbert: And his behavior was not what in an ordinary sense of the term one would describe as normal?

Gabbetis: That is correct.

Halbert: And he was inclined, to use the word in your evidence, to mumble?

Gabbetis: Yes, that is correct.

Halbert: And to wander off the subject.

Gabbetis: That is correct.

Halbert: And there are certain sections where you missed out chunks of the interview because he wandered off the subject completely?

Gabbetis: Yes.

Halbert: Did you find some difficulty in keeping him on the subjects that you wanted him to talk about?

Gabbetis: Yes, that would be correct.

Halbert: In fact, quite early on in your dealings with him you thought his condition and behavior so odd that you wanted to call in a social worker?

Gabbetis: Yes, I was really needing an opinion as to the best course of action in his circumstances.

Halbert: You did bring in a social worker?

Gabbetis: Yes.

Halbert: Somebody of his age, he is 28, you wouldn't normally, with a prisoner of that age, bring in a social worker to sit in on your interviews?

Gabbetis: No.

Halbert: You told us your notes were made two or three hours afterwards?

Gabbetis: Yes.

Halbert: And you wouldn't suggest that it was a word for word record?

Gabbetis: No.

Halbert: Especially with a rather odd conversation?

Gabbetis: No.

Halbert: Did you feel also that at times you were getting answers which didn't really relate to the questions?

Gabbetis: Yes, in some instances. As we mentioned earlier, he just drifted off the point.

Halbert: Some of the questions quite clearly appear to be answers to the questions you asked?

Gabbetis: Yes.

Halbert: But there were times, weren't there, when you asked a question and the answer did not relate?

Gabbetis: It related to the general subject but not specifically to the question. I wouldn't like to try and point out which ones were which at this stage.

Halbert: The first interview is whilst you are at Holyrood House, and at the end of the first section, which you recorded word for word, you then said he evaded the question and started talking about sexual matters?

Gabbetis: Yes.

Halbert: What do you mean by evaded the question? Do you mean he just went off the subject?

Gabbetis: He just went completely off at a tangent.

Halbert: You then asked him if he would go to the police station, and he refused, and then you carried on with the conversation and you cautioned him?

Gabbetis: Yes.

Halbert: And he said "I haven't raped anyone." And you said, "Who mentioned anything about rape?"

Gabbetis: Yes.

Halbert: You had, of course, told him that the allegation was that someone had been attacked on the Orme?

Gabbetis: Yes.

Halbert: And then again towards the end of that part of the conversation, you asked him about some photographs. Were you seriously going to get him to look through the photographs, or was that a device to get him to the police station?

Gabbetis: There was some doubt in my mind. I would say it was a little bit of both.

Halbert: You took him to Llandudno Police Station, and I think you said during the course of the morning you talked about various matters?

Gabbetis: That is correct.

Halbert: What sort of span are we talking about, roughly?

Gabbetis: I would imagine three quarters of an hour. I can recall that inbetween I had to make several long distance calls in connection with this matter and other matters.

Halbert: And then you brought him back on to the subject that you were enquiring into?

Gabbetis: Yes.

Halbert: And seven questions down you put this to him, "Let's be honest, did this woman offer sex to you that night?"

(He pursues the issue of my consent.)

Gabbetis: Yes.

Halbert: Why did you ask that question?

Gabbetis: Because we didn't have the benefit of speaking directly with the complainant at that stage.

Judge David: She was back in America by then?

Gabbetis: I believe she was, and in the circumstances I felt it only proper to ask the man had the woman consented to intercourse.

Halbert: And his response was, "She was pushing. She smelled right?"

Gabbetis: Yes.

Halbert: In fact that little bit of conversation, the implication is that they did have sexual intercourse to which she consented?

Gabbetis: You could read it that way, yes.

(What? Because he says I smelled right, that means I consented.)

Halbert: And then we have this odd comment - "She had a broken pelvis" - and then you terminated the interview?

Gabbetis: Yes, that is correct.

Halbert: And then you had one more interview, the last one before lunch, at the end of which you showed him the Royal Red brochure. And just before that you asked him, "Did you stay with her the rest of the night?", and his reply was, "Yes, and I helped her to the bus. This woman was aggressive on the bus." He was talking as if he got on the bus?

Gabbetis: It was difficult to understand whether he had got on the bus or whether he had just seen her to the bus.

Halbert: At the end of the next interview, the last one before you started taking contemporaneous notes, you say, "Forshile then went on to mutter about combat training and other irrelevant matters." Was he more or less talking to himself as if you weren't there?

Gabbetis: No, I wouldn't say as if we were not there, but if my memory serves me correct, I haven't got a note, he was talking as if he was an S.A.S. trained killer.

(Great. I'm attacked and raped by a man who thinks he is an S.A.S. trained killer, and I'm supposed to have consented?)

Judge David: He described a bizarre attack by a number of men, most of whom he had killed?

Gabbetis: Yes, he alluded to the fact that he was a government-trained killer, that he was a member of the Special Air Service, or something of the like.

Halbert: So he had really gone beyond?

Gabbetis: Yes.

Halbert: Would it be fair to say as the interview went on the degree of peculiarity and the distance he wandered off the point became steadier greater and greater?

Gabbetis: He would have quite lucid moments and then he would pass beyond, and for that reason we had a break and during that time he returned to his usual state.

Halbert: Referring to the contemporaneous notes, about two-third of the way through he said, "Before I went to Denbigh 21, 22, 23." Did you understand what he meant by that?

Gabbetis: I gathered from a conversation I had had with someone from Denbigh that he had been to the hospital there.

Halbert: The North Wales Mental Hospital in Denbigh?

Gabbetis: Yes.

Halbert: We are talking of the 21st, 22nd, and 23rd of July?

Gabbetis: Yes, if my memory serves me correctly.

Re-examination by Mr. Fairley

Fairley: Perhaps I can ask you about the difficulty you were experiencing to keep him on the subject, and the word you used in your evidence was "evading?"

Gabbetis: Yes.

Fairley: Did the questions and answers appear to you to be manipulated or free?

Gabbetis: When he spoke, he spoke quite freely. The difficulty one experiences in such circumstances is to find out what the motives were in his answers, whether he was attempting to be evasive or whether he was genuinely evasive.

Judge David: Was he putting it on or was he genuinely confused and irrational?

Gabbetis: I am not trying to evade your question but I don't know that I am properly qualified to draw that distinction. Better men than I have spoken to him.

Judge David: And those better men found it difficult, I can assure you!

Fairly: Thank you. I call Mr. James.

Terence Albert James, Sworn

Fairley: Your full name is Terence Albert James?

James: Yes, that is correct.

Fairley: And you are an approved social worker, operating from the area office Aberconwy?

James: Yes.

Judge David: You are a social worker with special experience in the care of mentally ill people?

James: Yes.

Fairley: And you were aware that David Forshile was being questioned.

James: Yes.

Fairley: And you had some knowledge of him, is that right?

James: Yes.

Fairley: I think you had been called out the previous evening to Llanrwst (Pronounced Clan - werst) Police Station where he had presented himself?

James: That's right.

Fairley: After having left the North Wales Hospital at Denbigh?

James: Yes.

Fairley: And he had no fixed abode?

James: Yes.

Fairley: On arrival at Llandudno Police Station on the evening of the 1st of August you were informed of certain matters by the interviewing officers, and so you remained present during an interview?

James: That is correct.

Fairley: Sergeant Gabbetis and Detective Constable Jones asked the defendant if he would accept your presence at the interview, and he agreed.

James: Yes.

Fairley: And after some preliminary questions - - -

Judge David: We have had the interview in detail, and it has not been challenged. The interpretation is for the jury.

Fairley: Yes.

Fairley: The fact remains that you accompanied the officers up to the point on the Great Orme where he said he had been, and you then returned to the police station and you were present during the interview?

James: Yes, that's correct.

Cross-examination by Mr. Halbert

Halbert: He took you to where something had taken place?

James: Yes.

Halbert: And the something he was describing was a terrorist attack?

James: On leaving the police station, Mr. Forshile directed the police officers to drive towards the Orme and gave directions "left" and "right," and at the site of the incident, where it was supposed to have occurred, he asked for the vehicle to stop, and said he thought this was the place. We alighted from the vehicle and crossed into the grassland at the side.

Halbert: But didn't he start to describe holding off the terrorists and pointing out where one of them had been shot when he came over the wall?

James: Very vividly.

Halbert: And after that you all went back to the police station?

James: Yes.

Halbert: And he was still very vividly carrying on with the description of the terrorist attack and the part he played in it?

James: His description when we got back to the police station, the on-going conversation became quite vivid and quite in depth.

Halbert: Did he appear to believe himself what he was saying?

James: Sitting as close to him as I was in the police station, he seemed in my opinion at times to believe quite totally in what he was saying. It seemed quite real to him.

Halbert: I think at one point he leapt to his feet?

James: The police officers had gone over the material a couple of times to make sure they were getting the correct information, and Forshile became quite incensed and leapt out of his chair, put his fingers before the officers eyes and said, "I could blind you." It had been a fairly lengthy interview, and my impression was he was becoming agitated and quite angry at the time.

(Even police officers were unprepared for his quickness, volatility and potential for violence when he considers himself frustrated.)

Halbert: Do you know his full name?

James: The name he gave me was David Forshile.

Halbert: I think at that point, or shortly after that, you had a conversation with Detective Constable Jones, and the upshot of it was there was no point in trying to interview him any further because of his unbalanced and deluded condition?

James: It became quite apparent that Mr. Forshile was becoming quite agitated and quite volatile, and there seemed to be at least the possibility of a nasty incident occurring. By this time he was on his feet and was trembling, and the interview was tending to break down, the answers were not tending to follow through with the story, and there seemed little purpose in it continuing.

(And can you imagine what chance a lone woman would have against such behavior? Is it any wonder I submitted?)

Judge David: It was all getting a little bizarre, was it?

James: Yes.

Halbert: In your statement that you made about this matter afterwards, you describe Forshile as being so unbalanced and deluded that any further attempt at conversation would be pointless?

James: The story he was giving us became more exaggerated.

Halbert: You would stand by this description you gave, unbalanced and deluded?

James: Yes, I would.

Halbert: Did you make enquiries concerning his history?

James: On the previous evening, having been called to the police station at Llanwst, the station officer informed me that the North Wales Hospital had been contacted and that Mr. Forshile had been discharged that morning at 10 A.M.

Judge David: From the hospital?

James: Yes. So I telephoned the hospital and asked to speak to the charge nurse on the ward, and asked what his condition was on discharge. He was unable to give me any more detail other than the name and that apparently he was discharged because there was nothing that could be done further for him, and he was free to go.

*(If the staff at this **mental** hospital had been unable to discover this man's true condition in a three day period, they were either not very discerniing or the defendant was covering himself very well. If he were, in truth, covering himself for three days in a mental hospital, then he had the capacity to knowingly do that. The question of his being knowingly evasive would then be answered. It could logically be deduced that he knew how to be knowingly evasive. That he knew when to use his illness and when not to.*

*My impression of the man was that he was genuinely deluded and unbalanced, violent, angry, and a cast off by society. On the other hand he knew **exactly** how to take care of himself. He smoked. He knew enough to pick up cigarette butts off the street. He knew enough to ask me for money. He knew he did not want me to catch my bus, so used the reason of my danger to keep me from going. He knew my face was dirty, and more than likely realized why. He told me to wash it. He then very gentlemanly waited outside until I came out, and observed and then reminded me that I had not washed my face. Once he had proved his power by assaulting and raping me, he then sat quite placidly outside my tent and talked for almost an hour. It was when his wants were frustrated that he moved into his deluded and unbalanced state. If he could fool mental health workers for three days about his state, perhaps he has fooled us all.)*

Fairley: Thank you. I call Detective Constable Jones.

Eifion Wyn Jones, Sworn

Fairley: Your full name.

Jones: I am Detective Constable 345 Eifon Wyn Jones of the North Wales Police stationed at Llandudno.

Fairley: You can confirm your colleague Sergeant Gabbetis over the earlier parts of your involvement with the defendant?

Jones: I can indeed.

Fairley: Together with the contemporaneous note that was taken.

Jones: Yes.

Fairley: And then passing on to the 10th September you were with Detective Inspector Colin Edwards when you went to Risley Remand Centre at Warrington?

Jones: Yes.

Fairley: And there in the presence of the Assistant Governor you interviewed the defendant?

Jones: Yes, I did.

Fairley: And did you keep contemporaneous notes of the interview which commenced at 1:27 p.m. and terminated at 2:44 p.m.?

Jones: Yes, I did.

Judge David: So this is six weeks later?

Jones: Yes.

Fairley: Are those the original notes which you took of that interview which I now hand to you?

Jones: Yes.

Fairley: Perhaps you would tell us how they read?

Jones: After the caution the interview went as follows.

Q. We want to see you about the thing we were talking about last time. The woman who was attacked on the Great Orme, Llandudno on 25th or 26th July. Were you living in Llandudno at that time?

A. Yes, for one night.

Q. Do you remember where you slept? Were you sleeping out?

A. Yes. I was living out I was living rough. I had the tarpaulin plastic sheeting.

Q. Where?

A. By the lighthouse in the cove, and I had a bag of food there.

Q. What food?

A. Steak and kidney pies.

Q. Do you remember a lady in a tent, an American lady?

A. I can remember a German and American lady and one in an electric wheelchair. I met a Swedish lady.

(He's consistent. I was Swedish.)

And then he began rambling on about matters nothing to do with the subject, and then the interview continued.

Q. Can you remember the American by the lighthouse?
A. The white house. I helped the lady with the electric chair.

Again he went off on a tangent.

Q. Do you remember the lady in the tent?
A. I asked her if she was alright.
Q. Did she give you a cup of water?
A. Yes. She was talking to a man.
Q. Did you leave then?
A. Yes.
Q. Did you come back?
A. The tent wasn't there.

And then again he went off on a tangent.

Q. She was about fifty wasn't she?
A. Thirty-five. There was someone in black leather there, I can't remember.
Q. What time?
A. About 2 or 3 in the morning. It was foggy. It rained.
Q. Did you have any conversation?
A. Yes, I asked for some water and I told her to be careful. She was crying her eyes out.
Q. Did she say where in America she was from?
A. No. Milwaukee. Indianapolis.
Q. What name did she use?
A. Many names. Mary. Not Vi. Different names. Jane and Audrey as well.
Q. The second time you spoke to her did she ask you to sleep with her?
A. She had something in your pocket, her pocket you know. I'm always worried about special visits. You don't get me on a rape charge. Not a rape charge.

(He has said this more than once. He clearly knows what the charge is. Is this more evidence of his wiliness?.)

Q. Last time I saw you, you said she had a cut mouth and black eye.
A. More than that. Bruised jaw - cheek.
Q. Did you help her the following morning?
A. Yes. Carried her bag and trolley, a tartan trolley. She went in the toilet and I borrowed five pounds or six pounds off her? I had another offer from someone to show them around Wales. I buried my jumper cause it was muddy. It had a hole in the right sleeve.
Q. What color jumper?
A. A black one.

Judge David: Was the jumper ever found?
Jones: No.

Q. What color laces did you have?
A. Blue cord. I had them and black cotton.
Q. The lady you helped out that night, did you tell her about people who might come from the hills or pubs?
A. Yes, there's nutters about.
Q. Did you help her in the morning?
A. Yes. There was a lady in green with a Honda 80. She had a blue windcheater.
Q. Did the American have a bike?
A. No, another woman.
Q. Did she shout for help that night?
A. Yes, she shouted my name. She had a revolver, an American Colt. She was an agent. She had a load of cards in her wallet. She opened it.
Q. Last time I saw you, you said you hit her?
A. Yes. I fell first and I had to slap her because she wouldn't get back in the tent. I said she put my life in danger.
Q. Did she behave herself after?
A. Did she fuck? A beige car nearly hit me down. When she came out of the tent she only had a shirt on. What's going on?
Q. Was she better?
A. No, she was in an abrupt mood next morning.

Q. Did you have sex?

A. No. Let's put it this way. I didn't smell it next morning.

Q. Did you hit her for a reason.

A. For a reason. I was dead serious. I ran back to talk to her. Smack - get back in.

Q. Did you sleep with her? Kept each other warm?

A. Does not ring a bell.

Q. Did you have sexual intercourse with her, with her consent?

A. I'm a man of the world.

Q. Did you?

A. No. Not one hormone will you find in her.

Q. Did she offer you sex?

A,. Yes, she offered. That's why she had a clout.

Q. How many times did you hit her?

A. Twice and I hit something else as well.

Q. She was putting her body to you?

A. Have you been sexually provoked? I got annoyed.

*(Consider this scenario. I did annoy him when he first came down to talk to me. I told him in no uncertain terms to leave, **and** I told him that I thought I was in more danger from **him** than from **any** Welshmen. From my work as a psychotherapist, I know that many men confuse violence and sex. These two acts begin to coexist in their minds. In this case, {as evidenced by his testimony} frustration causes the defendant's thinking to go off on tangents, whereupon he spews violent stories, and/or stories about sex. Therefore, when I annoyed the defendant and he became frustrated , he left, but then fabricated a violent story in his mind, became sexually aroused, returned, and did his deed.)*

Jones: At this stage the Detective Inspector read certain parts of Mrs. Savage's statement to him.

Judge David: You had got a statement from Mrs. Savage by now?

Jones: Yes. The relevant part was, "Take clothes off and brutal. Jeans off, thorns on ground. Let me do that. Pushed me back and came inside me. Took off pants and shorts off. Entered." I have abbreviated that part. The defendant replied, "Read middle part. Can't be right in a sense, but can be right in a sense. I had a track suit." He was asked, "Is it right you had sex?" and he replied, "No." And then he again went off at a tangent. The interview continued.

Q. Is she tight?
A. No, she can have organic and clitoral climaxes, either one. I didn't have
intercourse.
Q. If a woman put her body to you would you take her offer?
A. I'm not like that.
Q. What did you think about her?
A. She was a nutter on a mountainside. She was acting strangely. She gave me
flare matches.
Q. Did you have sex with her?
A. No. I thought she was going over the edge. I had to coax her away. I swear
she was going to jump. I don't want her death on my conscience.

These notes were then read over by myself to the defendant in the presence of
the witnesses present, and thereafter he signed them.

Fairley: In fact he did some drawings, didn't he?
Jones: Yes.
Fairley: Where are they? Hold them up? (Witness does so)
Judge David: They seem to be quite meaningless?
Jones: Yes.
Judge David: Did he do that at the time he was signing the notes?
Jones: Yes.
Halbert: They seem to be meaningless doodles and straight lines.
Judge David: Yes. Perhaps the jury ought to see them.

(Shown to jury.)

Halbert: I have no questions of the officer.

(Adjourned to following day)

*(After my morning's testimony I had thought the worst was over. I was never
more wrong. I had no idea what was in store for me for the rest of the trial. As I
listened to the testimony of the officers, my body felt like a wound-up spring ready
to snap, and my mind believed I was in a life and death struggle here. What was
most difficult for me was listening to the defendant come up to the truth and then
immediately back away . . . again and again and again. He would admit the truth,*

then follow it with a statement that made no sense. He did nothing but confuse the issues. I admired the officers' patience and fortitude in the process, and I also admired the defendant's ability to confuse.

I was in such a state of tension that night, that my friend, Sheryle, took me out and deliberately got me drunk. I had not had a drink for a long time, but I knew it was the only thing that would take the horror of that trial out of my body . . . and my spirit. And what I didn't know then, was that the worst was yet to come.)

The Case for the Defense

Witnesses for the Defense

(When court convened the second morning of the trial it began with a great hurrying and scurrying among the five major components of the trial: the two solicitors, the two barristers and the judge. Conferences were hurriedly held and there seemed to be a great need for an agreement of some kind. When the excitement was over Mr. Fairley came to me to explain. He told me there were problems in the way the trial was going. Because of these problems he had decided to enter a second possible charge, that of indecent assault. He explained the problem. The way the trial was going they may not be able to get a conviction on rape. Somehow, the fact that I had recognized the defendant as a schizophrenic was very damaging to the case for the crown and now they had to enter a lesser charge. He said he would rather try for conviction on the lesser charge than take the chance that the jury would free the defendant on grounds of insanity. He said, and I quote as nearly as I can remember, "We can't let this deviate back out on the streets."

After what I had gone through at the hands of the defense barrister the day before, I was not going to be satisfied **just** *to get the man off the streets. I wanted him convicted of exactly what he did. Rape! But then I wasn't asked for* **my** *opinion on that subject.)*

David Forshile, Sworn

Halbert: What is your full name?

Forshile: David Forshile.

Halbert: Is your family name Forsythe?

Forshile: Yes.

Halbert: Mr. Forshile, do you remember in the summer of last year, 1985, a time when you were on the Great Orme at Llandudno? Do you remember being there?

Forshile: 22nd of July, yes.

Halbert: Do you remember seeing a woman there who was camping on the Great Orme?

Forshile: There were several people camping on the Great Orme that night.

Halbert: Do you remember one woman in particular, the lady we heard from yesterday, being there?

Forshile: Yes, I do remember her being there. She was one of the nice looking ones who was by the camp site that night.

Halbert: How do you say you first came across her?

Forshile: I first came across her when I was walking along the coast road towards Colyn Bay or Little Llandudno. That is when I noticed the woman sitting by the side of the tent - Mrs. Savage. I wasn't worried about that type of thing, I was actually worried about myself. I asked for water and she refused to give me water at first when I asked. "I'm left out all night," I said and she offered water out of her goatskin container like you find in Spain that would carry wine.

Halbert: Had you seen anyone else near to where she was camping?

Forshile: Yes, there were several people.

Halbert: Was there anyone particularly passing on the pavement?

Forshile: Yes, there were people passing on the pavement and there were also cars going by.

Halbert: If I mentioned wheelchair to you would that help?

Forshile: It was like an electric motor driven car. The woman asked me to help her on to the opposite pavement where the hole in the wall was.

Halbert: We have seen the photograph where the gap in the wall occurs.

Forshile: It is the part where there is a dent in the pavement.

Halbert: There is a gap either side?

Forshile: A gap of about eight feet.

Halbert: You helped someone crossing in an electric wheelchair? Was it just after that you noticed Mrs. Savage camping down below the road?

(I don't know what this was all about, except perhaps to show the defendant as a man of compassion who would help a lady in a wheelchair, which of course would prove that he wasn't capable of rape.)

Forshile: This is prior to me meeting Mrs. Savage. I thought that was the least of my worries.

Halbert: You said that after you had done that you saw Mrs. Savage and asked her for some water?

Forshile: That is after I asked for water.

Halbert: Let us try to get it in order. You asked for some water and eventually she gave you some out of a container?

Forshile: She walked up to the wall and offered me water.

Halbert: Can you remember any more of the conversation at that time?

Forshile: I did not offer my name. There is one point I can't remember about, but I actually said I was travelling on that night to actually find a place to sleep myself. I actually left the woman walking back to the tent with her water and I proceeded around the cove. I was on the other side of the cove when I actually heard someone shouting, "David, David," so I came back no more than twenty minutes later.

(Interesting that I could have called "David, David," when he did not offer me his name.)

Judge David: You left her, you say, as she brought the water to you by the wall?

Forshile: By the wall.

Judge David: You were on the road?

Forshile: On the pavement.

Judge David: You say she then walked back toward her tent?

Forshile: Yes, she did walk towards her tent.

Judge David: And you walked away?

Forshile: I walked away.

Judge David: How far?

Forshile: About three-quarters of a mile. About twenty minutes walk.

Judge David: Then what?

Forshile: I was carrying a heavy bundle. I did take my time walking down, but I actually heard someone, similar to the voice I heard present yesterday, actually say, "David, will you come back?" I wasn't imagining things. I hope not, because it can be very lonely for a lady on the campsite with the mist.

Judge David: Was it a shout or an ordinary voice?

Forshile: It was like a shriek and then it was like an ordinary voice shouting.

(I was so desperate for him I was shrieking.)

Halbert: You thought it was the lady who had given you the drink that was calling?

Forshile: I thought so. In my wild imagination I thought my luck had gone up, but then I thought, "Well I don't think she's going to try anything like that. I will go back and my luck might be in." It sometimes happens that way, so I didn't really think. I ran most of the way back.

(Obviously his referral to "luck" here was sexual luck. He thought maybe I was calling him back, shrieking, so that I could have sex with him. Somehow, in the realms of male thinking, seeing a woman alone means first, that she is lonely and needs a man, and then, that she wants sex with that man. Why else would she be alone?)

Judge David: You thought you would go back as your luck might be in?

Forshile: Yes, I didn't know the circumstances of the woman - what she had been left in.

Halbert: How long do you think it took you to get back?

Forshile: At least ten minutes. I ran part of the way back.

Halbert: Where was she when you got back?

Forshile: I had already jettisoned the bundle of food I was carrying - I had something to eat. I left it by the side and walked on because I couldn't carry them any further.

Halbert: Where was the lady when you got back?

Forshile: She was halfway. I can't remember if she was inside or outside the tent. It is part of the story I can't remember.

(Had I really called him back I would have been outside the tent, panting, waiting for glorious sex.)

Halbert: You jettisoned your bag of food?

Forshile: Yes, it was too heavy to carry as it was farm produce. I thought I had better leave it because the more I went to Wales I thought the more danger I would be in carrying it. Someone might enquire about me and get the wrong idea thinking I had been robbing farms and I wasn't.

Judge David: You had jettisoned your bag?

Forshile: Yes.

Judge David: And got back to the tent.

Forshile: Yes.

Judge David: You can't remember if she was in the tent or not?

Forshile: I can't remember if she was in the tent or out. I have remembered part of the story when Audrey Savage did say that she climbed out of the tent without her jeans on. She said, "Hang on while I put my jeans on". I can't actually remember the incident vividly myself.

Judge David: She climbed out of the tent without her jeans on?

Forshile: Yes. She had a striped shirt on.

Halbert: Is that when you first get back do you say?

Forshile: When I first get back to the tent, yes.

Halbert: Take it steady and tell us, in your own words, taking your time, what happened after being called back?

(What? No "I put it to you that . . . '")

Forshile: Actually she mentioned something like, "I called you back," or something like that. She said something about water or something, I can't exactly remember. I called her a stupid thing and said, "What did you call me back for? I was set down for the night." I think she was offering me part of a Mars Bar. I can't remember. I don't think I actually struck her, but I might have pushed her and said, go away, or stupid thing. The language was not choice at that time of night especially when it was cold. I said, "What did you want?" She said, "What did you do that for? You could have it any time." I said, "What?" and she said, "Shut up," meaning not to speak and then she actually offered me sex.

(Now that's an interesting story. He makes it sound that I was so excited about him and his sex that I would have allowed him to push me and call me a stupid thing, and then insist that he have sex with me.)

Judge David: Just see if I have heard you correctly. It is not easy to hear exactly what you are saying. It is not your fault it is the loud speaker which makes it more difficult. You say that you got back to the tent, but you can't remember if she was in the tent or out of the tent. You do think you remember her climbing out of the tent without her jeans?

Forshile: Yes.

Judge David: She said, "I called you back," and something about water?

Forshile: Yes, something about water.

Judge David: You said you think she offered you part of a Mars Bar?

Forshile: It happened in the frenzy of the moment.

Judge David: You didn't think you struck her, but you might have pushed her?

Forshile: Yes.

Judge David: She said, "What did you do that for? You can have that any time." Then you had sex?

Forshile: Yes, outside the tent, sir.

Halbert: You had sex outside the tent with the woman?

Forshile: Yes.

Halbert: Whose idea was that?

(Now it's more than just consent. It's that I asked for it. I stood right out there in the middle of a cold night on the Wales coast in front of my tent with only a striped shirt on and asked a dirty, scruffy looking boy less than half my age, who says he pushed me and called me a stupid thing to have sex with me. Would you believe that if you were on the jury?)

Forshile: I think the first suggestion came from the woman herself, sir.

Halbert: Did you, in any way, force yourself upon her?

Forshile: I hope I didn't, sir, no. I was just asking for water that's all. I was more interested in travelling myself.

Halbert: She says that you hit her hard about three times in the face blacking her eye and as a result she gave in to you. Is that right?

Forshile: No, sir.

Halbert: After you had had intercourse outside the tent, what happened next?

Forshile: She actually climbed inside the tent and she told me to sleep inside the tent. I can't remember how it came about, but I actually had plastic outside the tent and she invited me into the tent rather than let me sleep on the plastic.

Halbert: She went into the tent?

Forshile: Yes, she had jeans on when she went into the tent the second time.

Halbert: You had a sheet of plastic you were sleeping on?

Forshile: Yes, it was by the side of the tent all night.

Halbert: She invited you into the tent rather than you sleeping on the plastic?

Forshile: Yes.

Halbert: What, if anything, happened inside the tent?

Forshile: Well, she moved her bundle out. She was facing the road where the zip was and she actually put the bundle there by the door and we actually settled down to sleep for the night.

Halbert: Did you have intercourse again inside the tent?

Forshile: Yes.

Halbert: Did you force yourself upon her on that occasion?

Forshile: Well, she invited me into the tent. I hope I haven't forced myself on anyone. The same as promiscuity. I can't understand all of it whether promiscuity is leading someone on or not. I don't know. She explained it to me.

(That must be the same as inviting a man into your apartment. Of course it follows that if you invite someone in, be it your tent or your apartment, a woman is inviting a man in because she wants sex. But then, of course, he conveniently forgets that I DID NOT INVITE HIM IN.)

Halbert: After you had intercourse the second time, whilst you were inside the tent, what happened then?

Forshile: Settled down to sleep for the night. I slept all night.

Halbert: You slept all night?

Forshile: I did wake one time in the night and she was actually fast asleep so I didn't disturb her and I went back to sleep myself.

(Now, isn't this the perfect picture of post-coitus bliss?)

Halbert: Do you remember the morning?

Forshile: Yes, we packed up the tent. All she had to eat was a steak and kidney pie and an apple. I asked, "Are you sure you're alright?" and she said, "Yes," so we packed up the tent into a green striped trolly thing on wheels, like a shopping bag, and we walked towards Llandudno. It took over three-quarters of an hour, or maybe an hour, to walk back. We were up about ten past six or quarter past six.

Halbert: Did you know where she was going in Llandidno. Did she say where she wanted to go?

Forshile: She said she had to catch a bus. I said, "I have nowhere in particular to go. Would you mind if I walked along with you?" She said, "No, I don't mind. The more the merrier the company." We walked back into Llandudno passed the cut away in the road where there were more campers asleep. There was a man going over the hillside that morning in a blue shirt, blue trousers and glasses. He walked directly past us as we went down into the castle area where you walk into Llandudno. We walked into Llandudno and passed a police officer. He didn't seem to be too bothered about us walking back. We got to the bus shelter and waited for the bus to London. I asked her to borrow six pounds because I needed to get some food that day. I can't exactly remember, but another girl with long black hair and a green trouser suit on came up and sat down and got on the bus at the exact same time as Dr. Savage. She was sitting just behind the first seat. That's where she seemed to be and the bus drove off. I left the bus stop area and actually proceeded to buy some cigarettes and something to eat out of the news agents stand.

Halbert: Let me ask you one more question about what you just said. Do you remember passing the ladies toilets?

Forshile: Yes, we had actually. There was a cart delivering milk at the time.

Halbert: Did she go in there?

Forshile: Yes. I went into the gents and used the gents myself. She alighted into the woman's toilet.

Halbert: She said that you told her to wash her face. Do you remember?

Forshile: I don't remember that. Not at that time of the morning.

Halbert: You told us about the policeman and also about borrowing six pounds from her?

Forshile: Yes, a five-pound note and a one-pound note.

Halbert: Do you remember writing your name on a piece of paper, a bus time-table?

Forshile: Yes, I said I would pay the money back. I said that when I got a place to live I would get in touch with her, or she could get in touch with me. I can't remember how it came about. It was stupid talk like, but I left my name and the name I wrote on it was not Forsithe, but Forshile. Probably I made a mistake at that time in the morning with being drowsy.

Halbert: May we see the exhibit. Have a look at it. Do you see a name on it?

Forshile: Written down one of the sides?

Halbert: Yes, there is a signature on it as well. Do you think you wrote that?

Forshile: I don't know, sir.

Halbert: It says, D. Forsithe, does it not?

Forshile: Yes, it has an i in the middle and I don't think I would make a mistake like that at that time in the morning.

Halbert: You wrote your name on something?

Forshile: Yes, that is my name.

Judge David: Is that your writing?

Forshile: I don't think that is the one.

Judge David: Is that your writing?

Forshile: I don't think that is my writing, but I could have wrote it.

Halbert: You remember writing your name on something?

Forshile: Yes, I did write my name on something.

Halbert: Do you remember a few days later the police coming to see you in the morning of Thursday the 1st of August - I know dates are difficult for you - at Holyrood House?

Forshile: They actually came about 9:30 or 10:00 o'clock in the morning.

Halbert: They spoke to you at Holyrood House first of all?

Forshile: Yes.

Halbert: And they asked you to go to the police station?

Forshile: They asked me to come along to help them with their enquiries. I seemed reluctant for the reason that my landlady was not on the premises and I was asking if I could actually stay in the hostel until my landlady got back before alighting to the police station, because she would get the shock of her life if she found out I had gone without saying anything.

Halbert: You spoke to the police at the police station. Do you remember going with them on to the Great Orme?

Forshile: Yes, the previous afternoon after meeting with the two police officers inside the room.

Halbert: You showed them the place on the Orme where all this had happened, did you not?

Forshile: I took a trip around the Orme, but I suppose I could see the response, they were showing me an air, I think it was more out of respectability. They were hoping to get a charge. There was one other thing. He showed me a knife inside the police station which was nothing to do with me and they also showed me -they never showed me the photographs, they mentioned the photographs afterwards.

Halbert: You have seen the photographs very recently. I showed them to you about two weeks ago?

Forshile: Yes. It seems the same type of coast road.

Cross examination by Mr. Fairley

Fairley: Mr. Forshile, today you have got a very clear recollection of what happened?

Forshile: I always have a clear recollection.

Fairley: You think you always did?

Forshile: I am not saying always, but up to a point. You remember as you go on. I did have nightmares for a while when I saw the first indictment.

Fairley: Did you?

Forshile: Yes.

Fairley: You see, you remembered when you saw the police officers, did you not?

Forshile: I was arrested in a white van with police written on the side with two police constables.

Fairley: I am not making myself clear. That was the second occasion after helping with the inquiries. Do you remember when you saw the police officers you had been up on the Orme?

Forshile: It probably would be. She was carrying camping equipment. It was certainly obvious.

(It's interesting, here, that all the while his own barrister was questioning him, he gave clear answers. As soon as he is questioned by the prosecuting barrister, he begins to get confused.)

Fairley: You remember when you saw the police officers you had been carrying paper bags?

Forshile: No. I don't think that is one thing I had on me. I don't think I had any paper bags.

Fairley: The one with the food in?

Forshile: It wasn't a paper bag. It was a crepe paper, about 100 wide.

Fairley: You remember that?

Forshile: I do remember that, because I would have to find food for myself.

Fairley: You remembered roughly where you left them up on the Orme?

Forshile: Yes. They did show me them. That is the reason why the police arrested me, because of where the food was left.

Fairley: You took them to where those bags had been left?

Forshile: Yes. I did show them the area.

Fairley: What I am trying to help you with is this. It is clear, is it not, you did remember being up on the Orme when the police officers saw you?

Forshile: I do know previous to the Great Orme I had been troubled by the police - I think it was after I had been introduced to the hostel - and then they actually arrested me for an assault on Mr. Henely, although he was confused over the dates that is all.

(Because the police in Llandudno had not yet received my statement at the time of the arrest of the defendant, they could only hold him for forty-eight hours. Then they were required to release him. After his release he cooperated very nicely by almost immediately attacking a man and his wife on the street, a Mr. and Mrs. Henley. The defendant accused the Henleys of reporting him to the police and getting him arrested in my case. This couple, after having been more than a little bit hurt, immediately reported the assault to the police. This gave the police the opportunity to pick up the defendant again and this time to hold him until they had my statement.)

Fairley: You remember being asked questions about the woman who had been attacked?

Forshile: No, they didn't say that when they first came to the hostel.

Fairley: Later they did?

Forshile: Later they did, yes. On a previous occasion the next day.

Fairley: It is the later bit I am asking about. Did they ask you whether or not you had met an American lady?

Forshile: They did that. They didn't say at first she was American. They actually said, "Did you meet a woman?" They didn't say what nationality.

Fairley: Do you remember telling them whether she was American or not?

Forshile: I can't remember, sir. I think I came out with the story that she was American. I don't think the police had that evidence at the time, because they only had the letter, unless they mentioned America in it. I wasn't allowed to see it.

Fairley: You knew the police officers had received a letter, did you?

Forshile: I wasn't allowed to see it.

Fairley: Do you remember saying to the police officers, "I haven't raped anyone?"

Forshile: Confusion, sir. I was totally confused that morning. The answers I gave I could have come out with a couple of things, but I doubt if I would have made a mistake like that, sir.

Fairley: What is a mistake about saying, "I haven't raped anyone?

Forshile: Well, it was when they arrested me. The occasion when they got me to go and help with enquiries. "Where is it right for a man to rape his wife?" I could not answer the question. I didn't answer the question, because I was scared. Perhaps why I was there was that I didn't answer. They helped me into an unlocked car with one of the hostel workers to Llandudno police station.

Fairley: You think you might have said that you had not raped anyone?

Forshile: I don't think the question was actually asked.

Fairley: You don't think it was asked?

Forshile: I have no recollection, no.

Fairley: You see what their note says is that you were the first person to mention the word rape?

Forshile: How could I, sir? They arrested me to help with enquiries on that charge. I hadn't mentioned it previous. It was the two police officers who mentioned it at the hostel that morning.

Fairley: Did you at the time have a beard?

Forshile: I was unshaven, sir.

Fairley: Did you tell the officers of a man with a beard?

Forshile: No, sir. I have no recollection of that.

Fairley: Did you tell the police officers that that man had raped her in the tent and then run off?

Forshile: No, sir. I have no recollection of that happening.

Fairley: No recollection of that?

Forshile: No.

Fairley: Did you tell the police officers that you had not had sexual intercourse?

Forshile: That question wasn't asked.

Fairley: What question was asked?

Forshile: The question was asked was I on the Great Orme that night.

Fairley: "Were you on the Great Orme?"

Forshile: No, they hadn't got round to that. I think rape came out in the Court of Law when my first solicitor, Mr. Roberts, was dismissed. I was given a solicitor, Mr. Roberts, and then Mr. Roberts did not seem to actually point out the case in court. After six months I received a second solicitor after being dismissed by the court and the second solicitor only dealt with one part of the allegation. Then I was appointed the learned gentleman **there** and he has been doing a great job ever since, because the other solicitor didn't seem to be interested in the case.

Fairley: I do not want to cut you short really, but perhaps we can stay with the questions that I am asking you. My question was, do you remember telling the police officers that you had not had sexual intercourse with the woman?

Forshile: No, sir.

Fairley: That was at a later stage when you were being interviewed in the afternoon, having been up on to the Orme and you came back and you were interviewed?

Forshile: No. I have never said anything like that.

Fairley: And you repeated it when you were at Risley. Do you remember them coming to see you, the Inspector and the officer who gave evidence?

Forshile: What are you trying to suggest? When I was going to Risley I don't think they would have known if I was frightened or not. They never asked for information about being clean.

Fairley: Do you remember the officers at Risley asking, "Did you have sex?" They asked you this and it was written down.

Forshile: I'm sorry I have no recollection of the question.

Fairley: And no recollection of the answer, "No, let's put it this way. I didn't smell it next morning." You don't remember saying any of that?

Forshile: No, I haven't got a clue.

Fairley: The next question that bears upon this is, "Did you have sexual intercourse with her, with her consent?"

Forshile: No.

Fairley: That was the question they asked you. Do you remember making the reply, "I'm a man of the world?"

Forshile: No, sir. This never happened. I didn't say anything of the sort. I actually said from the first allegation, "Where is it legal for a man to rape his wife, although he has to appreciate his vows of marriage. I don't think you have any right to rape a wife," and the next thing I was arrested.

Fairley: Do you remember being asked the question, "Did you have intercourse?" and the reply was, "No, not one hormone will you find on her?" Do you remember making some remark like that?

Forshile: It is very unusual, because she has plenty of hormones. She is female.

Fairley: You have no recollection of denying having had sexual intercourse, to the police officers?

Forshile: I never denied it.

Fairley: I am sorry.

Forshile: I never denied it.

Fairley: You never denied it?

Forshile: No. Dr. Lawson was at the Police Station. He was called in from the prison area I believe. That is before the case, or after the case came to court. I think it was on a previous remand date.

Fairley: Do you remember these interviews being read out to you?

Forshile: Interviews?

Fairley: Do you remember either of them being read at all?

Forshile: The interviews were not read to me. I was not allowed the prosecution evidence. I was only shown one particular statement and that was not to do with Dr. Savage, it was to do with the assault on Henely which was previous to that coming up. The grievous bodily harm.

Fairley: We had better not go into that. Let us stay with the question if we may. Do you remember reading these statements through later?

Forshile: I have not read defense evidence whatsoever. The solicitor went through part of the brief with me yesterday and on a previous day, not yesterday, in Chester. That was the first time I have ever looked at the defense evidence. I have never heard it before.

(Fairley is just not going to get a straight answer from this guy. Defense evidence, indeed.)

Fairley: Is any of it right then?

Forshile: I wouldn't know, sir. I am not in that position to say so.

Fairley: Let us just look at it from another point of view. From the point of view of what you told us today. You tell us that you saw this lady and she came up to the wall with some water?

Forshile: No, I asked her for a drink of water as I was thirsty. It is normal. I thought it was normal. If you see someone camping or something, it is normal if you are thirsty to ask for a cup of water. I thought it was the rule of the road if you are short of something to actually go to someone for help, for basic survival. I thought that was the rule of the road. She was sitting there crying her eyes out. I asked if she was alright. I said, "Is it alright to have a drink of water?" She went round and sniffed and said, "Get away" like so the first thing I thought was I'm getting out of here, but I will ask one more time for water.

Fairley: She said, "Get away?"

Forshile: She was sitting by her tent and I was fifteen yards away sitting by.

Fairley: What did you make of that statement, "Get away?" Was that an invitation to come down to her, or to stay away?

Forshile: Oh! I stayed away from her. I only asked for water. I wasn't stupid.

Fairley: You say you came back to her and she was in the tent?

Forshile: That seems to be unsuggestive when I said that she got out of her tent without her jeans on.

Fairley: You say that when you came down to the tent she was in it?

Forshile: She was getting out. I came back and I actually shouted her name.

Fairley: You told us that.

Forshile: And she actually came out of the tent.

Fairley: You say she came out of her tent without her trousers on?

Forshile: Yes. She proceeded to sit down saying, "Go away," and then, "Come back. If you want sex you can have it." When I talked about it previously she was actually standing .

Fairley: She said to you, "If you want sex you can have it?"

Forshile: "You could have had that." There was no question of that.

Fairley: She had said that previous?

Forshile: She said that when I actually came back.

Fairley: It was just that first time?

Forshile: It was just that first time.

Fairley: We know from other people that she got a black eye. She says she had a cut mouth as well. Did you hit her?

Forshile: I don't know, if she has stumbled, but I didn't actually hit her. I can't explain it, sir. If I actually hit her like that I would give you reasons for otherwise, because when I was actually arrested I only weighed about seven stone *(About 98 pounds)* I was grossly underweight, grossly frail. I wouldn't say that I was strong as an ox when I was arrested and she could have resisted any time when I feel she could have put me to the ground.

(But you all have heard the stories of how he pointed his fingers in the policeman's eyes and said he could blind him, and how he assaulted a Mr. Henely and put him in the hospital with a neck injury from which he is still suffering.)

Fairley: Mr. Forshile, if you hit her, why would that be?

Forshile: I don't think I actually hit her.

Fairley: You say you pushed her?

Forshile: I pushed her away, "Oh! Come off it," just joking - joviality.

Fairley: Where did you push her?

Forshile: I don't think I pushed her anywhere. I think she moved to one side.

Fairley: You did not lay hands on her at all?

Forshile: I don't think so, unless you are claiming something else rather than rape.

(Like for instance, wonderful intercourse with consent?)

Fairley: What was the point of trying to push her at all?

Forshile: I don't know. It's called common knowledge. It is really a point of being friendly with a person, if you can have a laugh about. It is usually called friendship, or something. Having a laugh - making a joke.

Fairley: It would not be friendship to give someone a black eye?

Forshile: No. I did have a black eye once through messing with a friend, but it does not mean to say he beat me up.

Fairley: Did she take her own clothes off?

Forshile: She must have done unless there was some else there undressing her.

Fairley: Did you try to take her clothes off?

Forshile: No, sir.

Fairley: Not at all?

Forshile: Why should I. She had already removed them.

Fairley: All of them?

Forshile: No, she still had her panties on. She wasn't wearing stockings.

Fairley: So what is rape?

Forshile: Rape is something that is physical, brought on by a person suggesting grievous bodily harm - like a psychopath. I should imagine rape is something that is so violent that it causes a woman grievous bodily injury in places where most people are not allowed to see, but there was no bruising, not that I have heard unless - I wouldn't mind medical evidence showing where the damage is of her pelvis, because I didn't see any.

Fairley: It is not suggested that her pelvis was damaged. It is suggested that she had a black eye?

Forshile: I didn't see no black eye. Maybe it's me and I may need glasses. I did ask for a hearing and an eye test which they said I was perfectly adequate. They said that they seemed alright and I seemed ship-shape, or I would be soon when I had had some decent food and that was as far as I can say. I went to Risley and they put me up in Court and then they took me to somewhere where I have never ever been before.

Fairley: You are better now?

Forshile: No, I'm not better. That's a matter for the medical journal.

(I wonder if he knows he can get out of a rape conviction by reason of insanity as long as he's not better.)

Fairley: Going back to rape. You say it is sexual intercourse that is with violence and force?

Forshile: That is what I was led to understand from the books and case reports. It is usually a very violent act.

Fairley: A violent act?

Forshile: Yes, more so than sexual. I believe it is a very violent act.

Fairley: What I was interested to know is why you were so keen to tell the police officers that you had not raped anybody?

Forshile: I have not offered that sort of information to anyone. I would not do that without counsel. I am not that ignorant.

Fairley: Do you remember that night, in the tent, how you slept?

Forshile: I slept beside her.

Fairley: She has told us that you had her arm under your head, is that right?

Forshile: If she wanted to turn she could turn. I was asleep at the other end of the bed, or bundle, by the door. She left it by the door the next morning saying that she had to get the bus at ten past seven, so the bundle was left by the door. She slept beside the bundle by the door and I was asleep at the bottom end of the tent. I had toweling on, like a sweatshirt with red and white stripes, jeans and under toweling and training shoes.

Fairley: Did you, in the course of the night, shortly after getting into the tent, have a further act of intercourse?

Forshile: Yes, sir, but 'further act' you say. It is an act, but I did not quote Shakespeare. She was actually very friendly.

Fairley: She was actually very friendly?

Forshile: Yes, she was very friendly.

Fairley: At no time did you think she was worried?

Forshile: I don't think I realized that at the time. I don't know if she was worried about the position or whatever. She did not seem worried about me being there unless she had a previous engagement with someone else and I interrupted her.

Fairley: Do you remember referring to the fact that there had been other people who had attacked her and telling that to the police?

Forshile: I have not said anything of that sort.

Fairley: You never said that whatsoever?

Forshile: No. Not whatsoever. I don't think so.

Fairley: You see, what I want you to understand is this, that your recollection today, you say, is the same as it has always been?

Forshile: Well, some days I remember more than others, but I have never been asked to give evidence before. This is the first time you have ever heard my side of the story, so any prior knowledge of that would only be hearsay.

(Ah, he knows the words hearsay, along with remand, and other legalese)

Fairley: However, you are remembering it today as you think you always remembered it?

Forshile: I don't know. I may think differently tomorrow. I can only be adjusted on the person I am that day. I could be different tomorrow.

Fairley: You had gone down to this lady?

Forshile: I have actually said that she came to the wall. I never went down to her .

Fairley: You have said that for a minute you had gone down to that lady and she had offered you sex?

Forshile: No, I'm not as naive as that.

Fairley: Can you explain that?

Forshile: Simple, sir. If I had seen a dog I would call it a dog and I would not call it a cat. You are treating me as a naive child. I can explain some of your reasoning, but I can't explain what you are trying to get at.

Fairley: Let me ask questions of you. You went down there and it was your case that she offered sexual intercourse.

Forshile: Yes.

Judge David: Can I speak clearly. We are speaking of two different things. The first time he says that she came up to the wall to him. Is that what you are saying, and she gave you water?

Forshile: She was carrying, like a goatskin bag.

Judge David: She went back to her tent; you walked away; you say that you heard her calling you, or thought you did, so you ran back. When you got back she was either in the tent or out of the tent, but you don't remember?

Forshile: I never seen her get out. She was sitting down and saying, "Go away," and then, "Come back," and all this.

Judge David: And you had intercourse with her outside the tent?

Forshile: Yes.

Judge David: Which time are you talking bout?

Forshile: That time.

Judge David: The second time when you come back?

Forshile: I didn't have intercourse when I was taking water.

Fairley: His Honor was trying to help. Let us go to the point where she comes out of the tent.

Forshile: Yes, she had a light striped yellow and fawn and brown shirt on.

Fairley: I want you to tell us exactly what she said to you.

Forshile: As far as I can recall she got out of the tent and I said, "Why did you call me back. I was here before. I was comfortable and settled down for the night, leaning with my back straight against the wall with polytene over me. I was warm and comfortable." If I didn't get into a warm comfortable position I would not get into a comfortable position for the night again and I would have to walk.

Judge David: At this point we will have a short break to give everyone a rest.

(Short adjournment)

(We broke for about ten minutes. As I remember, the defendant stayed on the stand and both the defense solicitor and barrister spent that time talking to him. That was interesting given his change in testimony when we came back. My suspicious mind leads me to believe that these two learned gentlemen suggested that he might own up to hitting me because that would give the jury the lead they would need to convict of indecent assault, rather than rape.)

Fairley: Mr. Forshile, I have only one or two more questions to ask you. I was just going back to the point outside the tent. We had got to where you have gone down to the tent and she has come out of the tent, you say, without her trousers. You sit down and have a talk with her?

Forshile: Well, I didn't actually. I went to sit down to talk and then she said, "The way I see this is I let you go and come back." I said, "What the heck are you on about? I was settled down for the night and there is no need to do that to me." She was rambling on. I don't know what she was on about at first. I thought I said, "Do you want me to sleep with you?", and she said, "You could have had that anyway. Let's talk about it. Let's be rational." I thought flipping heck. I lost my temper and actually slapped her, because she was acting hysterical.

(I certainly was hysterical, because I knew what he was on about.)

Fairley: This is a new piece you have told us, that you lost your temper and might have slapped her?

Forshile: I might have slapped her, but I never forced her to the ground.

Fairley: Why did you lose your temper and slap her?

Forshile: Because I made a mistake in the earlier part of the evidence I gave you. I asked for a cigarette, not water. I asked for a cigarette first. I said, "Have you got a smoke to spare, I'm all out. I'm cold and I'm travelling?" She said, "No". I said, "Can I have a drink of water then?" and she said, "But I don't know if I have much more water left. I went to move away and I said, "Can I have a drink of water?"

Fairley: Why did you lose your temper?

Forshile: Because I came back over, right round the cove and she said, "Go away," and then, "Sit down and discuss it. Let's be rational about it." I thought when I slapped her that she actually said - I could not repeat the language, I don't remember her exact words, "You know you could have that anyway." You know what I mean. She did not say that she was determined she would not let me off with it anyway.

Fairley: The slapping of her was before she said that to you?

Forshile: Yes, with the right hand.

Fairley: You slapped her before she said to you, "You could have had it anyway"?

Forshile: Yes.

Fairley: Just to make the point very clear for us, because you are telling us you had slapped her, for what reason?

Forshile: For the reason that she put herself in danger and me in danger. The weather was getting misty and cold. She changed her mind. I was coming back round the cove for the drink and I couldn't see the pavement because it was very misty. It was just like lights shining in my face. She was putting me in danger, because I would not be able to get to sleep that night and that would leave me in a decomposed state, if I didn't get down and get comfortable. She had risked my life I suppose. I wouldn't say she risked it, she would not have been convicted of anything. I wouldn't say I was really in danger, but when you get annoyed you say certain things and you suffer for it.

Fairley: Thank you, Mr. Forshile. I have no more questions.

(Here our stories are beginning to come together a little more. Now he says that in the beginning he asked me for a cigarette, not water. He says that it was later that he asked for water and I gave him some. We disagree as to where he

received the water. He says I came up to the pavement to give it to him, while I say I used it as a way to get rid of him once he was already in my territory. We are agreed that I didn't have much to give and I didn't want him to have it all. The idea that I called him back is a figment of his imagination. The truth is, he came back. We both agree that I was hysterical and he hit me. We both agree that sex occurred. I call it rape. The barristers call it intercourse. We both agree that the first time he raped me was outside the tent , after he slapped me. I say he blackened my eye and cut my lip. The second time was inside the tent. We both agree that together we walked to the bus in the morning. I say because it was the only way I was going to be free of him; he says because I invited him. There is evidence that he wrote his name on a brochure. I say he wrote it because he told me he was going to be famous some day and he wanted me to know his name; he says it was so he could return the six pounds he borrowed from me, all very friendly and nice. I say I continued to be hysterical until I was given "Rescue Remedy" more than thirty-six hours later, and he calmly went to the newsstand and bought something to eat.

If you were part of the jury in this case right now, which truth would you believe? Would you believe that this was a simple indecent assault with consent on my part? Would you believe that this was the beginning of what could have been a brutal beating, followed by submission on my part? Would you believe that there was enough insanity on his part that he didn't know what he was doing? What would you believe?)

Chandra Ghosh, Sworn

Halbert: Would you tell us your full name and qualifications?

Ghosh: I am Chandra Ghosh. I am a Bachelor of Medicine. I have a Bachelor of Surgery Degree. I have a Diploma in Psychological Medicine and I am a Member of the Royal College of Psychiatrists.

Halbert: You are a Consultant Psychiatrist at Park Lane Hospital, Liverpool?

Ghosh: Yes.

Halbert: Dr. Ghosh, how long have you known the defendant, David Forshile, or Forsithe?

Ghosh: Since the 21st of May, 1986.

Halbert: Have you also had the benefit of seeing earlier reports on him from fellow doctors?

Ghosh: Yes.

Halbert: And reports from Denbigh where he has been an inpatient?

Ghosh: I had the notes from Denbigh and also when I saw him in Risley Remand Centre I had the notes.

Halbert: Is he ill?

Ghosh: Yes.

Halbert: What is wrong with him?

Ghosh: He suffers from schizophrenia which is a form of mental illness.

Halbert: Is it possible to say for how long he has suffered from the illness?

Ghosh: His notes would suggest that he has been suffering from the illness since 1981. That is when he was diagnosed. He could have been ill before that, but certainly from 1981.

Halbert: You first saw him in May this year. Is he better now than he was when you first met him in May?

Ghosh: I am sorry. I saw him on the 17th of March in Risley and then I had him in my care since May.

Halbert: From the first time you saw him in March, or May when you had him in your care, is he better now?

Judge David: Has he been in the hospital under your care since?

Ghosh: Since May.

Judge David: A patient of Park Lane Hospital?

Ghosh: Yes, and he has been under my care. He is better now.

Halbert: Is there a great change in him?

Ghosh: Yes, there has been a considerable improvement in his mental state.

Halbert: The principal question I want to explore with you is this: Assuming from what you have said that he was suffering obviously from schizophrenia in July of last year - in other words at the time of the alleged incident - could his illness have affected his perception and judgement. I am not concerned with whether he knew what he was doing was right or wrong, or whether he was responsible for his actions - they are in issue in the case. Could his illness have affected or clouded his perception and/or his judgment?

Ghosh: Yes. Can I explain that? People who suffer from mental illnesses like schizophrenia do have an abnormal perception. They hear things. They hear voices of people when they are not there. They see things that normal people would not see and what they hear or see, or feel, actually influences how they think. It is possible, therefore, that if he were having abnormal perceptions at that time what he would think was happening to him would be influenced by that. Therefore, there would be a certain amount of clouding of judgment on the basis of abnormal perception.

Halbert: Yesterday, we heard that he described to the police a terrorist attack and that he killed one person and threw him into the sea and killed another this morning with an automatic in the road. Mr. James, the approved social worker, said that as far as he was concerned the defendant clearly believed what he was saying. Does that accord with what you would say of the condition of this nature? Will he be believing what he is talking about?

Ghosh: Yes, those are what we would call delusions.

Halbert: To him that is very real?

Ghosh: To him that is very real.

(Therefore, when he heard me call him back, it was real to him. Therefore, when he heard me say, "You could have had that any time," that was real for him. When he decided that there were seventeen Welshmen who were coming down from the hills to hurt me, and the only way I was going to be protected was for him to stay there and have sex with me, that was real to him.)

Halbert: Stop me if I've have got this wrong. I do not want to be interpreting something which I do not understand myself. He is reacting to the delusions? He is reacting to something he believes is actually happening?

(He had no problem saying things to me that were abjectly wrong. It's very considerate of him to be so nice now.)

Ghosh: Yes. He actually believes what he is perceiving and he actually thinks those things are true. His delusions are real to him.

Halbert: In describing them and saying that something has happened, he is not actually lying?

Ghosh: No, he is not lying.

(And in this point comes the issue, that according to English law, I didn't have to consent, but if the rapist thought I was consenting, then it isn't a criminal act of rape. So, under these conditions, when is a rape a rape?)

Cross-examined by Mr. Fairley

Fairley: Dr. Ghosh, perhaps you could help the jury with this: Schizophrenia in this particular case is a label. Could you put the meaning more simply?

Ghosh: Yes. Regarding schizophrenia, a psychiatrist would diagnose schizophrenia in someone we would consider to be mentally ill rather than a disordered personality. Someone who, when interviewing him, we would be able to elicit that they have got abnormal perception, as I described before. For example, they would hear things when nothing is being said, or there is no-body there. They would see things when nothing is actually perceivable visually. They would feel certain things when there is nothing to feel. Therefore, in the absence of real stimulus, they would be actually perceiving certain things. On the basis of that, they would then try to explain to themselves why they were seeing things, hearing things and feeling things that perhaps other people could not. The explanation of that would lead them to then come out of what I would diagnose, or call, delusions or disordered thinking. To someone who was looking at someone who was mentally ill, that person would be saying things which sound totally absurd. He would be claiming certain perceptions which you and I could not share.

Fairley: The next question is this: In such conditions there are varying degrees?

Ghosh: Yes.

Fairley: You know from his mental history that at the period immediately preceding the event with which the jury is concerned, he had been in Denbigh?

Ghosh: Yes.

Fairley: However, he had been in and out and taking his own discharge and also being discharged by Denbigh?

Ghosh: Yes.

Fairley: The difficulty, looking at the history and knowing as you do the history at the time, does it assist at all as to the question of degree of his schizophrenia?

Ghosh: No. Can I explain that?

Fairley: Yes.

Ghosh: The only history I have got out of the Denbigh notes suggested that they actually, if anything, missed a serious illness rather than diagnosed it. Therefore, no, it does not tell you how seriously ill he was at that time. He may have been, or he may not have been, but the diagnosis is not tenable.

Fairley: The next point to ask you is this: The fact that he was thought to be disordered at the time he saw the police officers, does that, in any way, answer the question of whether or not he knew at the time that the complainant was willing?

Ghosh: I do not know.

Fairley: Does it follow on because he was disordered by the time he saw the police that he would necessarily have been disordered in his appreciation at the time of the events?

Judge David: A week before?

Ghosh: No, it does not necessarily follow.

Fairley: Because the state fluctuates?

Ghosh: The mental state fluctuates. You can be very deluded and still at certain times perceive certain things which may have nothing to do with your delusion.

Fairley: The fact that he knew at the time he was being accused of attacking a lady and then was denying that he had raped her, does that suggest to you at all that he had any cognizance of what rape was about?

Ghosh: No, because I am not aware from the police depositions, or from what Mr. Forshile said today, that he actually understood what was being said to him.

Fairley: What he has told us today is very different from that which he told the police officers?

Ghosh: That is right.

Fairley: And what is more, today he has clearly indicated, you may think, that he understands what the offence of rape involves?

Ghosh: He understands what he means by it. He is clear about what he means by rape today.

Fairley: The fact that today at one moment, and also when he saw the police officers, he admitted to violence on the lady and then at the next moment he says that he has not, or it has been the other way round today, is that indicative of his level of understanding at the time that these events, with which we are concerned, took place?

Ghosh: No, because I would suggest that his level of understanding at the moment is perhaps better than what was going at the time. Can I explain that?

Fairley: Of course.

Ghosh: It is merely an assumption, but at the moment he has had treatment, so I would think that he is better now and more able to concentrate on what is being said. He would have more coherent thought processes. However, these are all assumptions based on the fact that I thought he was not being treated at that time I would have thought his mental state would have been much worse and, therefore, I cannot say anything definitive. I can only make assumptions.

Fairley: At the end of all this you are really unable to assist further than saying it is possible that his perception and judgment might have been affected by his condition?

Ghosh: That is right, and if what the police depositions say is correct, then he was thought to be disordered at that time.

Fairley: At the interview?

Ghosh: At the time of the interview.

Judge David: Dr. Ghosh, could you really, by way of reassurance to the jury, help on two points? Firstly, I am sure the jury would like to be reassured about this. Before this trial commenced very careful consideration was given, was it not, as to whether or not he was fit to stand trial?

Ghosh: Yes.

Judge David: Both you and a number of other consultants considered the matter and were all agreed that he is fit to stand trial?

Ghosh: He is fit to plead.

Judge David: And to understand his trial?

Ghosh: Yes.

Judge David: Another thing the jury would like reassurance on is this: With modern science, schizophrenia is an illness which can often, these days, be treated remarkably successfully?

Ghosh: Yes.

Judge David: It was not the case many years ago, but it is now?

Ghosh: It is now. It can be treated. You may not get cured, but you can certainly get an arrest of the illness and get a person back to virtually a normal state with treatment.

Re-examination by Mr. Halbert

Halbert: You mentioned Denbigh and you mentioned that it is possible to treat schizophrenia, but you have to diagnose it first before you can treat it?

Ghosh: Yes.

Halbert: As far as you are aware had Denbigh diagnosed schizophrenia, or something else?

Ghosh: The only diagnosis in the notes was not schizophrenia, but Munchhausen's Syndrome.

Halbert: Have you found from your own examination, when he does suffer, if that is the right word there, Munchhausen's Syndrome?

Ghosh: No, it is certainly non-tenable. That is a disorder where a person simulates (imitate, feign) physical illness not mental illness.

Halbert: That is something he does not do?

Ghosh: No, and there is nothing in the Denbigh notes which suggested he did.

End of the case for the defense

Barristers' Summaries

(These summaries are not taken from the official transcript of the trial of the Crown vs. David Forshile held on September 22nd and 23rd in 1986 in the city of Mold, Wales. The Barristers' summaries were never recorded. Therefore, I have rewritten them to the best of my memory.)

Summary **by Richard Fairley - Prosecuting Barrister on behalf of the Crown:** Ladies and gentlemen of the jury, we are here to assess the guilt or innocence of Mr. David Forshile in the alleged rape of Mrs. Audrey Savage on July 26, 1985, a little over a year ago today. On July 27th of that year, Mrs. Savage sent a written complaint to the Llandudno police department, which arrived there on August 1, 1985. This complaint stated that she had been raped while camping on the Great Orme. She described her alleged assailant and gave the name of David Forsithe. Later that day the Llandudno police picked up the defendant, David For-shile, interviewed him and have been holding him since that time until he was determined fit to plea.

Mrs. Savage says that she was quietly camping near the light house on the Great Orme near Llandudno and had been sitting with her back against a rock, reading. It was near 9:30 in the evening. While relaxing there, enjoying the sea and her book, she heard a voice from above. She thought the voice was saying that she should not camp there. Upon looking around she saw in the shadows of the evening what looked to her like a police officer, a man who was wearing a dark jacket or sweater. At any rate he was wearing something that made her think he was a police officer. She responded to what she thought were his objections to her camping on that spot. After some conversation he asked her for a cigarette. At that point she knew he was not a police officer, and she returned to her reading. Whereupon, he came down to her in an agitated state and began to talk to her about some Welshmen who would come down from the hills and put her in danger. She told him, angrily, that she did not think she was in danger from any Welshmen, but that she thought she might be in danger from him and would he go away. He agreed to go away if she would give him some water, which she did. Thereupon, he left, after having asked her name and telling her his name was David. She, not wanting him to know her real name, told him her name was Mary.

She was worried that he might come back and do harm to her and wondered about packing up and leaving, but she did not do so. She did take the precautions of hiding her money and checking her can of mace to see if it were working and it was not.

After about a half an hour, she decided she was safe and went inside her small tent to sleep, leaving her clothes on. Shortly thereafter she stated that she heard footsteps and knew he had come back. She heard him calling the name, "Mary, Mary" outside her tent, all the while trying to unzip the zipper. At that point she thought she would be safer outside the tent than inside and opened the tent door. She crawled out with her clothes on. She stated that she was a little unclear about what happened next but she knew he intended to rape her. She tried to stop him by pleading with him whereupon he struck her three times in the face, giving her a black eye and a cut lip. He then told her to take off her clothes. She, at that time, was afraid that he might continue to hurt her; therefore she decided to comply with his wishes.

Once on the ground he removed his pants, entered her and ejaculated into her.

When he had finished he wanted to get inside the tent with her, but she preferred that he not get inside the tent. She described the tent as small and she did not know what would happen if he were inside with her. She spent over an hour talking to him outside the tent until he again became agitated, and started talking about her ribs being broken. She then agreed to let him inside the tent. They both crawled inside the tent whereupon he raped her again, this time not able to ejaculate. He then forced her to wrap her arms around him and he proceeded to fall asleep, while she stayed awake.

In the morning she was concerned about catching a bus to London. She had her ticket with her. When it was light she asked if she could get out and go to the bathroom. He allowed her to do that. When she indicated that she wanted to go to Llandudno to catch the bus he told her it was unsafe to do so, and that she should stay there with him. She said that if he thought she would be in any danger he should walk along with her. He finally agreed. They then walked into Llandudno together, passing an outdoor toilet on the way. He advised her to go in and wash her face. She went inside and took care of her toilet needs, but failed to wash her face. When she came out he again told her that she should wash the dirt off her face. Later in the walk they passed two police officers, but she decided not to call out. She stated that all she wanted to do was to get away from him, and she thought the bus was the best way to do that.

When they reached the bus, they sat for about twenty minutes during which time he wrote his name on a bus schedule saying that he wanted her to remember him because he would be famous some day. Later he asked her for money. She gave him five pounds, all she had with the exception of one pound. When the bus came she got on, and he left the bus depot.

Arriving in London, she went to Victoria Train Station where she cleaned up; then she boarded another bus to Romsey where she was to meet some people. While waiting to be picked up by her friends in Romsey, she wrote a letter of complaint to the Llandudno police. Later she spoke with both Anna Marie Garden and Caroline Novarra. They both reported seeing her black eye.

On Tuesday next she boarded a plane for America.

Ladies and gentlemen of the jury, this is the story of Audrey Savage concerning her alleged rape by the defendant, David Forshile. In all due conscience, when you retire to deliberate this case, you must vote that the defendant, David Forshile did forcibly, and with violence, rape Audrey Savage on the night of July 26, 1985. Thank you for your attention.

Summary by Trevor Halbert - Defense Barrister on behalf of David Forshile: Ladies and Gentlemen of the jury, you have just heard the summation and arguments by my learned friend, Mr. Fairley. You have also heard the story as told by Audrey Savage, an American woman who was camping alone on the Big Orme close to the light house near Llandudno on July 26, 1985. You heard from both of them that on this night she was quietly reading with her back against a rock enjoying the sea and her book. Then my learned friend told you that she heard a voice from above, a male voice I presume, which she took to be that of a police officer. She says that when he asked for a cigarette she realized that he was not a police officer and returned to her book.

But let me put the story to you this way. Mr. Forshile was, indeed, talking to Mrs. Savage, being in need of some water to drink. When he asked for water she gladly came up to the road and offered it to him. There they chatted for a while. He then left, planning on bedding down for the night further on down the road.

Contrary to this, my learned friend said to you that first Mr. Forshile talked to Mrs. Savage from the road, finally asking for a cigarette, then came down to where she was sitting, talking about some Welshmen who were coming down from the hills to hurt her. This kind of talk frightened her, whereupon she asked him to leave. He did leave.

Let me ask you this, ladies and gentlemen. If she had been so frightened, why did she not pack up her things immediately and leave the area? Why did she stay, believing, as she says, that a man was near whom she was afraid might hurt her?

She claims that she did not try to get away because there was only one way out of the area. The only way out, she says, was up the hill and through the exact hole in the wall where he had passed. In other words she is claiming that she couldn't leave because she was afraid that he might still be up there hovering near the road, waiting for her. Yet, he had been gone for some time and she chose not to take the trouble to look to see if he had gone. If she had been as frightened as she said she was, wouldn't she have gone up to see if he was indeed gone? Wouldn't she have packed up her tent and left the area anyway?   Wouldn't she have gotten away somehow, if indeed she was afraid that this man might do her harm? But she chose to stay. She not only chose to stay but she got into her tent, with, she says, her clothes on.

They had exchanged names before Mr. Forshile left the area. She knew his name was David, although she, for some unexplained reason, told him her name was Mary. Mr. Forshile, having gone a short ways up the road, was bedded in for the night, when he heard her calling him back. "David," she called. "David, will you come back?" He thought his luck might be in so he hurried back, running part of the way. He found her inside her tent and she willingly came out without her jeans on.

Now let me put it to you this way. If she was as frightened as she claimed to be, wouldn't she have run away at that time? She states that as they faced each other she was facing the sea and was closest to the road. We have discerned that from where she was standing, it was no further than the length of this courtroom to the road. She could easily have run to the road and gotten away. She claims that she didn't run because she was worried about her equipment. Doesn't it seem strange that a woman who believes her life to be in danger, would worry so much about her equipment that she would not run at this kind of opportunity? Then she states that when he is about to rape her she willingly takes off her clothes and then she asks him if she can get her pad out of her tent to protect her from the thistles. Ladies and gentlemen of the jury, she willingly takes off her clothes, and politely asks if she can get her mat out of her tent to protect her from the thistles. What does that sound like to you, ladies and gentlemen?

Later, they spend an hour outside the tent talking. She claims she has just been brutally raped, but still she spends an hour sitting on the hillside with him chatting about the this and the that. And this is before she invites him inside the tent to sleep away the night.

Once inside the tent she claims that he raped her again, but she cannot remember whether she had her clothes on or not, or whether she took them off or he took them off of her. She thinks maybe she took them off. All of this in a tent so small that it is barely big enough for one person. This is the same tent that was so small that she had intercourse out in the thistles rather than allow him inside the tent with her.

And throughout the night, they sleep, wrapped together with their arms around each other. When she wakes at the first light she needs to relieve herself. They both come out of the tent, she goes a ways away from the tent, takes care of herself, and COMES BACK. She comes back, ladies and gentlemen. Even then, after having been, what she claims as, brutally raped, she comes back. She again chooses not to run away from a man whom, she claims, has beaten her, given her a black eye and brutally raped her. She comes back, again, claiming that she did not want to lose her equipment.

She explains to him that she has a bus to catch to London. She then claims that he told her it was dangerous for her to walk to town, and she says, "If you are afraid I am in danger you can walk with me, the more the merrier."

They then pack her things, and together they walk into town passing an outdoor toilet on the way. They both stop there to relieve themselves. She leaves her precious equipment outside the toilet while she is inside. Now, it seems, she is not afraid of losing this equipment. She has, she says, faced this man, whom she claims to be a rapist, all night in order to save her equipment. Now she leaves it outside the toilet where anybody could steal it.

Later, as they are walking through town they pass two police officers, standing as close to them as the width of this court room. She does not call out. She does not say, I am being kept by this man. She makes no indication that her life is in danger, or that she has been, what she calls, brutally raped. Instead she walks right past these two men with no indication that there was anything wrong. Here were two police officers who could have arrested her companion on the spot and gotten her out of, what she claims, was a life-threatening situation. In fact she says nothing. She claims that all she is caring about is getting on the bus. Not whether this strange man, who has beaten her and raped her, is arrested. Not whether they can get her out of what, she claims, is grave danger. No. They pass the police officers by with nary a sound.

They arrive at the bus station and he asks her for some money to carry him through. She gives him six pounds and he writes his name on the bus schedule so he can return the money to her. Now why would a man who has raped a woman leave her with his name? Just why, ladies and gentlemen? Because, I put it to you, there was no rape. Oh, yes, there was intercourse on that night. Twice there was intercourse, but there was no rape. Think about it ladies and gentlemen. There was no rape.

And even if **she** has deluded herself into thinking it was rape, he certainly did not think so. She called him back. She came out of the tent with nothing on but her shirt. She was pushing him. She willingly took off the rest of her clothes and lay down on the ground, asking for her pad to protect her, then invited him in to sleep away the rest of the night. He certainly would have been rightfully confused about her intentions, especially given his mental health at the time of the alleged incident.

So I put it to you, ladies and gentlemen of the jury. Was it rape, as Mrs. Savage claims? Was it a mistake on the part of the defendant as to her intentions? **Or** was it intercourse with total consent? Look at the evidence, ladies and gentlemen. Yes, look at the evidence and then you decide.

Thank you for your attention.

(I was a wreck. I was trembling. I was numb. I was so tense that I thought I was going to leap right into the middle of that court room. My stomach was tied into knots. My hands were cold and clammy. I was holding on to Sheryle's hand so hard that halfway through she had to pry me loose, or she would have had no circulation.

It's hard to explain what happened to me. It's hard to describe the state of my being. Somehow I felt as though I had disappeared. I knew my body was there. It had not changed. It was sitting next to my friend on a bench at the side of the court room looking to all events and purposes as though nothing were happening. But going on inside of me was a holocaust. With every word spoken by Mr. Halbert, the "I," the "me," was being destroyed. That's the only way I can put it. Perhaps the best word I can use for it is that piece by piece, word by word he was destroying my soul.

I was listening to this man take my words and twist them to suit his own purposes. I was listening to him distort and misrepresent what I had said. I was listening to him malign my person and my character. I was hearing him belittle me with his tone and with his words. He had taken my truth and used insinuations and innuendos to distort it until it was almost unrecognizable. It seemed as though he had taken my person and turned it inside out, saying, "This woman is a liar."

All I knew from the moment David Forshile struck his first blow was that I was going to die if I didn't submit. This man could and would kill me to get what he wanted. He wanted to have what he wanted and my body, my person, my soul were only there for his purposes. I was his prey. And he was willing to use his superior physical strength, his violence, his ability to terrorize, to get what he wanted. Trevor Halbert was willing to use the results of my terror to get what he wanted.

The first man, David Forshile, took my body by force. The second man, Trevor Halbert, took my integrity by force. Together they took my soul and twisted it for their own ends . . . until I felt as though I had no soul left.

*Invasion. To take me and force me to be yours. That's what rape is all about. To have no regard for **my** body, **my** person or **my** truth. That's what rape is all about. To trample over the very essence of me to get to your ends. That's what rape is all about.*

And it is in my essence that my soul resides.

And when Trevor Halbert finished telling a jury about his truth in a courtroom in Mold, Wales in the United Kingdom on September 23, 1986 I had no soul left. By taking my truth and twisting it into what he wanted it to be, he had forced me. By having no regard for my fear of death at the hands of a madman, he had forced me. By using his superior tone to twist, insinuate, and outright change the truth, he had forced me. In other words he had taken my very soul from me . . . and left me with knots in my stomach, a sense of being crazy and a friend with no circulation in her hands. And that's what rape is all about - - - Now there were two.)

Judge's Summation

(The Judge's Summation is taken word for word from the trial transcript. The emphasis, however, is mine.)

Judge David: Ladies and gentlemen of the jury, on the night of Thursday, the 25th of July, of last year, Doctor Audrey Savage, a middle-aged American professional woman, was on vacation in the United Kingdom and was camping alone on the Great Orme. She was approached by the defendant; and it is common ground that during the hours that followed, sexual intercourse occurred between the two of them twice. The defendant spent the night by the tent, or in it; and the following morning the two of them walked together into Llandudno so that she could catch the bus back to London.

Those are the bare bones of the very strange story which you and I have listened to during the last two days - the story being strange and at times bizarre. One of the worrying features of the case - I am sure it has worried you, as I assure you it has worried me - is that the defendant is ill. It was obvious to Mrs. Savage on the night. It was obvious to the police and the social worker when they interviewed him a week later, and obvious, I suspect, to you and me as he gave his evidence. Doctor Ghosh has told us that, in fact, he suffers from schizophrenia which is a mental illness.

You would, I am sure, like to know a little bit more of how you should approach a case when the defendant you are trying is mentally ill. The broad picture is this: in this country the first consideration of any criminal trial is that it should be a fair one. If the defendant is ill to the extent that he is not properly able to defend himself on a serious criminal charge, he is not put on trial. It would not be fair to try a man who was not able to properly defend himself. However, as you will appreciate, if that happens, the person who is charged is not simply allowed to go. The practice is that he is detained in a mental hospital until he is either fit to be tried, or fit to be discharged from the hospital.

If he is fit to be tried, or fit to be discharged from the hospital, the Home Secretary decides whether he shall, or shall not, be put on trial. So much depends upon how serious the case was and how stale it has become. A person who is on a charge which is not terribly serious, who has been kept in the hospital for five years by reason of mental illness, and has now thankfully recovered and is fit to be discharged, is unlikely, after that period of time, to be put on trial. However, that is the decision of the Home Secretary.

Pause with me for a moment, and in doing so I am sure you will realize that there are many people who, whilst being ill, are not so ill that they cannot be tried. Of course, it is very desirable that a person should be tried as soon as possible after the events, providing he is fit. It has been decided in this case, you know, from the evidence of Dr. Ghosh and by colleagues of hers with consultancy status, that this defendant, whilst still being ill, is fit enough to be tried and is fit enough for a fair trial. Therefore, you and I now have to proceed to consider carefully the evidence; and you, the jury, have to decide whether either of these charges has been proved. Let us first of all take stock of the law. It is for me, the Judge, to give you, the jury, directions on the law. It is supposed, with a confidence which I hope is well placed, that I am more likely to get the law right than you. You have to listen to what I say about the law and act upon it in this case. Traditionally, Judges try to help juries by reminding them of some of the evidence and perhaps make some observations upon the evidence to help the jury with their task, which is to judge the facts in the case. That is why a decision of fact is left to the jury and not the Judge so that each of you can bring your common sense and experience of life to bear on what is going to be a very important decision.

It is all the more important that it should be trial by jury in a case such as this which involves intimate personal relations. And is it not obviously right that the jury should consist of both men and women, each sex being able to assist in reaching a sensible and fair decision? Therefore, when you deliberate in your room after this summing-up, **please remember not to let your common sense and experience of life desert you when reaching your decision.**

As I explained to you first thing this morning, there are now two charges in this indictment. It started with one; but there are now two. It makes no real difference, because it would have been open to you to return a verdict on the second count in the alternative without adding it to the indictment, but I thought it was better to have it added so that we can all see exactly where we stand. The first charge is one of rape. Members of the jury, rape occurs if a man has sexual intercourse with a woman, but, at the time of the intercourse, she does not consent to it; and at the time of the intercourse, **the defendant knows that she does not consent to it.**

Let us pause and take stock just for a moment. "Consent," that word is to be given its ordinary meaning; and **do remember that there is all the difference in the world between consent and submission.** Consent means consent freely given by a woman who truly is agreeing to have sexual intercourse. A woman who submits in fear is not consenting within the meaning of this act, so do bear that in mind, because **that is very important in this case.** The second point, you will remember was, 'and the man who at the time of the intercourse knows that the woman is not consenting'. Surprising though it may seem, there are some situations where sexual intercourse can take place without the woman consenting, but the man not realizing that she does not consent. To be rape, both points must be proved.

On the second point, the question of does the defendant know, or did he know at the time of the intercourse, that she was not consenting. The Act of Parliament, which is the recent Act of Parliament, passed as a result of careful deliberation by a committee presided over my Mrs. Justice Heilbron, provides specifically that when you are considering whether at the time the man knew the woman was not consenting, the presence or absence of reasonable grounds for such a belief is one of the matters which you the jury should take into account. This is one of them. **Does it really mean nay more than this: that you should approach it from a common sense point of view? I do not think it does.**

If the sexual intercourse that took place that night - it does not matter which of them - was without the consent of Mrs. Savage - and if the defendant, at the time, knew that she was not consenting, he is guilty of rape. If those facts are proved, you must not shirk from doing your duty of convicting him of rape. Supposing, however, you are satisfied - it is entirely a matter for you, but it may be without much difficulty - that sexual intercourse was without her consent; but you are not satisfied that he knew she was not consenting, then you could not convict him of rape - because both have to be proved. However, you could, if you thought fit, convict him of indecent assault; and I will explain why.

When considering the question of indecent assault, the test is an objective one. Indecent assault occurs if a man uses force to a woman, any force will do in that regard, and does it deliberately and unlawfully and in circumstances of indecency.

If viewed objectively, the defendant did by force, because that is the allegation here that he hit her first, have intercourse with Mrs. Savage; **but you are not satisfied, perhaps because of his mental illness, that he really knew that she was not consenting,** it would be open to you to convict him nevertheless of indecent assault. Because on those facts it would be difficult to conclude it was other than an assault and difficult to conclude that the circumstances were other than circumstances of indecency.

It seems to me, in reality, that if both the points that I have been explaining to you are proved, he is guilty of rape. If the first point only is proved (that is to say sexual intercourse without the woman's consent at the time) but the second one (his knowledge) is not proved, it seems to me almost certainly you would then be right to convict of indecent assault. However, do not forget in all this that the defendant's case is that she consented. He said, "She called me back," and indeed he did, at one stage, suggest to you that she was inviting him.

The defendant's case clearly is that this was sexual intercourse with consent . If that is so, of course, he is to be acquitted altogether of both charges. Try to remember that. Bear in mind this point that arises on the two charges of this indictment: that they are, of course, alternatives. If you convict of rape, you will not be asked for any verdict in respect of indecent assault. However, if you find him not guilty of rape, you will be asked for your verdict on the charge of indecent assault. So much for the charge.

Let me now tell you something else. We have found in these courts over the years and indeed over the centuries, that in cases that involve sexual behavior of men and women, one needs to be extremely careful to start with. This is really obvious when you pause to reflect that acts of that sort almost invariably occur in private. Almost invariably there is no third party to give the jury an independent account of the events. All too often you have two people, the only two people who were there, one giving you one account and one giving the other. How is the jury to be sure where the truth lies?

Is it not the case that over the years it does sometimes happen that people lay false charges? Women make false allegations of sexual molestation and men do too. Therefore, that means that we have to view this case with greater care than others. **As a rule of practice, it has been held for many years that it is generally unwise and unsafe to convict a defendant of a sexual charge unless there is some independent confirmation of the evidence of the prosecutor or prosecutrix.** In other words, in this case is there some independent evidence which tends to support, in some material respect, the evidence of Mrs. Savage, and does it tend to show that the defendant is indeed guilty of the charge he faces?

I have to make this plain, also: that it is open to you, if you come to the conclusion there is no independent evidence to convict. You have heard and seen them both; and if, bearing in mind this warning, you the jury are sure that the defendant is guilty of one or other of the charges on the evidence of Mrs. Savage alone, it is open to you to convict on that evidence alone provided you bear in mind my warning. However, you should look, of course, to see if there is some independent confirmation.

My duty is to draw your attention to the evidence which could fall into that category; and it is for the jury judging the facts to say if it does, and whether you the jury regard this as supporting evidence of Mrs. Savage. It goes without saying, of course, that you do not get to the stage of looking for independent confirmation unless, having heard the parties, you are disposed to accept the evidence of Mrs. Savage. If you are, you look to see if there is confirmation.

Now, the matters that could fall into that category are these: first of all, she was injured and she says so. Two witnesses, whose evidence was read to you, say so; and the defendant, at various stages, said so. She had, we know, a black eye. She says that she had a cut lip as well; but there is no independent confirmation of that. However, there is independent confirmation of the black eye. **How did she come to have a black eye if this was consensual intercourse?** That is the first question you might choose to address your minds to. That is something that could provide confirmation of her account.

Secondly, during the course of the interviews between the defendant and the various police officers, at various stages he did admit to the use of violence. He did admit to striking her. Of course, you will have to bear in mind his mental state at the time he was being interviewed. In that connection, it is clear that his symptoms at that time were pretty florid. The account given by the officers is obviously at times utterly bizarre, so you need to be a little careful. You heard him give evidence today and we know now that he is much better than he was then. He is now in expert hands and it would seem he is responding gratifyingly to the treatment he is now receiving. However, in evidence today, you may feel it is a matter for you, **he did at times admit that he struck her** . That is another matter you will consider that could fall into this category.

In much the same way, you will remember, **at various stages of the interview he denied having had sexual intercourse with her - a fact he now admits.** In a normal case I would have no hesitation in saying to the jury that such a denial shown to be a false denial, assuming you are satisfied that is what was said, could amount to this sort of confirmation. However, one needs to be so much more careful in this case because of his mental state. Bear that in mind as it is still open to you if you think right. There it is, members of the jury; those are the matters, it seems to me, you should address your attention to on the question of independent confirmation.

One thing which may have been going through your minds as I have been talking is the letter of complaint which Mrs. Savage sent to the police in Llandudno. Bear this in mind: that it is, of course, permissible for you to know that when she got to Romsey that evening she sat down and wrote to the police in Llandudno, complaining. It does not provide independent confirmation, because the letter comes from Dr. Savage herself.

It cannot be regarded by you the jury as independent confirmation, but you can take it into account in the rather limited sense of showing consistency on the part of the witness in question.

You have been told by both counsel, and it is my duty to repeat it, that the burden of proving this case is on the prosecution. You do not convict Mr. Forshile on either count in the indictment unless you are sure that the charge has been proved. The defendant is not under any obligation of proving his innocence. The law in this country is that it is for the prosecution who brings the charge to prove it if they can. The standard which you the jury apply is this: if you are sure the charge is proved, you convict. If you are not sure, you acquit. That is the approach you should adopt.

I do not think it is helpful to go into the refinements about what you are going to think about when you get home; because if in your jury room you are sure that the charge has been proved, one of either of these charges, you say so. At least you will have the satisfaction of knowing you will have done your duty and that is the way to approach it. If you are sure he is guilty of rape, you say so. If not, consider indecent assault. If you are sure he is guilty of indecent assault, you say so. If you are not sure of either, then you say not guilty.

Let me now go back to yesterday when Mrs. Savage was giving you her account. One difficulty in this case, which I and the shorthand writer who sits in front of you had, was that Dr. Savage at times spoke softly, and at times quickly, in an accent not wholly familiar to all of us. Therefore, it is possible that I may not quite have got down exactly correctly some of the evidence she said. When the defendant in this case was giving evidence you will remember he spoke very fast indeed, much too fast at times to get down what was being said. However, I take this view: if you say to the witness, "Stop, give your evidence at dictation speed." the witness cannot do it. Witnesses do not think or talk like that and it is not fair to them. It is better that you take the risk of perhaps missing small bits in order to allow a witness to give simply a coherent account at his or her own speed.

Mrs. Savage is a lady in her mid-fifties, a psychotherapist and a Doctor, presumably, of Philosophy. She is not a medical doctor. She was on holiday in England in July last year; and on Thursday the 25th of July she was on the Great Orme. She had set up her tent, a one-woman tent, and she was sitting in front of her tent reading in the evening light. She showed you from the photographs where it was. She said that she heard from behind someone speaking to her. She said, "He was telling me that I should not be camping there. I did respond because I thought he might be a policeman." She said, "He was wearing something dark at the top and later when he came down he was wearing a dark sweater. I thought he had a stubbly beard and he was carrying what I thought were two plastic bags carried over his shoulder. There was sort of straw sticking out of one of them. He was warning me about Welshmen drinking in the woods and that they would come down and harm me. He said that he would stay and protect me. I said that I was not in danger and I did not want him to stay. I did not wish him to stay and I repeated it several times. I said that I was going to pack up and leave unless he left."

She continued, "He asked for some water and I said, 'If I give you water will you leave - will you go away?' He said that he would, so I gave him some water and he went away. As he was leaving he asked me my name and I said that my name was Mary." Members of the jury, you know that it is not her name; and she told you why she gave that name. She said, "I said that my name was Mary and he said that his name was David. He went up the road and out of my sight."

She said "I was very frightened. I wondered if I was really in danger and so I hid my money." She said that she hid it in the bottom of her sleeping bag. She said, "I waited quite a while to see if he would come back. I did not think I could get the tent down and get away so I went into the tent and closed it. Later I was aware of footsteps walking around and I had a horrible feeling. I knew he was back. Next thing he was calling, "Mary," but I did not respond at all. He came to the door of the tent and he tried to open it. I did not want him to come in. He started to open it and I thought it would be safer outside than in, because it was dark by then."

She explained about the spray can which they carry in America and which they use. She said that she had had it with her for years and is it not the story we hear all the time in life that when the time came to use it it was empty. She tested it, but it was not working. She said, "I was not undressed and I came out of my tent. I was very frightened. He was standing opposite and I remember telling him, 'Please don't do this'. I don't remember what he had said, but I remember trying to tell him not to do it."

Now to the vital part of her evidence. She said, "He hit me very rapidly and very quickly in the face three times - I think like **that**," and she indicated the two-way slap of the face. She said, "The next day my lip was swollen and I had a black eye." Members of the jury, can I ask you to pause and to think about this piece of evidence which may **provide the clue to the first count in the indictment; because if this were an immediate prelude to sex - and you may think on the evidence that it clearly was - if this evidence is true, that he hit her to have sex, could he possibly, at the time, have thought she was consenting? If he thought that she was consenting, why hit her? It is very important that you should consider that part of the evidence.**

She went on, "I realized that he could be very brutal - no way could I fight. I thought that I had better give in or I would be brutalized. He was tearing at my clothes. I said, 'Are you going to rape me?' I said, 'I'll take them off,' and I took off my jeans and my underpants. He told me to lie down and I did. There were some thistles there and I asked could I get my pad and I just got it. He pushed my legs apart and took off his pants. I still had my shirt and sweater on. I remember seeing him standing there. He got on top of me and entered me immediately. I laid there and he thrust three or four times very quickly, ejaculated and rolled away."

Again a little later she went on, "He wanted to get into the tent with me. I knew he was going to try and stay. I didn't want him in the tent with me. The tent is very small. I decided to try and talk to him so we sat outside quite a long time, at least an hour." **She is a psychotherapist, so she must have been good at talking to him** . She said, "By now he was calm. He had been very, very agitated, but he insisted on going into the tent. I was very frightened and he was talking of my ribs being broken, not that they had been broken, but I feared he would do that. In the tent he tried it a second time. He entered me." Then she went on to describe the act of intercourse.

She said, "He accused me of not being co-operative and I said, 'It's hard to be co-operative when you are being raped'."

She described how he had gone to sleep with her arm under him and his arms around her. She said, "We were sort of locked together for the rest of the night. He slept but I didn't." She spoke of her bus ticket, or the schedule - they call it a schedule across the water - which she had got with her and she was obviously worrying about catching the bus. Defense counsel made the point, which you will have to consider, what was she worrying about, worrying about catching a bus, or worried about being in a tent with a person who raped her twice?

She said, "About five o'clock I had to get up and go to the bathroom." The Great Orme is liberally provided with the type of bathroom she was looking for at that stage. "It was getting dawn and I told him earlier about catching the bus. He tried to talk me out of it and then said that I would be in great danger going for the bus so I said, "Why not walk with me?'" What, in effect you may think she was saying was this: that she wanted to go and catch the bus, he did not want her to go and the way in which she got round that was by suggesting that he should go with her. *(An absolutely accurate statement.)* She told you that there was a lot of curious conversation and one can believe that from what one has heard in this case.

By six o'clock the tent was packed and they were walking towards Llandudno. They passed another bathroom of a more substantial nature, I suspect, on the outskirts of Llandudno, and went towards the Bus Station. She said, "We passed two bobbies and I thought should I yell out; but I made the decision not to do that as he could have turned on me at that point and hurt me again. I was very afraid of that." The defense, of course, makes the point that if this had been as she describes, it must have been utterly harrowing. She had plenty of time to think that there were policemen there, so why not yell out and seek help? That is a point you will have to consider, bearing in mind the defendant's case is that she had had intercourse with him with her full consent.

She said, "At the Bus Station he asked me for money and I have him five pounds. Whilst sitting waiting for the bus he wrote his name down on the schedule. I left on the bus about twenty past seven and I went to London. I went to the Train Station at Victoria, showered and caught the coach to Romsey." She arrived early at Romsey and spent the hour or so, which she had to wait, writing a letter to the police at Llandudno.

She said that in the early states she was more irritated than frightened when he came on the scene, but by the time he left she said, "I was very frightened." She went on to explain three things. She said, "First of all I hid my money. Secondly, I checked my aerosol, and thirdly, I seriously considered running away, but I had to go up the hill towards him - that is towards the way he had gone - or down the hill which was very rocky. Anyway, it would take a long time to pack up." When it was put to her by defending counsel, who had to put the defendant's case to her, **that she called him back, you will remember her reaction was, "That is ridiculous. I did nothing of the sort. I didn't want him around and I told him repeatedly to go."**

She told you that her view of him that night was that he was a full-blown paranoid schizophrenic. Again, it is for consideration if you think there is really the remotest possibility that a middle-aged professional woman would have sexual intercourse willingly, on the hillside, with someone she regards as a full-blown paranoid schizophrenic .

The two witnesses I referred to who spoke of an injury to her were the two women at Romsey. Anna Marie Garden was one and in her statement which was read to you it included these words, "I noticed she had a bruise under one of her eyes." The other woman was Caroline Novarra who said this, "Under her eyes on the left there was a bruise." So much for those witnesses and now let us turn to look at the defendant's own version of these events before we look at the other evidence; because that enables me to put side by side the account given by Mrs. Savage and the account given by Mr. Forshile.

His account, given this morning, was that he was walking along the coast road and noticed this lady sitting by her tent. It was getting dusk. He said that he was worrried about himself. He said, "I asked for some water and she refused at first. It was like a shriek and then like an ordinary voice shouting. I thought I would go back. **I thought my luck might be in. " I think we all understand what was meant by that.** He said, "I ran most of the way back. It took more than ten minutes to get back. I jettisoned my bag with the food in it. I can't remember if she was in the tent or out."

He continued. "She climbed out of the tent without her jeans on. She said, 'I called you back.' I said something about water and I think she offered me part of a Mars Bar. I don't think I struck her, but I might have pushed her. She said, 'What did you do that for? You could have that any time,' and then we had sex." He might have thought that "that any time" presumably was a reference to sexual intercourse. But if this is so, what he describes of the incident of pushing immediately preceded sexual intercourse and you may think was clearly connected and related to it. Mrs. Savage, you recall, said that she was struck three times and immediately after that he had sexual intercourse with her. You may think, therefore, both of them are relating to violence that occurred prior to the sexual intercourse on that first occasion.

He then said, "We had sex outside the tent. The first suggestion came from the woman herself." There, almost in a sentence, is his defense. "It was her suggestion and she climbed into the tent and invited me to sleep in the tent rather than on the plastic outside. She put a bundle down and we settled down to sleep. We had intercourse inside the tent. She invited me into the tent."

He then went on in response to a question, "I hope I didn't force myself on anyone. I slept that night. In the morning we packed up the tent and walked towards Llandudno. She had to catch a bus. I said, 'Shall I walk you back?' and she said, 'Yes, the more the merrier.' We walked past a police officer in Llandudno and walked to the bus shelter. I asked to borrow six pounds from her." You will recall the reason why he wrote the name down on the brochure was so that he could let her have the money back. He said, "The bus drove off and I bought some cigarettes and something to eat." That was the end of the story that day as far as he was concerned.

He was interviewed by the police a week later and I will deal with that in a moment or two. Amongst other things in cross-examination he said this, "I don't think I hit her. I pushed her away." He was asked in what circumstances and I think I caught him correctly when he replied, "Jollity. I don't know if I pushed her. I might have lost my temper and I might have slapped her." Later he went on, "I slapped her before she said, 'You could have that anytime.' "

What happened when he was seen by the police a week later? You will remember that the police had received the letter on Wednesday and on the Thursday he was interviewed, first of all, by two police officers who went to the hospital where he was staying in Llandudno itself. Let me take you to that part of the story. I am not going to go through all the interview, as it would not be helpful to you. You have the note of interviews which were written down at the time; but you have not got any note of interviews which were not written down until after the event, because then it is simply the officer's recollection of what was said and then writing the note down - on most occasions, something like two and a half to three hours later. In those circumstances, no one could pretend that the note made would be a verbatim note.

He was seen just before half-past ten on that Thursday morning and after a few opening, fairly illogical exchanges, came this question, "Have you been in Llandudno before, David?" Answer: "No." Question: "Are you sure? Weren't you here on Friday last?" Answer: "No, I wasn't. I haven't been here before." Later, still, at the hospital came this exchange, "Did you meet the American woman?" Answer: "She wasn't American, she was Swedish. I haven't raped anyone." Question: "Who mentioned anything about rape?" Answer: "She did. I didn't see anything until I heard a small voice like moaning over the wall. He ran off then." Question: "Who ran off?" Answer: "The man with the beard. He'd raped her in the tent and then he ran off." **You will remember, that night, he was unshaven himself.**

Again there were some more questions and answers which did not take the case very much further and he is now at the police station. Whilst at the police station he is asked this question, to which he gave a rather long reply, the last part of which is relevant. Question: "Let us get back to this woman you met on the Orme. Had you met her before?" Answer: "She was German. It was late and she was crying. I had to get her to safety. They were after her. She wouldn't lie still. She would have given our position away. I had to hit her. She was going to walk towards them." Question: "How many times did you hit her?" Answer: "Across the face so she'd come down. You've got to persuade people somehow."

A little later still he was asked, "So you did have sex with her?" He replied, "She took her tights off." Question: "Did you force her to have sex?" Answer: "Not me, she wanted it. I could tell." Question: "So you did have intercourse with her?" Answer: "Yes. It wasn't very good though, she had a broken pelvis." Question: "What did she say to you?" Answer: "You're trying to catch me out now. I'm not going to be charged."

In view of the somewhat bizarre conversation on the part of the defendant, the police, very sensibly you may think, got hold of a social worker with expertise and experience in Mental Health cases, Mr. Terry James. In the afternoon the interview was continued with the same two officers and with Mr. James present. He was asked a question about people he was speaking to on the Monday and he was asked who. He replied, "Don't know, they looked like terrorists to me. There were fifteen or thirteen of them coming down on us. Band. Killed one and pushed him over into the sea. I killed another six on the road with my automatic and she got her head up so I hit her like that - smack - smack - Get down." I had to hit her. She wouldn't stay down." Question: "Where did you hit her?" Answer: "Her head and face. Had to or she'd be killed. They know what they're doing, you know."

Of course, that piece of conversation is utterly bizarre; but you will have to bear all that in mind when considering whether to pay any attention to the admission of hitting her which was contained in that exchange. Certainly, you may think his condition, when being interviewed by the police, was pretty florid. Members of the jury, it does not mean that he was like that on the night on the hillside the week before. It does not necessarily follow. Certainly, there was ample evidence on the day he was questioned of the schizophrenia from which unfortunately he suffers.

Then came some more interviews. You have one there which I think was at twenty-past five, the one which starts, "Do you understand?" Answer: "Yes." I do not know if that interview helps very much. A little bit more than halfway down you see this exchange, "Did you have sex with her at all?" Answer: "No, because her pelvis was broken." Question: "Did she invite you to have sex with her?" Answer: "No. I've never seen her before."

Over the page, the question towards the top: "Did you have to hit this woman at all?" Answer: "She came out of the tent and I manhandled her." Question: "Did you have to hit her hard?" Answer: "I just made sure she went down arm up her back. She had something in her hand." Question: "Did you have to hit her on the face?" Answer: "I hit her on the side of the cheek with a slap. She had a gun; her head was up. I had to slap her."

Then right at the end, over the page again, the last few exchanges: "What were you wearing that night, a black pullover?" Answer: "I haven't got a clue. Some of my clothing has gone missing." Question: "Where is your black pullover now?" Answer: "I told you, I buried it somewhere. I know where it is. I can pick it up anytime. It's a safeguard." Question: "Against what?" Answer: "Simple, someone had been picking on me." Later on, to fit the story of the pullover, he did say that it got very dirty, and there was a hole in one of the sleeves, and that's why he buried it.

Some six weeks, or thereabouts, went by and he was interviewed at Risley Remand Centre. You have a note of that interview, but there is not really much in that which is going to help you one way or the other. If you turn to the third page, about ten lines down, "Did you have sex?" Answer: "No. Let's put it this way, I didn't smell it next morning." Question: "Did you hit her for a reason?" Answer: "For a reason. I was dead serious. I ran back to talk to her. Smack. Get back in." Question: "Did you sleep with her. Keep each other warm?" Answer: "Does not ring a bell." Question: "Did you have sexual intercourse with her with her consent?" Answer: "I'm a man of the world." Question: "Did you?" Answer: "No. Not one hormone will you find in her."

As far as those interviews are concerned, members of the jury, you will remember the defendant told you in evidence that he did not agree with some of these answers. Some of the answers he did not remember. Bear all that in mind. Bear in mind that as far as the interviews are concerned of which you have not got a record, that those were not verbatim and, therefore, are only of limited value. Finally, before I leave this case entirely, just let me remind you that Dr. Ghosh, the consultant in charge of this case, told you that her patient suffers from schizophrenia. He was diagnosed as such as far back as 1981. She cannot say whether the diagnosis indeed pre-dated that or not.

She said that he had been in her care since May, and had been in her care in the hospital where specialized treatment can be given to him. There had been a considerable improvement in his mental state. She told you that with the mental illness there would inevitably be a certain amount of clouding of judgment. She explained that, to him, his delusions are real when, for example, he is speaking of being on the mountainside with a gun killing someone and throwing him into the sea and killing six more on the road. That sort of account is obviously rubbish to you and me; but that is the sort of thing which in his illness, to him, would be totally real. Therefore, he would be telling of something which to him was real and actually happened - although you and I know it did not.

The doctor also said that with his condition of schizophrenia, the symptoms do fluctuate from time to time. In other words, a person at one stage can be obviously ill and at another stage can be much nearer normal. The condition varies from time to time. There it is, members of the jury.

It has just gone three o'clock and I will ask you to go to your jury room and sit down round the table and weigh up this case. It is an important case from every point of view. When you get to your room let me give you this piece of advice: You ought to first of all elect one of your number to be foreman of the jury. It does not matter at all whether it is a man or a woman. We have no sexual discrimination in the Crown Court. I simply use the word "foreman" because I am afraid I do not find the word "fore-person" falls happily from the lips. Bear in mind that this person you elect should be a person who seems to you to have the sort of qualities of chairmanship; because the person elected will have to take the chair in the jury room to give each of you the opportunity to put forward your own point of view, your own recollection of the evidence, your own impression of the witnesses, and your own view of the case.

You will find that having sat in patience and in total silence throughout this case, when you get to the jury room and the door is closed behind you, and the Judge is not to be seen, you will all want to start talking at the same time. I advise against it. Please make sure that once you have elected a foreman, he or she sees to it that each of you speak in turn so that you can arrive at a carefully considered, logical and fair conclusion. When the jury bailiff has been sworn, would you retire and consider your verdict?

(And so ends the trial of The Crown vs. David Forshile. I felt ever so much better after hearing the judge's summing up. I clearly felt heard by him and as though he knew the truth. I felt as though I could breathe easier now, or perhaps I started to breathe at all since the beginning of the trial. Since the judge had heard the truth, I was sure the jury had too.

If you were a member of the jury after hearing the judge's summation how would you vote? Would you vote to convict David Forshile on the first charge, the charge of rape? Would you vote against the charge of rape, but for the charge of indecent assault? Would you decide that he was guilty of neither charge and vote that he was not guilty? How would you vote?

I waited.

There was a short recess and then the court reconvened to try the defendant on his other charge, the charge of assaulting Mr. and Mrs. Henely on the day he had been released from jail on the charge of rape. They were just ushering in the new jury when Sheryle and I arrived back in court. There were eighteen people sitting in the two rows of benches just across from us. I looked at this group of people and wished that this had been the group of people chosen for my jury. They looked like a much more mature group. The women, especially, looked as though they had some experience with life.

*That jury was seated, both Mr. and Mrs. Heneley testified as to the circumstances of their attack, the defendant pleaded not guilty, the judge gave his summation in much the same manner as he had used in my case, the jury retired and the whole thing had taken not more than fifteen minutes. I had the distinct impression from the Henely's testimony that the defendant had deluded himself into believing that Mr. Henely was the one who had caused his arrest in the rape case, and the defendant was going to take care of **him** in his usual brutal manner. It seemed another piece in the proof of his guilt. However, my jury had not heard this case.*

When this case was over we retired to the prosecution's witness room to await the return of the jury in my case. We were not there more than five minutes when they announced that the jury had returned. They had been out just a little over a half an hour.

We returned to the court room.

I do not have the transcript of this aspect of the trial, so this is as close as I remember.)

Judge David: Has the jury reached a decision in Regina vs. David Forshile?

Forewoman of the Jury: We have your honor.

Judge David: What is your decision on the first charge?

Forewoman of the Jury: We, the jury, vote the defendant not guilty on the first charge of rape.

(I *must admit I barely heard anything beyond those words.*)

Judge David: What is your decision on the second charge?

Forewoman of the Jury: We the jury vote the defendant guilty on the second charge of indecent assault.

(Judge David thanked the jury for their work and dismissed them. He then discussed with Dr. Ghosh the conditions of the defendant's sentencing. By this time the second jury was back. They had taken about ten minutes. They pronounced the defendant guilty of assault and they were dimissed. Court was then adjourned.

Bedlam commenced. It was like a T.V. trial. I was surrounded by people wanting to know how I felt. I didn't mince words. I had just been subjected to my third rape, the rape by the jury. I was furious. I said I thought the jury had copped out, a favorite American word. I had been raped, plain and simple. I had been beaten and raped. I had two witnesses who had seen the black eye, and one who had given me rescue remedy in order to stop my inner craziness. I had done what few women choose to do, just because of this kind of trial and this kind of decision. I chose to prosecute. I had stayed with the case for over a year, and had flown back from America to England to testify. I had lived through, although just barely, the horror of cross-examination, and the even more horrible summation by the defense barrister. I had listened to him say in every way that he could that I had wanted sex with this crazy man. I had been through inner hell and back since the rape. My ability to trust, my social relationships, my feelings toward men - all men - my sexual feelings and responses, even my ability to work, had all suffered, and this jury pronounces this man, "Not guilty." It was beyond belief. Yet I had to believe it. It was there, in front of me. Indecent assault. Not the same. Not a vindication for what I'd been through because of this man. Not a vindication for all the other women I knew who had been raped and had been unable to prosecute. Not a vindication at all.

But the judge wanted to be fair. He didn't want to convict an innocent man. Yet how could a jury believe this man was innocent of rape in the face of the evidence? It took this jury approximately thirty minutes to decide that the defendant had not raped. Assaulted me indecently, yes. Raped, no. What could have been going on in this jury's collective mind?

First of all, there could not have been much discussion, not much difference of opinion, or it would have taken them longer to reach a verdict. Or, if anybody had been in favor of convicting of rape, rather than indecent assault, they were easily dissuaded. Four women and eight men. What could have gone on in their minds?

My thoughts ran wild. Possibility: I was an American. Americans are not universally loved around the world. Perhaps this jury did not find me likable, did not find my situation sympathetic. Possibility: The jury actually believed that I had consented. Possibility: The jury believed that the defendant believed I had consented. Possibility: The jury believed, perhaps subconsciously, that I had no right to be an independent woman, traveling alone, camping alone, preferring to be alone, and therefore, whatever happened to me was what I justly deserved. Possibility: Perhaps the jury believed, again perhaps subconsciously, that a man has a right to sex with a woman under whatever circumstances he chooses because woman is in reality the possession of man, no matter what the status of the man or of the woman.

*As a whole, I had the impression that this particular group of twelve people were not inclined toward independent opinions. I have since learned that rape convictions are not very popular among juries. I have learned, that no matter what the evidence, juries rarely convict of rape. Possibility: That this jury took the easy way out. Convict the man of indecent assault, put him in a mental hospital where he can get treatment. Then they could go home knowing that they had done the right thing, and still not stir up controversy among their peers. Convicting a man of robbery. Good, because personal property is at stake. Convicting someone of murder. Even better, because human life is at stake. But convicting someone of rape. Not good, because the woman probably deserved it, and the man was provoked. End of that discussion. This jury did not have the balls to go against this type of public opinion. They copped out. They went for indecent assault. They chose to believe that the defendant didn't know that I was **not** consenting. He knew I was hysterical. He knew he had to hit me. He knew what he was after; after all he ran all the way back thinking his luck might be in, but he did not know I was **not** consenting.*

The rape was complete. I had lost my right to my own body. I had lost my peace of mind. I had lost my trust in human nature. I had lost my openness and ability to talk about who I was. I had lost my credibility at the hands of the defense barrister, and now I had lost the right to be vindicated. Yes, the rape was complete.

People told me differently. The prosecuting solicitor told me that they rarely got convictions in rape cases. I was very lucky to have gotten a conviction on indecent assault. The policemen told me they were very happy with the decision. All they needed was to get the man put away so he could rape no more. They told me, after it was all over, that another woman had been raped two nights prior to mine, and the man who had raped her answered the description of Mr. Forshile. She, however, had declined to prosecute. They were delighted that I had prosecuted, and that the man would be in a hospital for a long time. Mr. Halbert was happy because he had won on the question of consent. He had convinced the jury that even if I hadn't consented the defendant didn't know that I hadn't consented. All Halbert cared about was to win. Not my state of mind. And the reporter was happy because he got an interesting story to send out to his newspapers. AMERICAN WOMAN FURIOUS WITH JURY'S DECISION IN RAPE CASE. That head, or a similar one, ran in six different newspapers.

What happened? On the surface a woman was raped, the man was caught, jailed, treated for his mental illness, a trial was held in front of two extremely competent barristers, a very fair judge, and a jury of twelve men and women. The man was convicted of indecent assault. He would be in a maximum security mental hospital at her majesty's pleasure under the mental health act, section 37 - 41. This means that they could keep him until they were absolutely sure he was well - probably a long time. I should be happy. Everybody else was.

But something else had happened, too. The whole center of my being had been devastated, and was not so easily appeased. What is it when a woman has been raped? What is it when her body, not even her body, is her own, when it is subjugated to a man's pleasure? What is that? What does it do to a woman? What did it do to me? The jury is not yet in on that trial, because not all the evidence has been heard. But it will be, believe me. It will be. Halbert, and the like, may have won the battle, but they haven't won the war.

Sheryle and I drove back to London that night. I was both exhausted, and still reeling. I talked all the way. She talked all the way. We both knew what had happened. We both knew that the wrong thing had happened. We both knew we were victims again. We both knew that there was no more fight to fight.

The next morning she put me on a plane for New York and from there back to Indiana. The stewardess had to remind me to buckle my seat belt, because I had started to write. I wrote . . . and I wrote . . . and I wrote . . . half way across the Atlantic. No, the jury is not yet in on this case. I am still writing.)

Principles of Rape
A Potpourri

I have attempted to portray the theory of rape as it has never been portrayed before. I often find the theory of anything to be dull and uninteresting. Instead, I wanted to make this theory captivating and inspiring. Hence, you will find two plays, two collages, a parable and an inspirational piece . . . along with the few necessary statistics.

Question:

What is Rape?

I define rape as the violation of body, mind and spirit perpetrated by a man against a woman for the purpose of gaining power. To do this he uses violence and his sex organ. This process causes women psychological helplessness and shame and is followed by blaming the victim. Within society the very existence of rape keeps women submissive to men whom they think will protect them. The fear of the violence and the degree of violation of rape creates a need for women to pretend it does not exist. Men rape because they think they have the right.

Webster defines rape as: 1) An act or instance of robbing or despoiling or carrying away a person by force. 2) Sexual intercourse with a woman by a man without her consent and chiefly by force or deception. 3) An outrageous violation. (Webster's Ninth Collegiate Dictionary, Merriam-Webster Inc., Springfield, Mass. 1983)

The F.B.I defines rape as carnal knowledge of the female forcibly and against her will. (U.S. Common Law and the F.B.I. Criminal Code)

Question:

How does a victim prove rape in court?

The law says that the prosecution needs:

> Identification of the rapist
>> The use or threat of force
>>> Penetration against the victims will

In actuality, to prove in court, the victim needs:

> Strength and determination enough to report it and
> suffer through what will be inevitable.

> An unblemished reputation

No sexual history beyond an impeccable marriage

>>> Proper dress

Rational Behavior at all times

>> No history of drinking or drugs and no use
>> of them at or near the time of the incident

To overcome the negative attitudes of the police in order to
get the incident reported as a rape rather than a lesser charge

Forbearance to stay with the process when all looks impossible

(Does this kind of proof seem like the good old American system of justice - or does it seem as though something else is going on?)

Question:

How many rapes are there in the United States in a year?

The F.B.I. publishes figures each year and in 1987,the last year for which there are complete statistics, 92,000 rapes were reported to the police.

From there on in it depends on the way you want to look at it.

For instance, there is the question of how many raped women actually report it? Most statistics and research say about 10%. Therefore, to get a more accurate number of rapes actually committed in the United States multiply 92,000 by 10.

Result: 920,000

Then there is a question of how the police record reported rapes. According to statistics and research approximately 50% of reported rapes are "unfounded" (recorded as a different crime) by police. Therefore, multiply 920,000 by 2.

Result: 1,940,000

This would give an estimation of actual rapes in the year 1987 as **1,940,000.**

A survey on rape published by the Uniform Crime Reports gives a different number yet. This statistic, for 1988, is 167,000 rapes, up 12% from 1987. Multiply that by 10 and then by 2 and the number is over 3 million.

Question:

How many rapists in the United States are caught?

In 1987, the last year that this figure was published by *The Uniform Crime Reports*, the estimate is that approximately 28,000 were caught.

Question:

How many men went to trial and were convicted?

Of those caught, 19,000 went to trial and were convicted.

Of those who went to trial, 88% were sentenced to incarceration in prison or jail.

Use any figure you want: 92 thousand, two-million, or over three-million, appallingly few men (approximately 16,000) are ever forced to be accountable for their crime.

No wonder men don't worry about the consequences of rape.

Question:

What if it had been robbery instead of rape?

What If It Had Been Robbery, Mr. Halbert?

A Fantasy in one Act

by

Audrey Savage, Ph.D.

Cast of characters

T. Halbert: Defending attorney

A. Savage, Ph.D.: Victim of Robbery

Scene: An American courtroom

Time: Anytime a defending attorney cross-examines a woman

Act One

Halbert: Now, it has been established by my learned friend that you were indeed robbed on the great Orme on Thursday night, July 26th, is that not correct?

Savage: Yes, he took all my money and almost everything else I needed to take care of myself. I was left destitute.

Halbert: Yes. And it has also been established that it was indeed this defendant who robbed you.

Savage: Yes. I have identified him without question, right down to his shoe strings.

Halbert: My learned friend also showed that you were beaten at the time of the robbery.

Savage: Yes. I was left with a black eye, a split lip, two broken ribs and a broken pelvis.

Halbert: Now, my question to you Mrs. Savage, is . . . .

Savage: You may call me Doctor.

Halbert: Yes. Now, Mrs. Savage. My question to you is . . . .

Savage: I'm not married.

Halbert: Not married?

Savage: No.

Halbert: That is very important information to this case, Mrs. Savage. I will look into this later in my questioning. Right now I would like you to stop interrupting me and answer this question. Just what were you doing on the Orme that night?

Savage: I was camping.

Halbert: Alone?

Savage: Yes.

Halbert: Now, what this court, and I'm sure this jury, would like to know is just why you were camping alone?

Savage: I enjoy camping alone.

Halbert: (Winks at one of the male members of the jury) So you do not enjoy camping with someone else?

Savage: I didn't say that. I said I enjoy camping alone.

Halbert: Wouldn't you have been able to prevent this robbery if you had been camping with someone else, perhaps your husband?

Savage: As I explained to you, I am not married.

Halbert: Then, perhaps, you were looking to get married.

Savage: No. I do not wish to be married. I only wanted to camp alone. I wanted peace and quiet.

Halbert: Do you realize that you set yourself up for exactly what happened to you that night by camping alone?

Savage: Are you suggesting that the reason I was robbed was because I was camping alone?

Halbert: I'm asking the questions here. Your job is to answer them.

Savage: Yes, sir.

Halbert: Now, back to my question. Is it not right that you would not have been robbed of all you own if there had been someone else, perhaps your husband, to defend you in case someone had wanted to rob you?

Savage: That is quite possible.

Halbert: Good. I would appreciate it, Mrs. Savage, if you would answer my questions more directly. I dislike taking these circuitous routes.

Savage: I'll try, sir. I want to cooperate with this court.

Halbert: Yes. This court wants justice even more than you do.

Savage: Yes. I can see that.

Halbert: Now, what were you wearing on the night of the robbery?

Savage: I was wearing a pair of jeans and a black pullover sweater.

Halbert: Tight jeans?

Savage: Not particularly. Just jeans.

Halbert: Tight sweater?

Savage: No. Quite loose actually. It was heavy and meant for warmth.

Halbert: I put it to you that you were wearing clothes meant to entice a robber.

Savage: I was not! I was wearing clothes to cover me and keep me warm.

Halbert: None the less a tight sweater and tight jeans are very enticing to a robber. (Winks again at one of the male jurors.)

Savage: I told you, my clothes were not tight.

Halbert: Now, I'd like to know a little about your marriage. You are a good looking woman, have a positive personality, and seem intelligent. Why are you not married?

Savage: I prefer not to be married.

Halbert: I put it to you that you go out in public places by yourself, wearing suggestive clothing so you can entice a robber, who can then satisfy you in the ways of a man?

Savage: That's ridiculous. I do nothing of the sort. Why would I . . . ?

Halbert: I'm asking the questions here.

Savage: I'm sorry. I forgot.

Halbert: Now, about this robbery. You say you were robbed of all your money and almost everything else you had?

Savage: Yes. He left me with only the clothes on my back, and a few little things the defendant decided were of no use to him.

Halbert: And you say that the defendant beat you and left you with a black eye, split lip, two broken ribs and a broken pelvis?

Savage: Yes, and no money to get to a hospital, or to pay for it if I did get there.

Halbert: What I don't understand, Mrs. Savage, is why you didn't run away.

Savage: He was very threatening. He frightened me. I felt paralyzed. I was afraid he would kill me.

Halbert: Those don't sound like good reasons for not running away. There was plenty of space between you and the road in which to run.

Savage: I was also hoping I could save some of my things.

Halbert: You mean, you were facing a man who was threatening you, frightening you, and whom you were afraid would kill you and you were thinking about your things?

Savage: Yes, I . . . It was all I had.

Halbert: Now, as I understand it, you managed to get a ride into town and then you got on a bus and rode to another town. I repeat, you got on a bus, Mrs. Savage. Why didn't you go to the police station and tell them you had been robbed?

Savage: I still had my bus ticket. I just wanted to be with people who would care about me, who would take care of me. I didn't have the strength to deal with it any more.

Halbert: So you allowed this robber, as you call him, to go free with all your worldly possessions when you could have stopped at the police station, made your complaint, and probably been taken to the hospital?

Savage: I wasn't thinking that way. All I wanted to do was get away from him and to where there would be people to care for me.

Halbert: I say again . . . you let this robber, this man who had brutally beaten you and stolen all your money and worldly possessions, go free, because you wanted to be where people would care for you?

Savage: Yes.

Halbert: I put it to you that that was not the case at all. I put it to you that you had second thoughts about what happened?

Savage: What do you mean?

Halbert: Because you were robbed by consent, the night before.

Savage: No!

Halbert: If you actually had been robbed as you said you were, you would have been in such a state that you would have gone immediately to the police station to report such a thing. Not waited until you got to where people cared for you, as you say, to write a letter.

Savage: I wanted to get away, that was all I cared about.

Halbert: (Winks again at the jury, at several of the male members this time. One of them winks back.) Now, Mrs. Savage, what with camping alone, and wearing those tight clothes, let's assume that you were not robbed by consent, but how was the defendant to **know** that you weren't consenting. Just how was he to know, with that much provocation? Just how, Mrs. Savage?

Savage: I told you, my clothes were not tight.

Halbert: But you were camping alone, is that not right?

Savage: Yes.

Halbert: I have no further questions of this witness.

(After hearing from two witnesses who corroborated Dr. Savage's physical condition after the robbery, two policemen who had interviewed the defendant whereupon he took them to the place where the robbery had taken place, the defendant himself who denied everything and a psychiatrist who stated uncategorically that the defendant was crazy and could not have known whether the woman was consenting or not, the jury took fifteen minutes to pronounce the defendant, "NOT GUILTY.")

**Question:
What if it had been murder instead of rape?**

What If It Had Been Murder,
Mr. Halbert?

A Play in One Act

by

Audrey Savage, Ph.D.

(**We** are sorry but this play can not be enacted, due to the death of one of the characters. It was hoped to be shown that the complainant, Dr. Savage, had enticed the murderer by being alone when she should have been with a man to protect her; had enticed him by wearing lewd and exciting clothes and had actually consented to the murder. If she had not consented, then it was meant to be shown that the murderer had not known she had not wanted to be murdered. However, due to the death of Dr. Savage .... Well, you know the rest.)

Question:

What do rapists say about their crime?

Rapists Say:

I abused young children. I would drive around the neighborhood until I found one. Kids are innocent. I would tell myself nobody liked me. I would get depressed and that was when I did it.

It was fun.

When I couldn't handle the stress I just went out and raped.

I raped my step-daughter. Once I got started I couldn't stop. I didn't care about her. I cared only about me.

When I feel horrible, I have to bring someone else down to my level. That's when I rape.

It was exciting - the fear of getting caught, the fear of their telling, the evil of it.

I was like a drug addict. When the effects of the drug wore off (effects of the last rape) I'd have to have more of the drug. I'd have to rape again.

All my life I had to prove I was a man. A man is sexual with women. Part of being tough is being sexual with women.

I take my anger out on women because I know I can get away with it.

How can she be so selfish? I did nothing wrong. In one evening, all I've worked for in a lifetime is shattered.

Some of the women who work for me have accused me of sexual harassment. I was ordered by the court to get some therapy. I don't think I did anything. I just teased them a little bit, you know how it is? But they say it was sexual harassment, so here I am.

I might get sexual with you. I hope you don't mind.

You'd better watch out because I'm going to kill you. Just you watch out. (Phone warning to me.)

I go to movies and I masturbate. Then when I'm all excited, I go to shopping malls and I get out of my car and when I see a woman coming toward me, I pull it out and masturbate in front of her. They never do anything. They just look scared and almost run to their cars. It's fun to watch them trying to unlock it and keep an eye on me at the same time. I don't do anything. I just stand there with it out, having a great time. It's small, though. I don't like it because it's so small. When I was in High School all the guys in the locker room used to laugh at me because I was so small. My father? He used to pick on me all the time.

I was fearful of women - their rejection, the humiliation. I didn't get involved emotionally. I wanted to humble them and make them powerless. Degrade, defile, ejaculate over, make them feel like scum.

I viewed women as a threat. Then I focused my anger toward them. In that way I didn't have to be accountable. I just didn't want to suffer any consequences.

To put these statements into other words, "I'm looking for power, control, dominance and self-esteem."

(Some of these statements were made by clients of mine, some by clients of a male rape therapist who was interviewing them for the police forensic department. The names have been withheld to protect the innocent and the guilty.)

Question:

What do victims say about their ordeal?

Victims Say:

A client's story (one who had been a previous rape victim.)

At 1:30 a.m., having been asleep about three hours, I woke up to hear, "Here, let me take your hand. Help me."; and to the feeling that my right hand was being placed on a fully-erect penis. In the first semi-awake thought there was a rather slow dawning of reality. I saw a tall, skinny white male standing over me. I had an instantaneous response. "No you won't. Not this time." I came up punching, knocked his hand free from my arm and threw him backwards. We banged into each other trying to get out.

At 1:38 a.m., rage seeping in, shaking, in shock, I called 911. The dispatcher was dispassionate, unbelieving. He asked "Do you want an officer to come by?" Asked, would you believe? Asked! It took twenty minutes for them to get there.

Approximately 2:00 a.m., a white female officer made a casual entrance. Her whole body said: disdain, skepticism, amusement, disgust . . . WITH ME! She took down the facts. She questioned me primarily about where I worked, how long I'd lived here, how he got in. She was far more interested in my stability than in the event. I had to ask her to walk around the side of the house to be sure he was gone. Never once did she show any interest in how I might be feeling.

A week later I was called down to the police department to look at mug shots. When I left his office, I was so shaky I stopped at the victim's assistance office. In a half-hour conversation with the supervisor there (who was wonderful), she told me that their belief is that only 20% of all sex offense crimes are even reported because of exactly the kind of "mind-fuck" I'd been through. She said sex offense cases trigger a policeman's or woman's own "crap."

I feel real helpless. Not much chance of catching him.

Kathi's story (Minneapolis Star and Tribune, Sunday July 6, 1987) -

SUICIDE ENDS KATHI'S FIGHT FOR DIGNITY

Three prominent hockey players sexually assaulted Kathi at an out-of-town hockey game in 1985. Two years later she commits suicide.

"Boys will be boys." (Some officers of the Youth Hockey Association.)

"Kill the bitch. She took our friends to court." (Scrawled on her locker at school.)

Those three boys were at a suburban mall bragging to their friends and Kathi's friends that they had screwed Kathi. (Friends of Kathi.)

Kathi is undergoing promiscuity counseling. (Someone from Kathi's community.)

There was a question. Surely the boys were thrown off the hockey team? Answer: Quite the opposite. The boys have gone on to become hockey heros. The coach even spoke positively about the "hungry" and "aggressive" style of two of the assailants. They have been nothing but cheered. The coaches even tried to change the **court** calendar so the boys could play hockey. It appeared to Kathi that hockey heroes were more important than accountability. More important than justice. More important than Kathi. (Reporter for the Star and Tribune.)

Look at him. Do you really think he could do anything like that to your daughter? (Mother of one of the assailants)

"Don't you remember when you were 16? You liked that when the boys did it to you. You may have slapped their face, but you liked it. My sons bring girls to the house all the time and I know they do that and I know the girls like it." (An officer of the Hockey association)

"I've got 200 kids who were late for school. I've got to arrange for their detention. Clean the locker yourself." (The vice principal when Kathi complained about the obscene writings on her locker.)

My client's stories -

I was studying for my medical boards. I had been up late every night, and I suppose he kept seeing my light in the window. I don't know how he got in, but suddenly there he was. He was standing over me with a huge lead pipe. He was huge, brawny. He forced me into the bedroom and he raped me again and again. He wouldn't go. It was morning before he finally left. I had my boards two days later. I don't know how I did it, but I took them. I still have nightmares about it. And when my husband and I have sex, I still see him over me. I still see him there. Over me. I've never talked about this before. (This conversation took place at least five years after the event.)

It was my mother. I remember, I was real little. She used to stick things up me. I would cry, and then she would cut me with a razor down there. I have all kinds of scars. (This client became narcissistic.)

The first time I was forced I was about five. It was a man who lived next door. He used to babysit for my mother while she worked. I couldn't understand it but I knew it was bad. I knew I was bad. I told my mother, but she wouldn't believe me. She said I was making it up. I thought maybe I was. So when my uncle started doing it when I was eight, I didn't even tell her. I just let him. When he stopped, it was the man my mother was living with. It never stopped until I was grown. Now I'm married, and I really love my husband, but I can't have an orgasm. Can you help me have an orgasm?

I think maybe I was a victim of incest. I don't remember it, but he was always shouting at me. He beat me when I didn't do exactly what he wanted. I don't remember sex with him, but I keep thinking there was. (Client who became anorexic.)

I've been to the doctor and he says the problem is lubrication. Every time I try to have sex I can hardly stand it, I hurt so much. It started after I was raped. The man beat down my door. He forced me. Then he came back the next day and the next. I finally went to stay with my sister, and then moved out of there. I'm still afraid every time anyone comes to my door. And I'm so scared for my little girl. I don't know what to do. I've got to have that man I live with for protection, but he's going to leave me if I can't have sex with him.

It happened the first time with some people I was living with. My mother had left me with them and just never came back. They just made me into their plaything. It was both the man who owned the house and his son. If I didn't do it, I wouldn't have any place to stay. They kept telling me they'd put me out if I didn't do what they wanted. Then my aunt came and rescued me, and took me to live with her. I was so happy with her. I loved her, and she loved me. Then you know what happened. When my mother found out I was happy, she came back and got me. She used to have her lesbian friends over all the time and she would make me have sex with them. I'm married now; but I can't tolerate sex with my husband. I keep having dreams about women; but I don't want to be a lesbian like my mother. I want to be married.

My father was a fundamentalist preacher. He would preach all Sunday about the sins of the flesh, then he'd come home and molest me and my sister. I hate God. I hate the church. I hate all men. God isn't about love. He's about violence and hate. Spiritualism isn't worth shit. No Male God is going to tell me anything.

My father was very strict. I had to do absolutely everything he told me to do. So when he started to tell me I had to play with his penis, I did. I remember him sitting in his chair, drinking beer, and calling me to him. I knew when he called it was time. I hated it, but I knew I had to do it. I had to do everything he said. I got really fat. Then, when I went away to college I went on a diet and I lost all that weight. Now, I'm really careful about how much I eat. I weigh it all out and only eat so many calories a meal. (This client was anorexic and weighed only 86 pounds when I first started working with her.)

I knew it was going to happen one day. I was so careful, but I was always afraid after my husband went to work, and he left at four o'clock in the morning. On this night, I heard something at the window, and there he was. He was wearing a stocking cap over his face. I don't know what I did, but he got in the window somehow. He had a gun. He forced me onto the couch. He did it right there. All I could think about was I hope my daughter doesn't come downstairs. I don't want him to hurt her, too. Please God, let her sleep through this. I don't care what he does to me, but spare her. When he was through, he left. I think it is a guy who lives just down the street from us. He had kind of a gravely voice, and that guy keeps stopping to talk to me in his car. He has the same voice. Now we have to move out of our house. We have to sell it and buy another one. I can't stay there. I don't know how we're going to afford it, but we have to do it. I can't stay there. I just knew it was going to happen some day.

It was my brother. We used to band together against my father, because my father was so awful. I loved my brother a lot, but when I was about 14 he started sneaking into my room. I couldn't believe it. I just turned over and pretended to be asleep, but he did what he came for and left. He came about three times, then I finally started locking my door. I thought my father was going to have a stroke. He carried on and on about my locking my door. It was after that that I started getting fat. (This client weighs nearly 300 pounds.)

(And the worst story of all. I run a women's group consisting of ten highly developed and mostly professional women. One day I asked them how many of them had been raped or sexually molested. I was appalled when 100% of them answered in the affirmative.)

To put it in other words, "I was afraid, defiled, and made to feel helpless."

Question:

What do the Courts say?

Courts Say:

When one chooses law as a profession, he has dreams of always defending the innocent and advancing righteous cause. Then when you start to actually practice, you find yourself defending people who are not innocent and, in fact, have done truly abhorrent things. The result too often is emotionally numbing cynicism. If I ever start to forget the human side of the case I am involved with, I will think of Kathi. (Attorney for one of the accused hockey players, *Minneapolis Star and Tribune*. July 6, 1987.)

I'm afraid most men still think of women as their property. In the case of rape, the property value goes down. (Attorney for the vicitm from movie, *Lipstick*.)

Be prepared to be abused again in court.

Not guilty on the charge of rape. (Judge in movie, *Lipstick*.)

It's not like she was tortured or chopped up. (Judge commenting to reporter after giving a very light sentence to a rapist, *New York Daily News*.)

She's still alive isn't she? (Attorney for a member of a gang who left their victim for dead.)

I will do anything to the alleged victim to get my client off. I will malign her, accuse her, blacken her reputation, dig up dirt on her, confuse her on the stand, accuse her of lying, remind her that she has a slim to no chance of conviction or anything else I need to do to get him off. (Personal communication from the Defense Attorney for the rapist of one of my clients.)

Question:

Why do men rape?

WHY MEN RAPE

A Play in Five Acts

by

Audrey Savage: Rape Victim

Act One

Cast of Characters

Father: A typically-concerned father, works hard for the establishment, comes home at night to his beer and his T.V., plays golf on weekends when he's not watching football, basketball, or baseball, and mows the yard on Sundays.

Son: Somewhere between the ages of three and sixteen: in his formative years when he learns everything from his role model, his father.

Scene: A typical living room in a typical suburban home

Time: Anytime

Premise: (From Anne Wilson Schaef, *Women's Reality,* pp. 7 - 13)
"The four great myths of the 'White Male System' are:
   1) The white male system is the only thing that exists.
   2) The white male system is innately superior.
   3) The white male system knows and understands everything.
   4) Within the white male system it is possible to be totally logical, rational and objective.

These myths can be summarized by another:
                  That it is possible for one to be God."

Act One

Father: I have some things to teach you, my son.

Son: Yes, father.

Father: What I have to say to you is very important; and you must remember what I say to you today for the rest of your life.

Son: I will, father.

Father: To begin with, when you grow up you will be a superior being, superior to anyone and anything.

Son: Yes, father. I am a superior being, superior to anyone and anything. Does that mean I'm superior to mother?

Father: Especially to your mother, my son. Superior to your mother, to your sister, and to all women. You must remember that. To your mother, to your sister, and to all women.

Son: Yes. I am superior to my mother, to my sister, and to all women.

Father: As a matter of fact, the only entity more superior than you is God; and you will grow up to be so much like God that the two of you will be indistinguishable.

Son: I will be indistinguishable from God.

Father: You will win at all things. You will train yourself to that end. You will hone your body until it is a fine instrument. You will train your mind; and you will never forget your purpose in life. Remember, always, that your purpose in life is to win. If you can be nice and still win, that is good. If you can't win by being nice, win in whatever way you can. Do you understand, my son?

Son: I understand. My purpose in life is to win. And I should do whatever I need to do in order to win.

Father: Good. Now listen carefully, my son. In order to win, you will need to be aggressive and to understand violence. There are two ways to do this. First, you must learn to fight. The best way to do that is to learn to play sports, always playing with the spirit of aggressive winning - remembering that nice guys finish last. Next, you must watch as much violence on T.V. as is available to you. The violence on T.V. will show you how it's done. You must then practice aggression whenever you can.

Son: I think I'll like that, father. I'll feel good learning to fight. That way I can be sure of winning all the time.

Father: That's right. When you know how to fight and you know how to win, then you can be powerful. It is more important than anything else to be powerful. You see, all other men will also consider themselves superior beings, consider themselves the same as God, and be out to win. Therefore, in order to win, you must be more powerful than they are. It is always a rule, my son, that in relationships with other men, one of you must win and the other must lose. Therefore, you must be powerful enough to be the winner. You must not lose to another man. Do you understand that, my son?

Son: I think so. I must be powerful at all costs; otherwise another man will be more powerful than I, and he will win. I must not let that happen.

Father: You have it my son. You are very intelligent. You can use that intelligence to obtain your power and to keep it. The way that you do that is to control **everything.** Let nothing get separated from your control. Not your house, not your money, not your business, not your wife, not yourself, not anything. What you can not control, you need to learn to control. As a matter of fact, when you grow up, why don't you learn to control this blasted weather. I'm getting tired of it raining every time I want to play golf.

Son: I should control everything. And my first job when I grow up is to learn to control the weather.

Father: Yes. And you need to be very very careful not to show any emotion. When you show emotion, you just might get out of control.

Son: Like mother does.

Father: Exactly. Always keep your emotions under control. Never, and I want you to listen very carefully to this, never let anybody know how you feel. If you allow anyone to know how you feel they will think you are weak. If they think you are weak, they will take advantage of you; and then they will win. You must not let that happen. No, you must not let that happen. If you feel afraid, act tough. If you feel more afraid, act tougher. If you feel tears coming to your eyes, get rid of them.

Son: I am to show no emotion.

Father (Clears his throat): Well, there is one emotion you can show.

Son: And what is that, father?

Father: Passion. Sexual passion, my son. You can have all the sexual passion you want. And you deserve it. It's a hard world out there, my son; and when you get finished fighting the good fight, you should have your little piece of ass. It's a reward for all the fighting and the winning you will be doing.

Son: Right! I can have all the sex I want. Right!

Father: Yes, because sex fixes everything. If, by any chance, you should feel weak, or afraid, or unjustly treated, just get yourself a piece of ass; and that will fix it. Or, if somehow you don't get to win like you're supposed to, sex will fix that, too.

Son: Right! Sex fixes everything. If I don't feel good, I can always fix it with sex. I'm glad you told me that, father. I wouldn't have thought of it myself. So if you're through with me, I just think I'll go and check that out right now. I don't mind telling you that I don't feel so good right now.

Father: Wait. There is one other topic we must discuss before you go.

Son: It won't take long, will it? I'm anxious to get started.

Father: Well, you had better know about this before you start on sex; because I have not yet talked to you about women.

Son: Oh, yes. I had forgotten about that.

Father: Well, you'd better not forget that. If you don't understand how to control women, you might not win. That would be most serious. So I will tell you what you need to know. First of all, it is very important to have a woman. We need them to take care of our house, cook our food, wash our clothes, bear and bring up our sons, and to feel all those stupid things we can't be bothered to feel.

Son: Are you saying, father, that we need them to take care of all the things that we don't want to do?

Father: Have I got an intelligent son, or haven't I? That is exactly what I'm saying. We have very important things to do, you and I, and very important things to think about. We can't be bothered with all of those stupid little things that they enjoy so much. Their minds are only fit for the little things anyway, so we just let them do it. Do you get the drift, my son? (Winks slyly at the boy)

Son (Winks back): I sure do.

Father: Now about sex, my son. It is your right; and you get it any way you need to. That means you can just take it when you want it. But, sometimes it's easier if you warm the little woman up a bit. Women's minds are small. They think about love, and feeling good, and talking intimately. When they get into one of those moods, they need to be humored. We know those things aren't important. We know they just interfere with getting to the business at hand; but go ahead and humor her if it will avoid a fight. Sex is easier without a fight. And ... oh, yes. Be sure to tell her you love her. You don't have to mean it, but that's a sure way to get her into bed. It gets them every time.

Son (Winking at his father): Tell her I love her. Yeah. I can do that. I can even convince her I mean it.

Father: That's it. That's it. Convince her you mean it. You have to play their little games now and then to be sure of winning. But you won't have to play for long. You see, women aren't very bright. They believe it when you tell them you love them; and once they believe it, they're hooked. Then they'll hang on you like a leech. It'll take the Chicago Bears to shake them loose. Just keep telling them you love them once in a while, and you'll have them for life.

Son: You mean I only have to play her game until I win? I only have to tell her I love her until she's convinced, and then I can forget it?

Father: Umhmm. That's absolutely right. Then you can go back to the important things in life: your work, Monday night football, and nights out with the boys. Then the only thing you'll have to worry about is some other son-of-a-bitch coming along and trying to take her away. You must not allow that.

Son: I have to be very careful that some other son-of-a-bitch doesn't come along and take her away.

Father: Yes. You see, once you've won a woman, she is your property. She belongs to you. Your job, then, is to see to it that no one interferes with your property. You see, she gives you your immortality.

Son: My immortality, father? I don't understand.

Father: Your immortality. It's just what I said.

Son: You mean I don't have to die?

Father: Of course **you** have to die. But she will give you **sons,** you see. It's those sons that will make you immortal. They will grow up to be just like you. That's how you will live forever.

Son: Oooooh, I hadn't thought of that.

Father: It's our job, as men, to live forever. That way we can keep control of everything. Remember, I said that when we first started this little talk. If we leave the decisions to anyone else, things won't come out the way we have decided they should. Always remember that, my son. Things won't come out right unless we live forever.

Son: Being immortal is the same as being God, isn't it, Father? If we're immortal and always completely in control we can be the same as God, can't we, Father?

Father: That's right, son. We can control it all. And don't you ever forget it.

Son: I certainly won't, father; because now I know that you are the strongest and the smartest and the best man on earth. I will always do as you say.

Father: That's my boy. Say, do you think you could put that sex off a bit and watch the game with me? Detroit is supposed to **kill** Chicago in this one.

Act Two

Cast of Characters

Mother: A typical working housewife - works all day at a menial job, comes home to all the housework **and** the care of her three children; her daughter, her son, and her husband. She is tired all the time, but feels that she is doing her duty.

Daughter: A girl somewhere between the ages of three and sixteen, untried in the world, trusting. She believes she must learn from her mother - but not everything.

Scene: A typical living room in a typical suburban home

Time: Anytime

Premise: (From Anne Wilson Schaef, *Women's Reality*, p.23)

"In the reactive female system women are born under the original sin of being born female."

Act Two

Mother: You must sit down, my daughter, for we need to talk.

Daughter: Yes, Mama.

Mother: There are some things I need to teach you that are very important. They are so important that if you don't learn them, you may not survive in this life.

Daughter: Yes, Mama. If I don't learn them, I may not survive in this life. But I don't understand, Mama. Who would want to hurt me?

Mother: There are men out there who want to hurt you. Of course, not your father or brother, but other men. These other men want to do things to you that are very bad. So you see, it is most important to your life that we talk right now. You must learn to always keep in mind that these men want to do bad things to you; and that you must always protect yourself from their harm.

Daughter: But what will they do to me? What is so important that I must spend my whole life protecting myself against it?

Mother: They will hurt you, my child. They will brutally hurt you; they will take your soul and annihilate it; they will force your body to do what will make you vomit; and they may even murder you if they don't get what they want.

Daughter: Mama, that's horrible! If that is true, I'll do whatever you say.

Mother: What I say is true, so listen very carefully.

Daughter: I'm listening, Mama.

Mother: First and foremost, you must understand that you are inferior to all men. By being female, you were born inferior. This is the first and most important thing you have to remember in order to protect yourself.

Daughter: I am inferior to all men. This is the most important thing to remember. But, Mama, I don't feel inferior. I am better than brother in school. I talk more than he does and say more important things. I am more fun to play with. **And** I am better at most things. Why am I inferior?

Mother: Because he will grow up stronger than you are. **And** your father has taught him that because he is stronger he **should** beat you up if he thinks you are better than he is. But even more important than that, you are inferior just because men say so.

Daughter: You mean I am inferior to men because they say so?

Mother: That's right. And because they will beat you up if you say anything different.

Daughter: And because they will beat me up if I say different.

Mother: That's it, now you understand.

Daughter (Furrowing her brow): I'm not sure I understand. From what you say, it would seem that father and brother are no different than the men I need to be afraid of - the men you said I needed to protect myself against.

Mother (Horrified): Oh, yes, they are! They are here to protect us.

Daughter: Now I'm really confused. You say that there are men out there that will hurt me; and father and brother will protect me from those men. But then you say that father and brother have decided that I am an inferior being; and if I say differently, **they** will hurt me.

Mother: That's why you must **never** say different.

Daughter: You mean in order to protect myself, and to have father and brother protect me, I must never say that I am not an inferior being?

Mother (Convincingly); That's right. And not only that, but you must **believe** with all your heart that you are an inferior being; and that whatever **they** say or do is right.

Daughter: I must believe with all my heart that I am an inferior being, and that whatever father and brother say or do is right.

Mother: Yes, do you believe that? You must believe that **now,** or I will never rest easy.

Daughter: I guess I have to believe it, if that is the only way I can keep myself from being brutalized, annihilated, or even murdered. And I wouldn't want to upset you, Mama. If you think it's that important, I will believe it. Yes. I believe it.

Mother (Relieved): Good. Now I can rest easy. **Now** we can go on to the rules of playing this game.

Daughter: There are rules?

Mother: Oh yes. There are definite rules. The men have made up definite rules, and we must abide by them.

Daughter: I must abide by the men's rules.

Mother: Yes. First of all, as an inferior being, you must find a man to protect you. You **must** always have a man to protect you. You are not safe at any time unless you have a man to protect you.

Daughter: I must find a man to protect me and be with me at all times.

Mother: Yes, and in order to have this man to protect you, there are certain things you must do. First, **you must be beautiful.** That means you must spend most of your time being sure you are beautiful. You must buy the best and most expensive clothes, clothes that will make him pay attention to you. You must keep your hair in ways that he will like. You must make up your face so it is extra pretty, and so he won't see anything about you that he might not like. And most of all, you **must** stay thin. Men won't like you and they won't protect you if you get fat. Do you understand all of that?

Daughter: I think I do. I have to spend a lot of time making myself beautiful; because If I'm not beautiful, he won't protect me. I especially have to stay thin.

Mother: Whew. I'm glad you understand that; because the rest of you is relatively unimportant in comparison to that. Being beautiful and thin comes first and foremost, after being sure that you know you are an inferior being.

Daughter: The rest of me is unimportant. Now, I don't understand that, either. What do you mean, the rest of me is unimportant?

Mother: I mean your personality, your intelligence, your talents. Those parts of you are not important in comparison to being beautiful.

Daughter: But mother, I know I'm more intelligent than brother. I do much better than he does in school. I think much faster and better than he does. I know I'm more talented, too. I've been in the school play, I can play the piano and the guitar, and I sing. I won the badminton tournament at school, and I was on the winning volleyball team.

Mother: None of those achievements are important. You see, he plays football.

Daughter: You mean football is more important than grades, singing, the school play, badminton, and volleyball?

Mother: Yes. That's exactly what I mean.

Daughter: But why?

Mother: Don't argue with me. It just is. That's one of their rules.

Daughter: Oh, I see. It's one of their rules I have to abide by in order to be protected by them. I just have to believe it.

Mother: Now you've got it. Pretty soon, once you have a man to protect you, you will forget about singing, guitar playing, and certainly playing badminton and volleyball. You'll forget that you're smart. You will learn what's important in life.

Daughter: I will learn what's important in life. What's really important in life is to have a man to protect me, and to follow men's rules.

Mother: Exactly.

Daughter: Exactly, she says. Exactly. Mama! What you're saying is ridiculous!

Mother: Yes.

Daughter: Then why are you saying it?

Mother: Because if you don't learn this, my child, you will be annihilated. Your will not live to tell the tale. Your soul will be dragged through the mud, spat upon, rejected; and you may not even live to have a soul.

Daughter: But, Mama, if I do all that you say, I might as well not have a soul.

Mother: Yes. That's what it feels like. It feels like a great hole where your soul should be. You'll feel it right here below your heart. You'll have it all your life. You will never fill up that space where your soul should be.

Daughter: Mama! How can you say that I should do this if it means giving up my soul? My very soul!

Mother: Because I can't rest easy unless I know you are protected. I brought you into this world to live. You **must** live; and I know you won't live unless you are protected.

Daughter: Oh, Mama, you sure do ask a lot.

Mother: You know I wouldn't ask this of you unless it were a matter of life and death.

Daughter: I know you wouldn't. So if you think it's that important, I guess I can pretend that brother is smarter and more talented than I am.

Mother: Not pretend. You must really believe it.

Daughter: All right. All right. I'll really believe it. But does that mean I have to give up getting good grades, and singing and playing the guitar and stuff?

Mother: No, you don't have to give them up, but you must let your brother believe that he does those things better than you.

Daughter: But Mama, **he** doesn't do them at all.

Mother: Then you have to make him believe that what he does do is better than what you do.

Daughter: Like football is better than badminton, right?

Mother: That's it. Now you're getting the idea.

Daughter (Sarcastically): Now I'm getting the idea. Now I'm getting the idea.

Mother (Ignoring the sarcasm): And now that you understand that rule, there is another rule to learn, too.

Daughter: Another rule?

Mother: Yes, it has to do with sex.

Daughter: Sex?

Mother: Yes. The men have gotten together and have decided when women are going to have sex and how.

Daughter: But I thought sex was a mutual thing. I thought it had to do with love and romance and intimacy.

Mother: Then you are misguided, my child; and you had better learn what sex is all about right now. Sex is for **his** pleasure, and has nothing to do with you.

Daughter: Wait a minute! I'm not crazy about it, but I can accept all of those other rules. This one is too much. Sex has nothing to do with me?

Mother: That's right. And the sooner you get yourself straight on that one, the better off you are going to be. Oh, you may get a little pleasure out of it, and sometimes you might get a lot; but that's only accidental. You are really there for two reasons. The first is to give him his pleasure, and the second is to give him sons.

Daughter (With a flash of anger): Now you're being old-fashioned, Mama. There's been a sexual revolution, you know; and things are different now. Now I can have pleasure, too. I can even initiate sex if I want.

Mother (Knowingly): You just think there's been a sexual revolution. There's only one thing that is different now. Now men think **you** should have sex as often as **they** want to have sex. Now you have less right to say no. That's the only thing that's different.

Daughter (Not wanting to fight about it): Okay. Okay. I give. I am to have sex at his pleasure and be sure to give him sons. Anything else?

Mother: Yes. There's one more thing. One more extremely important thing. Men lead with their penises.

Daughter: Now that's crazy, Mama. I don't understand that at all.

Mother: Well, I don't exactly understand it, either; but what I do understand is that they think of it as their power. I guess they think of it as their power because it produces pleasure and it produces sons. One thing I'm sure of is that they think about it all the time. Just listen to them talk if you don't believe me.

Daughter: Yes, they do talk about it all the time. I've heard the boys at school. They give it names, like Peter, or Dick. They say things like, "I'd like to ram it up her cunt," or, "I wonder what she'd be like if I stuck it in her."

Mother: You've heard it? Oh that's nasty. You know you shouldn't listen.

Daughter: Mama! Which way do you want it!

Mother (Embarrassed): Oh, yes. Well, there are some things you shouldn't listen to. You've got to be a lady, you know. Now, where was I?

Daughter: You were teaching me about men's penises.

Mother: Yes, I was teaching you about their penises. What's important here is what they presume that you believe about these instruments. They, somehow, think that their penises are so powerful that you will do anything for them.

Daughter: I will do anything for a man's penis?

Mother: Yes. Some men even believe that we want one.

Daughter (Laughs): Want one! What would I want one for? They do nothing but get in the way. They're so exposed. The only time I'd want one would be if I had to piss off the side of a boat.

Mother: Careful of your language, daughter. Ladies don't talk about pissing.

Daughter: Sorry, Mama. I forgot.

Mother: Right. Now, where was I? Oh, yes. It's the pleasure. They think those penises give us pleasure. It gives them pleasure so they think it gives us pleasure, too. As a matter of fact, they get downright paranoid about it giving us pleasure, always asking about whether we 'came' and like that. But I'm getting ahead of my story. You see, they believe that as long as it gives us pleasure, we will want it. And since their penis really represents **them** - their power so to speak - they want to be sure we covet it.

Daughter: You say their penis is them. It's their power - so they want to be sure we covet it.

Mother: Yes, then they can use it to control us.

Daughter: How do they do that?

Mother: They refuse to use it for pleasure; they hurt us with it instead. They use it when we're not ready. They use it and then don't pay any attention to us afterwards, when we really need attention. And sometimes they force us to submit to it when we abjectly say no. Then it becomes their weapon.

Daughter: And they can do that because they are stronger?

Mother: And more intelligent, and more talented, and more understanding of how the world works, and bigger, and more forceful, and louder, and more violent when they don't get their way. You see they can hurt you. You must let them have the right to lead with their penises.

Daughter: I must let them have the right to lead with their penises. But won't they think about me and my feelings at all?

Mother: No. They don't understand that you have feelings. All they know is what's important to them. And what's important to them is themselves, their work, and their penises. Anything that doesn't fit into those three categories doesn't exist.

Daughter: So when it comes right down to it, I don't exist?

Mother: That's right.

Daughter: I am not intelligent, I don't have talents, I don't have any abilities, I don't have any freedom to do what is important to me, because I have to do what is important to them. On top of that, I don't have a soul; instead I have only a hole in myself, an empty place that can never be filled. And I do all this so I can be protected from annihilation by men; and I have to have one or more of these men to do the protecting.

Mother: Now I think you understand.

Daughter: What I understand is that they are bigger and stronger than I am; and therefore I must follow their rules. If I don't, they will annihilate me somehow.

Mother: Yes. They are bigger and stronger than you as well as more intelligent, and more talented, and more understanding of how the world works, and more forceful, and louder, and more violent when they don't get their way. So you see, you must let them lead with their penises.

Daughter: I will, I will. I will let them lead with their penises. I don't want to be annihilated.

Mother: Now I think you understand fully.

Daughter: Yes, I understand.

Mother: And don't ever forget it.

Daughter: No. I won't forget it, Mama. You and me together. We have to keep ourselves from being annihilated. I love you, Mama. I'll do this for you. Yes, I'll do this for you.

Mother: Now I can rest easy. Come on then, we've got to go in the kitchen and make dinner for your father and brother. They'll be hungry after their busy afternoon watching the football game.

Act Three

Cast of Characters

Rapist: Everyman

Rape Victim: Everywoman

Scene: A park, a parking lot, a woman's bedroom, inside a car, the street, a man's bedroom, a dark alley, anywhere the rapist thinks he can perpetrate his crime.

Time: Anytime

Premise: It is always women's sexual feelings that cause men's brutality. Their feelings are like "sirens" which lead men to rash actions against their wills. (Paraphrased from Susan Griffin, *Rape: The Politics of Consciousness*, 1986, p.76)

Act Three

Victim (Is minding her own business when she looks up to see a man bursting in upon her. She looks frightened but acts calm.): What do you want?

Rapist (As though he has every right to be there): Relax sister, I'm just doing my job.

Victim (Confused): What do you mean, "job"?

Rapist (Walking around her in a menacing way): Just what I said. I'm just doing my job. The dirty work for all the rest.

Victim (Sarcastically): And just what is the dirty work, if I may ask?

Rapist (Raising his fist in the sign of power): Being sure you stay in your place.

Victim (Still believing she has some control): Well, do your dirty work some-place else. I'm busy right now.

Rapist (Moving closer, intimidating her): Listen, bitch. You don't understand. From this moment on you do what I say.

Victim: You're right. I don't understand. Just get out of here.

Rapist (Looking at her appraisingly): Well now, you're a pretty piece of ass. I won't mind my work tonight. No. I won't mind one bit.

Victim (Beginning to understand that she might be in some danger): But what are you after?

Rapist: Power, lady. That's all. Power! I want power over you. I want to make you do exactly what I want.

Victim: But why? I do what you want already.

Rapist (Waving a tire iron at her): Not enough, bitch. Not enough. You wheedle and manipulate and weasel. I know you. I know your weasel-like little ways. You don't give me what I want.

Victim: You're scaring me. I'll give you what you want if you just tell me what it is. Don't hurt me. I don't want to be hurt. Just tell me what you want.

Rapist: Yeah. Now you're talking. You're scared enough to talk, aren't you? I'll tell you what I want. Yeah, I'll tell you what I want. You are my property. You belong to **me.** You will dress like I say; believe what I tell you you can believe; and do what I want and only what I want. You will keep my house the way I want my house kept. You will bear sons. You will raise my sons the way I want them raised. You will have sex when I say you'll have sex. And you will keep your mouth shut!

Victim (Laughs behind her hand): He wants me to treat him like God. He isn't any god to me. (Drops her hand) All right. I'll do all that. Just don't hurt me.

Rapist: And you'll love me and serve me no matter what I do, just because you are my woman. Understand?

Victim (From behind her hand): Fuck you. You don't deserve my love and my service. (Drops her hand) Oh, yes. I'll do that. Just don't hurt me.

Rapist (Roars): I heard that. I heard that. Now we'll see about "fuck you." I'm going to kill you, you little gutter snipe. (Simultaneously whips out his two weapons of power: a gun and his penis. He drops the tire iron with a clatter.) Git over there. Git over there, I say. And git your knickers off.

Victim: No. I'm not going to take my knickers off for you. You're ugly. You're vile. Get away from me.

Rapist: I'll show you what you're gonna do. Git over there and git your knickers off.

Victim: No.

Rapist (Brandishing his gun): Oh yes, you will. Now do it.

Victim: I won't. I hate you. I hate you. Now leave me alone.

Rapist: You're not hearing me, you - you bitch. I want your cunt. I want it now. We'll see who's boss. (Advances on her, waving the gun while the erect penis points threateningly at its target.)

Victim (Backs away):

Rapist: Do as I say. Do it now.

Victim (Covers her face with her hands): No.

Rapist (Tears the victim's hands away from her face and with the butt of his gun and his free hand, beats her face until her eyes are black, her mouth is bleeding, and she has fallen in a crumpled heap on the floor.) I said, do as I say. Do it now.

Victim: Please don't kill me. I'll do it. I'll do it.

Rapist (Standing over her with the penis swaying in her face, and the gun pointed at her head, talking through gritted teeth): I said git your knickers off and do it now.

Victim: Yes.

Rapist: Faster.

Victim: Yes. As fast as I can.

Rapist: That's not fast enough.

Victim: I'll do it faster.

Rapist: Right, bitch! Now we'll see who's boss.

Victim: Yes. You're showing me.

Rapist (Stands over her with his penis pointed at her head and laughs): You thought you could win, didn't you, you little slut. You can't win. You're nothing but a whore. You can't win over me. I'll always win. I know exactly how to do it. All I have to do is this, and I'll scare you **and** your sisters into doing exactly what I want. This is all I have to do. Now see this (Pulls at his penis.)

Victim (Disappearing into psychological oblivion): Yes.

Rapist: You know what this is?

Victim: Yes.

Rapist: Look at it. I said look at it, you slut. Because that's what you are. The worst kind of slut. I said look at it.

Victim: I'm looking.

Rapist: This is power. This is all the power I need. I can make you do anything I want, with this. I can make anyone or anything do what I want with this. I can win any fight. I can do whatever I want. I can win ... win ... win. With this I can win. Isn't that right, slut?

Victim (Is silent):

Rapist (Hits her across the face): I said - isn't that right?

Victim: Yes. Yes. That's right. You can do anything with it.

Rapist (Needing her agreement): I have all the power, don't I?

Victim: Yes. You have all the power, now.

Rapist: That's not what I said, bitch. I have all the power all the time. That's right, isn't it? All I have to do is brandish this little tool of mine, and I can get you to do anything. Isn't that right, slut?

Victim (Silence):

Rapist (Hits her on the top of the head with the butt of his gun): Answer me, whore. Answer me now.

Victim: Yes! Yes! You can do anything with it. Yes.

Rapist: And you want one just like it, don't you?

Victim (Silence):

Rapist (Grabs her hair and pulls her head back until she screams out in pain): I said, "Don't you?" Answer me when I talk to you. You like this little tool of mine, don't you? As a matter of fact, you'd like one just like it, wouldn't you?

Victim (Screams again): Yes. Yes. I'd like one just like it.

Rapist (Relaxing): That's right. I knew it all the time. And since you don't have one of your own, you want mine, don't you? (He laughs like a hyena.) You want what it will do for you, don't you?

Victim (Silence):

Rapist (Clicks off the safety on the gun and points it into her ear): Aren't you hearing me? You want what it will do for you, don't you?

Victim (Shudders, and curls over into the smallest figure she can become, trying to protect her very soul): Yes. Yes, I want it. I want it.

Rapist: I knew it. You want all that pleasure. It makes you a woman ... doesn't it?

Victim (In the tiniest of voices, knowing now that she is lost): Yes, it makes me a woman.

Rapist (Pulling back on the trigger of the gun): And you want me now, don't you?

Victim (Looks out of the corner of her eye at the penis): You or that weapon of yours?

Rapist (Hits her with the butt of the gun, opening a gaping wound in her head): Don't get smart with me. It's the same thing.

Victim: Yes.

Rapist: Now say you want it.

Victim (In an even tinier voice): I want it.

Rapist: Louder!

Victim (Louder): I want it.

Rapist: Right! (Crashes down on her, opening her body, pushing her legs apart, thrusting, mauling, pushing, until she is bleeding.)

Victim (Has lost all contact with her body, her mind, and her feelings. She is laying, inert, while his body sways above her. Her soul begins to emerge out of her, and is seen seeping away, into the horizon. She is left with no body, no mind, no emotions, and now no soul.)

Rapist (In the throes of ecstasy): Oh, yes. Oh yes. You like it. I know you do.

Victim (Lies without moving):

Rapist (He gets up, and thrusts his weapon back inside his pants. He looks at the victim with disgust): You're a slut all right. You're nothing but a slut. (Kicks her with his booted foot.) Git your knickers back on. You look like a whore.

Victim (Lies without moving):

Rapist: I said, git your knickers on, whore. Git 'em on.

Victim (Feels about for her underwear, finally finds them. Groans as she tries to sit up and put them back on.):

Rapist: I'm going now. But I'll be back. And don't you tell no one about this. Understand? Because I'll be back. I'll see to it that you don't talk to no one. If you say one word, I'll cut your throat out, and then your talking days will be done. Understand?

Victim (Holds her bloody head):

Rapist: I said: Do you understand?????

Victim (Through swollen lips, barely mumbling): Yes. Yes, I understand.

Rapist: Good. Now clean yourself up, whore. You don't want nobody seeing you looking like this. Filthy bitch. (Strides out the door, slamming it hard enough that she shudders.)

Victim: (Is last seen sitting on the floor, a forlorn and pitiful pile of rags and bruises - blood flowing from the cuts on her face and her head, and now running with impunity onto her underwear. She sits for a long time doing nothing, bent over, holding herself with both arms around the knees. Her bleeding head rests on her knees. After many minutes without moving, a tear slowly rolls down her cheek and drops onto the floor. Her hand, which had been clasped around her knees changes into a fist and she lifts it toward the closed door. She screams with all the force she can muster.) I hate you! I hate you! I hate you!

Act Four

Cast of Characters

Prosecuting Attorney: One of the good old boys

Defense Attorney: One of the good old boys

Scene: Outside a court room, any court room

Time: Anytime

Premise Number One: "A trial is only an adversarial contest between barristers. Neither you nor the defendant is of importance to them. The only important thing is which one wins and which one loses." (Sheryle Geen, personal communication, September, 1986)

Premise Number Two: "In the White Male System relationships are conceived as being either one-up or one-down. In other words, when two people come together or encounter each other, The White Male System assumption is that one of them must be superior and the other one must be inferior. There are no other possibilities for interaction." (Anne Wilson Schaef, *Women's Reality*, 1981, p. 104)

Act Four

Prosecuting Attorney: Well, my learned friend, are you ready for **our** battle?

Defense Attorney: Of course. I'm **always** ready.

Prosecuting Attorney: I've got you beat this time. It's an open and shut case.

Defense Attorney: Oh, ho. That's what you think. I've got public opinion on my side.

Prosecuting Attorney: That's not going to work this time. I've got all the facts and they're all documented.

Defense Attorney (With contempt): Facts! What are facts in comparison to what I've got? I've got the jury, old man. The Jury. The jury will win my case for me.

Prosecuting Attorney: Not this time. Not after they hear my facts. No. This time there will be no question.

Defense Attorney (Laughs): Sorry. Not so. Just wait until I get that victim on the stand. I'll give her my triple whammy, and she won't know what hit her.

Prosecuting Attorney: Your little tricks won't work with this one. She's as strong as they come. You won't shake her.

Defense Attorney: Ha! There isn't a woman alive I can't shake. And the stronger they are, the harder they fall. Just you watch.

Prosecuting Attorney: She's not only strong, but this one was really raped.

Defense Attorney: By the time I get through with her, she won't know whether she's been raped or not.

Prosecuting Attorney: No, I've got you beat this time. She knows what happened and she's very good with words. God knows I've lost to you often enough with that little trick, but not this time.

Defense Attorney: Of course you'll lose. This time is no different than any other. By the time I get through with this victim, she'll actually believe she consented.

Prosecuting Attorney: Um hmm. I know your tactics. You'll try to confuse and mislead her, then cause her to be so emotional that she won't know what she's saying.

Defense Attorney: Right. You've got it. That's exactly how I win. How else? She's already all emotional over what she thinks happened to her; so I'll just make her believe that she was wrong - that what happened didn't happen. Women are patsies for that kind of treatment. Get them all confused, and they really don't know what happened.

Prosecuting Attorney: Your old "you can't stick to your story routine," right?

Defense Attorney: Right. And then I'll start asking her questions about **her** sex life. She knows she's no "lily white," but she doesn't want anybody else to know it. And if there's anything that makes a woman feel like a bad woman it is to imply that she likes sex. That she goes after sex. That she has less than a pristine sexual history. And there isn't a woman alive who's pristine. If she thinks her life has been pristine, I can always go after her fantasies. Believe me, her fantasies won't be pristine. One way or the other, I can get her upset. You bet. I can get her all upset.

Prosecuting Attorney: And then the jury stops believing her story, right?

Defense Attorney: Right. Then she becomes questionable. She's violated the rules. She's not done what every upright Christian woman is supposed to do: "Love, honor and obey" her husband. That'll set the jury off. Everybody knows that a woman is supposed to love, honor, and obey her husband. She's clearly not supposed to be gallivanting around on the streets where she sets herself up to be raped.

Prosecuting Attorney: This one wasn't out on the streets. She was in her own bedroom.

Defense Attorney: Doesn't matter. She set it up. He probably saw her sashaying around on the street in some tight sweater, with her skirt up to her ass. Every red-blooded male is going to react to that.

Prosecuting Attorney: Now I've got you. She's a professional woman and wears nothing but business suits.

Defense Attorney: Professional woman, huh? Well, that's how I'll get her then. Probably marches around with her nose up in the air thinking she's better than him. Aggressive type. I know that kind. Probably got him all upset acting smart. Uppity. No man is going to let a woman get away with that.

Prosecuting Attorney: No, actually, she's very quiet. Does her job, and lives a quiet life.

Defense Attorney: Mysterious type then. Won't share her treasure. Sits on it and keeps it all to herself. A man can't let her get away with that. A man can't let a woman keep her treasure to herself. She should share it. You know what I mean? (Winks suggestively at his adversarial partner.)

Prosecuting Attorney: Sounds like you've got it all figured out.

Defense Attorney: Well, my learned friend, it sounds as though you don't know much about rape defense. I don't have to have it all figured out. The woman will do most of the work for me.

Prosecuting Attorney: Now that **is** news to me. How do you get her to do that?

Defense Attorney: She is the architect of her own defeat.

Prosecuting Attorney: Yes?

Defense Attorney: Yes. First of all, she doesn't **know** whether she caused the rape or not. She literally doesn't know. Somewhere deep in her **little mind,** she thinks she probably did. All I have to do is play on that and I've got her.

Prosecuting Attorney: You mean you can make her a willing participant in her own defeat?

Defense Attorney: You betcha. If that's the only way I can win, that's exactly what I'll do. I can make her believe that she asked for it.

Prosecuting Attorney: Now you know that's bullshit. No woman is going to ask to be beaten up.

Defense Attorney: Women do! Have you seen any porno movies lately? Women do. All the time. That's what they want, when you get right down to it. Domination. They're only happy when their dominated; and then they can submit, the way they're supposed to. That's the only way they're happy, my learned friend. Perhaps you'd better do a little more studying about women. If you did, then you'd know.

Prosecuting Attorney: No. That, I'll never believe.

Defense Attorney: Well, just in case you're right, I won't make a big thing about her wanting to be dominated. As a matter of fact I won't even bring it up. But the jury knows. The jury knows what women want. Both men and women on the jury know that a woman wants to be dominated. They know she really wanted to submit, no matter what she says . . . no matter what all those women's liberators shout about. Take my word for it. A woman wants to be dominated; and if she brings a man to violence in the process, that's the way **she** wants it.

Prosecuting Attorney: Well, you may be able to get **her** to act against her own best interests, but your defendant won't convince any jury of his innocence.

Defense Attorney: What's so different about **this** defendant? He's a man, isn't he?

Prosecuting Attorney: He's a man who brutally beat this woman, and then raped her.

Defense Attorney: Oh, wait a minute, my learned friend. You know as well as I do that every man deserves his little bit of sex when he wants it.

Prosecuting Attorney: Of course, but . . . .

Defense Attorney: And if he has to get a little bit violent to get it, why . . . that's a man's way.

Prosecuting Attorney: Yes, but . . . .

Defense Attorney: Women get a bit obstreperous around sex now and then, you know. They use it for a weapon to get their way.

Prosecuting Attorney: I know, but . . . .

Defense Attorney: So that's what happened in this case. Every man on the jury knows that; and it won't take much to convince the women.

Prosecuting Attorney (Looks down and away, as though defeated):

Defense Attorney: So you see, you haven't won this case. You may have all the facts on your side; you may **think** it's an open and shut case, but I've got all the good Christian morality on my side. A woman belongs to a man, and that's the way it is. He, then, can do with her what he wants.

Prosecuting Attorney: Including rape her?

Defense Attorney: Well, he'll try not to do that; but if she gets out of line, yes. Including rape her. There's nothing better than a little rape to keep a woman in line.

Prosecuting Attorney (Realizing an important truth, standing up straight again, realizing he is not defeated): You're right, there. It does keep a woman in line. But, my friend, it's against the law, and this is a court of law.

Defense Attorney: With the decision made by a jury of his peers. That jury is my best ally, believe me.

Prosecuting Attorney: And the judge is my best ally. It will be he that instructs the jury.

Defense Attorney: So we both have our team, old sport. I have twelve, plus the woman, on my team. What have you got?

Prosecuting Attorney: I've got the judge, and he's more powerful than all. He has to be fair. He has to uphold the law.

Defense Attorney: But he's a man, isn't he?

Prosecuting Attorney (Refuses to answer the question): It's time to start. All I've got to say is, "May the best **man** win." In a few hours we'll know which one of us it is.

Defense Attorney: Just like our old college days, isn't it, old sport, when we used to play football - you for SMU and me for MU?

Prosecuting Attorney: (Smiles) And you were a son-of-a-bitch on defense then, too. But S.M.U. still beat the shit out of you.

Defense Attorney: Let's shake on it.

Prosecuting Attorney: Shake on it.

Defense Attorney: Let's go.

(Together, the two men enter the court room and take up their adversarial positions, knowing that the best man will win.)

Act Five

Cast of Characters

Jury: Eight men and four women

Jury Members 1 - 8: Eight upstanding, moral, Christian men, who belong to the good old boys' club

Jury Members 9 - 12: Four upstanding moral, Christian women, who belong to the good old boys

Judge of the Criminal Court: A senior member of the good old boys' club

Scene: The room set aside for jury deliberation in any court

Time: Anytime

Premise: In a rape case "defense rarely ever waives a jury trial **knowing** that the jury is an ally, not an enemy. Juries, which are often male-dominated, are extremely reluctant to convict. Juries are allies of male defendants and enemies of female complainants for reasons that run deeper than their poor grasp of the law or their predominantly male composition. They are composed of citizens who believe the many myths about rape, and they judge the female according to these cherished myths." (Susan Brownmiller, *Against Our Will: Men, Women and Rape*, 1975, p. 368)

Act Five

Jury Member 4: We are here to decided this case of rape. I suggest we elect a foreman.

Jury Member 9: Stanley, why don't you be the foreman, since you spoke up first.

Jury Member 11: I second the nomination.

Jury Member 4: All in favor say, "Aye."

All Jury Members: Aye.

Jury Member 4: I think this is an open and shut case. The defendant is no more guilty than the man in the moon. I think we should just vote on it and then we can go home. I'm supposed to bowl tonight; and I don't want to be late.

Jury Member 7: We can't do that. The judge said that everybody should have their say. Now, if we're all quick about it, you can get to your bowling, Stanley. Let's just be quick about it.

Jury Member 4: Alright. Everybody be quick about it. Let's just go in order. Men first.

Jury Member 1: I know he didn't rape her; she obviously consented.

Jury Member 2: She's just a loose woman. The defense attorney showed that. There's no question in my mind. She's just a loose woman.

Jury Member 3: Yeah, did you see the way she wiggled her ass when she walked up to the stand. Anybody who wiggles their ass like that is asking for it.

Jury Member 5: And she's married. I wonder how her poor husband is taking this?

Jury Member 4: He probably feels cuckolded. But we aren't supposed to worry about him. Our job has to do with her.

Jury Member 10: But what about . . . ?

Jury Member 4: Lucille, you know we decided. Men first. You have to wait your turn.

Jury Member 10: Oh, yes. I forgot. I'm sorry.

Jury Member 6: I don't think that woman was even sure that the defendant was the right man. I think she's accusing the wrong man. She doesn't even remember what he looked like. She said it was dark.

Jury Member 7: The prosecuting attorney did present evidence that she was beaten. He had pictures of her with a black eye, and a bandage on her head.

Jury Member 4: Anybody could put a bandage on their own head for a picture. That doesn't prove anything.

Jury Member 10: But what about the black . . . ?

Jury Member 4: Lucille, I **said** men first. You'll get your turn.

Jury Member 10: Sorry.

Jury Member 4: Now, just don't forget again.

Jury Member 8: Well, what I think is that those two certainly told different stories. She said he broke into her room, beat her up, and raped her. He said she invited him over for a drink, then asked to have sex with him and said she wanted to be tied up. Some women like it that way, you know. I don't understand it. Now my wife, Myrtle, would never put up with anything like that; but then Myrtle doesn't put up with much sex either. Sometimes I get a little pushy when she gets that way.

Jury Member 4: Now Harry, we're not here to talk about Myrtle. You could do with a little more pushing with that woman. If she were my wife, she wouldn't get away with what you let her get away with.

Jury Member 8 (Hangs his head): You're right, Stanley. But then, I know where to get mine - you know what I mean (Winks at Stanley). I can let Myrtle have her little ways. I know where I can get mine.

Jury Member 4: Now Harry, forget about Myrtle, I said. We're here to talk about this other woman.

Jury Member 3: And a mighty pretty woman she is. I'm sorry it wasn't me got to her first.

Jury Member 10: . Can I talk now?

Jury Member 4: I said wait your turn, Lucille. There are two still ahead of you.

Jury Member 9: - I thought that man was such a nice man. I can't imagine him doing anything like what she said. He's just such a nice-looking young man.

Jury Member 11: Yes. He certainly does look like his mother raised him right. It's such a shame he's in all this trouble.

Jury Member 10: Wait a minute - this woman says he forced his way into her room, menaced her with a gun, told her to "get your knickers off" in no uncertain terms, beat her in the face, and hit her on the head with his gun until she was almost unconscious, and then raped her until she bled; and you're talking about what a nice man he is. I can't understand it. You all are trying to say it was her fault. What's going on here?

Jury Member 4: Don't forget now, Lucille, I've got my bowling tonight. Don't stir things up and make me miss it, now.

Jury Member 10: Just what's important here? Your bowling game, or the fact that this woman was raped.

Jury Member 12: Now Lucille, don't you get all upset here. We don't know that she was raped. She only said she was raped.

Jury Member 5: Yes, now, Lucille. Haven't you ever had sex with a man and then decided you shouldn't have done it and thought about accusing him of raping you? I bet you have, loose as you are.

Jury Member 10: Wait a minute. My sex life is not on trial here.

Jury Member 4: No. And let's not put it on trial. My bowling, you know.

Jury Member 10: Stuff your bowling. This is a case of rape.

Jury Member 2: Now, now, Lucille. Don't get all riled up. Don't act out of sorts here. We're all just trying to do what's right.

Jury Member 10:   What's right! What's right! You all are trying to railroad that poor girl into having caused her own rape. She didn't do it. She's not responsible for what he did to her. He did it. What about his responsibility?

Jury Member 9: Now, Lucille, just calm down. We don't know that he's responsible. We only know what she said he did. We don't know that for sure.

Jury Member 10: Just because she's a woman, you aren't going to believe her? And just because he's a man, you **are** going to believe him?

Jury Member 5: No, no. That's not the case at all. We're just trying to get at the truth here. I know that any woman who wiggles her ass like she does can't be trusted. Those kind never tell the truth.

Jury Member 10 (Holds her head in her hands): Oh, my God.

Jury Member 7: That's a good idea. Let's pray about it. God will tell us what's right.

Jury Member 10: No. We're not going to pray about it. Didn't you hear what this woman said? Didn't you hear her tell about how she missed four weeks of work before she was cured of her concussion. Didn't you hear her talk about all the mental torment she's been through since the rape? Didn't you hear her tell about the money it's cost her in doctor and hospital bills? Didn't you hear her talk about how she hasn't been able to concentrate on her work since it happened and how she is in danger of losing her job? Didn't you hear all that?

Jury Member 8: - Some women are sickly, you know. Now take my Myrtle .

Jury Member 4: Harry!

Jury Member 8: Sorry, Stanley. But my Myrtle now, she's just the sickly kind, you know - like this here woman.

Jury Member 4: I think we should take a vote. The innocence of the defendant seems clear to me. That woman, she consented, without a doubt.

Jury Member 10: I don't think we should take a vote. The innocence of the defendant is not clear.

Jury Member 12: I think Stanley's right. He's got his bowling, you know; and I have to be home to fix supper for Archibald and little Hal.

Jury Member 5: You know, Lucille, now that I look at you, you look a lot like that woman out there. Are you related? You can wiggle your ass pretty good, too. Are you her sister? I bet you're her sister. That's why you're shouting and carrying on this way.

Jury Member 9: Lucille, you wouldn't want to put that poor boy in jail, would you? Think if it were Freddie. Think if he were your son. He'll have to spend four or maybe five years in jail. Think of how hard that will be on his wife. He's married, you know.

Jury Member 10 (Hysterically): He raped a woman, don't you see that? He raped her. He took her very soul.

Jury Member 2: What are you talking about, Lucille? Soul. A woman like that doesn't have a soul.

Jury Member 10 (Again, with her head in her hands): Oh, my God. Oh, my God. I knew none of you were very smart; but I didn't think you were this stupid.

Jury Member 4: Lucille! That's enough. I will not have the honor of this jury debased. I will not have it.

Jury Member 10 (Shakes her head in disbelief):

Jury Member 1: Lucille, I didn't want to say anything about this, but you're just forcing me to it. Stanley's got his bowling and I want to watch the football game tonight. You're just bent on obstructing justice.

Jury Member 10: Yes, Albert? What is it you want to say?

Jury Member 1 (Clears his throat): I really don't like to say this; but, Lucille, you're just forcing me to it. I saw you last Friday night in that little bar right around the corner from your office. I saw you sitting at that bar just having a high old time with some young man. Dancing and snuggling, like you were ready for a fling in that bed yourself. And Fred Senior was nowhere to be seen. Tell me, Lucille. Where was Fred Senior? Never mind. I know where Fred Senior was. He was at his lodge meeting, and you out there having a high old time with another man?

All Jury Members (Look in horror at Lucille):

Jury Member 1: Now what would Fred think if I told him about you dancing and snuggling like that?

Jury Member 10 (Staring at the group with her mouth open): He was just a friend. He was a man I work with. And we weren't dancing and snuggling. I danced one fast dance with him. There was no snuggling to it. I've worked with him for five years. Sometimes we go out for a drink together when we've been working hard and are tired.

All Jury Members (Continue to look in horror at Lucille):

Jury Member 10: And my having a drink with a friend has nothing to do with this case.

All Jury Members: Oh, yes it does.

Jury Member 4: Now that you have seen the light, Lucille, I suggest we take a vote. I suggest that we vote not guilty of rape. Right, Lucille?

Jury Member 10: No, I . . . .

Jury Member 1: Right, Lucille?

Jury Member 4: My bowling.

Jury Member 1: Remember? My football game?

Jury Member 12: And I've got Archibald and Hal.

Jury Member 8: And I'm sure Myrtle would be interested in knowing about your little affair with that man. She always feels better after a little gossip.

Jury Member 10 (With her head in her hands): Right.

Jury Member 4: Everybody who votes not guilty raise their hands. Good, it's unanimous. I'll get home in time for a good supper before bowling.

(The jury gets up and files back into the courtroom. The judge and the principals return for the verdict.)

Judge of Criminal Court: Has the jury reached its decision?

Jury Member 4: We have, Your Honor.

Judge of Criminal Court: Bailiff, would you please bring the decision of this jury, of these twelve right men and women, to me.

Judge of Criminal Court (Reads): This jury declares unanimously that the defendant is not guilty as charged of the rape of this woman. He is cleared, in our collective minds, of all responsibility for any sexual act that may or may not have taken place between the two of them.

Judge of Criminal Court (To the Jury): You are unanimous in this decision?

Jury Member 11 (Whispering to the woman next to her): Hush, Lucille.

Jury Member 4: We are, Your Honor.

Judge of Criminal Court: I want to thank you men and women of the jury for your time and your careful deliberations in this case. Go now, to your homes - knowing that you have discharged your duty in a righteous manner.

Jury Member 4: Thank you, Your Honor.

(As the jury members file out, on their way home, on their way to their various activities, there is a flurry of activity in the courtroom as the Complainant falls to the floor, blood gushing from her vagina.)

Question:

Out of what culture does rape emerge?

RAPE'S STAGE

or . . . variously titled

Billions for Defense But Not One Red Cent For

The People Being Defended

A Collage

Woman *is the Nigger of the World*
Words and Music
by
John Lennon and Yoko Ono

Woman is the Nigger of the world
Yes she is - Think about it:
Woman is the Nigger of the world -
Think about it - Do something about it.

We make her paint her face and dance.
If she won't be a slave, we say that she don't love us
If she's real we say she's trying to be a man -
By putting her down for pretending that she's above us.

Woman is the Nigger of the World
Yes she is
If you don't believe us - take a look at the one you're with.
Woman is the slave of the slave.
Ah, yes. If you believe me, you'd better scream about it.
We make her bear and raise our children.
Then we leave her flat for being a fat old mother hen.
We tell her home is the only place she should be.
Then we complain that she's too unworldly to be our friend.

Woman is the Nigger of the World
If you believe me - take a look at the one you're with.
Woman is the slave to the slave.
Yeah - If you believe, you'd better scream it.

We insult her every day on T.V.
And wonder why she has no guts or confidence.
When she's young we kill her will to be free.
By putting her down - we put her down for being dumb.

We make her paint her face and dance.
We make her paint her face and dance.
Dance . . . Dance . . . Dance
Dance . . . Dance . . . Dance
We make her paint her face and dance.

And from the Media:

Judge Finds three men, ages 21, 25, and 19, guilty in the rape of a girl 16. The three men raped the girl as they drove along various roads during a three-hour period. The suspects threatened her with a knife and beat her. The victim was left naked in a ditch. The attorney expects to appeal. (Minneapolis Star and Tribune, Feb, 7, 1987.)

Wilding
        Skin Heads
                "Youth Gone Wild"
                        Satanic Worship

Evening T.V. lineup of cop shows where the tough out-tough the tough and their women stand by and applaud the toughing.

Wednesday, Bloody Wednesday (Headline from *Time*, Aug, 31, 1987)

A Rambo-like killer devastates a quiet England country village. (Public Broadcasting System , *All Things Considered.*)

He was a quiet fellow except when he talked about guns. Last week he used his shooting skill to deadly effect, turning his neighbors into targets in the worst massacre in modern British history. He wore a headband, a combat jacket and an ammunition belt slung over his shoulder. He looked just like Rambo. The savagery was as swift as it was deadly: 13 people died between 1:05 p.m. and 1:15 p.m. Final toll: 16 dead, 14 wounded. (*Time*, Aug. 31, 1987.)

Demolition Sale

"Overkill," shrieks the young fan, as the heavy-metal quartet by that name begins a number at a Chicago hellhole called Medusa's. "Overkill! Excellent!" he shrieks again over the triple-digit decibel din, his hand aloft in the devil's horns salute. *(U.S. News and World Report,* Sept. 7, 1987.)

Cutting edge of the teenage subculture . . . "Heavy Metal" . . . material revels in satanic imagery and expounds on effective methods of torture and disembowelment. Lyrics unprintable, or deliberately disgusting . . . . (ibid)

Ripping apart, severing flesh, gouging eyes, tearing limb from limb. (ibid)

Teenage nihilism, complete with liberal doses of violent sex and occasional thoughts of suicide. (ibid)

Friday night and I need a fight. (ibid)

My motorcycle and a switchblade knife, but what I need to make me all right are girls, girls, girls. (ibid)

Mosh: Young boys slamming shoulder to shoulder with abandon . . .some engage in bizarre ritual called "stage diving" . . . the kids get more and more unrestrained . . . diving off balconies onto the heads and arms of kids below. (ibid)

"They're nuts," says promoter Chris Williamson approvingly. "It's great." (ibid)

Movie scene:

The woman is beautiful,
voluptuous and always ready.

She wants it from any
man within range.

She is always thinking
about men and sex.

When there is no man available to satisfy her insatiable
sexual craving, she masturbates, licking her lips, and
emits groans of ecstasy.

When a man shows up she terminates
her self excitation and attacks him.

She does everything to excite him,
to get him to satisfy her craving.

Eventually interested, but not committed,
he succumbs to her insatiable demands.

After she pours herself all over him,
he eventually becomes excited and
has an unemotional orgasm.

She goes her way to find
another sexual encounter.

What movie? **Any porno movie**

She's a real knockout. She is a beautiful lady from head to toe. Those 37-inch breasts drive me wild. (Letters to the Editor, a porno magazine.)

I love a woman's body hair. A full jungle of untrimmed bush, unshaved legs and thighs, hairy underarms and a "beaver trail" leading south from a woman's belly button really makes my cock jump. (ibid)

I loved Misty's tits. I also loved the dirty cartoons and the filthy letters. The serious writing spoiled it, however. (ibid)

Just sex . . . and pussies. (ibid)

I know that I'm a sexist pig and treat women like meat. (ibid)

I have long blond hair which reaches my shoulders, full lips, blue eyes, and a body that measures 37-24-36. My body frequently gives men an instant erection. (ibid)

Movie Titles

Succulent

Any Time, Any Place

It's Everything You Want

Devil's Ecstasy

Liquid Assets

Primal Rage

Squalor Motel

Fox Holes

Sex Busters

Stud Hunter

Fast Chick

Rear Entry

In Heat

Corrupt Desire

Etc.

Etc.

Etc.

Man kills five before taking own life. (*Wisconsin State Journal*, Aug. 31, 1987.)

Sixty-five police officers treated for chemical dependency. As many as ten times that many have dependencies but are afraid to seek help. (ibid)

Three university basketball players cleared of rape charge. (*Minneapolis Star and Tribune*, Aug, 31, 1986.)

Murder, suicide pact - a cult leader called Benevolent Mother and 31 disciples took drugs and strangled each other. *(Wisconsin State Journal*, August 31, 1987.)

Students allowed to read Godless books, *The Wizard of Oz*, and *The Diary of Ann Frank*. Federal Appeals Court overturns rulings set forth by fundamentalist seeking to remove "secular humanism." (*Wisconsin State Journal*, August 31, 1987.)

Man with history of molesting children requested to post signs on his home and on both sides of vehicles in letters at least three inches high: "Dangerous sex offender, no children allowed." American Civil Liberties Union taking case on appeal as cruel and unusual punishment. (*U.S. News and World Report*, Sept. 7, 1987.)

Interpretation of the Koran prohibits the execution of virgins, therefore convicted virgins are raped before being put to death. (*New Age*, July, 1985.)

He is one of a long line of sneak weenies and covert-action weasels who have - from the Berline blockade to the present day- changed U.S. foreign policy from "Speak softly and carry a big stick: to talk bullshit and carry a wad of American Express travelers' checks. (P. J. O'Rourke, in *Rolling Stone*, Sept 10, 1987, p.35.)

Sex Pistols

Demolition Sale

Pit Bulls

Ollie North for President

Raped her and beat her and slit her throat with a knife. Shot her in the stomach with a .25 caliber pistol. The two hours of viciousness ended when he dumped her body on the city's east side and set the body afire to cover his crimes. (*Time*, Sept 7, 1987)

Play guns are a $200 million a year market for U.S. toy makers. (ibid)

Nine Cop movies grossed a half a billion dollars in the summer of 1987.(*Variety Magazine*)

It's drugs, drugs, drugs. Drugs and murder. Selling, buying, possessing for sale and often enough, killing someone in the process. (*Insight*, July 6, 1987)

A man charged with stabbing a deadbeat customer over $15.00 of stolen steaks. (ibid)

Twenty-seven-year-old woman who stabbed her sixty-nine-year-old landlord ninteen times, apparently because he refused to lend her money for heroin. (ibid)

A man is charged with sodomizing all four of his girlfriend's daughters. (ibid)

A ninteen-year-old is a major dope dealer. (ibid)

Many of the cases, technically misdemeanors, were actually hard-to-win serious assaults and rapes turned down by the district attorney's office in a continuing turf war between the two prosecutorial agencies over conviction rates. (ibid)

I Want Your Sex. (Song title)

Erotic hostility

Current TV shows depicting murder after murder after murder.

Terrorism

Bombings

Wife Battering

Child Abuse

Incest

Three Indiana men - including a retired Indianapolis policeman and a Little League coach - have been indicted by a federal grand jury on child pornography charges (*Indianapolis Star*, Sept. 15, 1987.)

Making Crime a Career

Twenty-six-year crime veteran views himself as victim. (Headline in the *Indianapolis Star*, Sept. 15, 1987 - from the above three part story.)

As he sees it, he is a minister of God, an author of novels, a father of teen-agers and a friend of man. (ibid)

In this world he is a cunning predator, a psychopathic prowler of inner-city streets who feeds on the defenseless. (ibid)

He's a monster. (ibid)

Arrested more than 70 times on close to 100 criminal charges. (ibid)

Typical career criminal - the hard core offender who commits two of every three crimes. (ibid)

He will blame everybody but himself. (ibid)

She was the perfect victim. When she refused his sexual advances, he punched her in the face, knocking her to the ground and causing her nose and mouth to bleed. As she screamed, he warned her: "I'm going to give you to the count of three. If you don't shut up I'm going to hit you again." (ibid)

I find no evidence of mental illness in this man. (ibid)

He is a predator that preys on others who can't defend themselves. (ibid)

The judge gave the defendant three years in prison; he was out in 18 months. Almost a year to the day after he was released he was arrested again. The charge? Rape. (ibid)

How many criminals go to jail? There are 51,600 estimated crimes committed; 53% reported, 5.6% arrested, 3.6% prosecuted, 3.4% convicted, 2.5% imprisoned. (ibid)

Victims say pursuing criminal case was a "waste of time." (ibid)

I did everything the law told me to do and I didn't get anything out of it. (ibid)

If this happens again, I'll just take matters into my own hands. But they say then I'll be the one to go to jail. (ibid)

Movie Titles

The Great American Bash

Cobra - It's a disease. Meet the cure.

Strike Force

Cocaine College - Sex, drugs and rock 'n roll . . . a deadly combination.

Impulse - The madness inside us all.
 Imagine what would happen if every desire,
every urge, every passion, locked deep inside
you suddenly exploded on impulse.

Bad Boys - Is tense and exciting.

Harem

Angels Die Hard - Their battle cry . . ."kill the pigs."

Savages

Exterminator 2

A View to Kill

Rage of Honor

Warbus - The only escape from death was a ride through hell.

Pray for Death

Killer in the Mirror

Etc.,   Etc.   Etc.

A critic comments on the new Billy Idol video - *Straight out of the devil's workshop . . . a grisly mix of vampire and Nazi imagery . . . depraved, decadent posturing . . . leather steel spikes and crucifixes, snarling and shadowboxing.*

Had enough? I have.

Question:

What are the deep psychological processes that cause men to rape?

A Parable

In the beginning was the word and the word was God and God made Man in his image. Unfortunately, he made Man in his image and not exactly like him. He made one mistake and one mistake only; that of giving him psychological vulnerability and weakness. When God realized his mistake he called Man to the mountain top and gave him a lecture. "Listen well, my son, for this is important," said God. "Your life depends on your following my instructions to the letter."

"I have heard those words before," thought Man. "From my father. Maybe I don't have to listen this time."

"Listen up," said God, who had the power of knowing what Man was thinking. "Listen up, this is different than what your father told you. I have made you into a superior being, superior to all living things. I have made you physically stronger than most and more intelligent than all. When you meet creatures who are physically stronger than you, use your wit and you will always be superior."

"I already know this," thought Man. "I hope I can stay awake for this lecture."

God decided to ignore this thought, knowing that from now on his words were new. Man would stay awake. "Now, I have made one mistake and one mistake only," he continued. "Well, two really. I have made you as psychologically vulnerable as woman. I have given you emotions. I have given you the emotions of grief, tenderness, hurt, and sadness, along with a few others. But the worst one I gave you is fear. I did not mean to do that, but I forgot. And I made you vulnerable in one area of your body, your penis."

I've noticed that," thought Man. "I banged it the other day and I thought I would die. I hope God is going to tell me what to do about that."

But God wasn't worried about Man protecting his penis. He **knew** Man would take care of that. What he wanted to talk about was his other mistake. He went on. "Now, in order to rectify my oversight you must do as I say."

"Just like my father," thought Man. "I have to do what he says, too."

"Yes you do," said God thunderously. "And here is what you must do. You must always pretend that you are not vulnerable, even when you are. You must always pretend that you do not have any emotions. You see, if anyone finds out that you are really afraid, or that you ever cry, or that they can hurt you, then you will be vulnerable and they will think of you as weak. If you appear weak you will give my image a bad name; therefore you must not appear weak."

"I'm a good actor," thought Man. "I can do that. I can pretend I am not vulnerable."

God was pleased with that thought so he went on. "The woman that I made for you will be the biggest cause of your feeling vulnerable and weak. When you want to be silent she will want to talk. When you want to be distant she will want to be intimate. When you want to be free she will want you near her. When you want sex she will want affection. When you need her love and nurturing and acceptance she will reject you."

"Reject me," thought Man. "Oh, yes. I had better listen up."

God continued. "I did not give woman much power but unfortunately I had to give her one piece, a mind of her own. Most of the time her mind is weak and she will do what you want, but sometimes she gets out of your control and will not. It is when she will not do what you want that she is rejecting you. Remember that. Rejection is what you must control at all costs. Rejection is not acceptable. Always remember that. Rejection is not acceptable."

"The more vulnerable you feel, the more likely women are to reject you. Therefore you must nip this in the bud immediately before it has a chance to get started. Now here are some lessons in what you must do. Pay close attention. Learn them well. And never violate them, or you will give my image a bad name. Do you understand?"

"I understand, and if it is important to you it is important to me," said Man.

"Good. Here are the lessons. Some of them I have illustrated with examples of how other men have handled similar situations. Pay close attention to what these other men have done because this will help you a great deal."

"Your First Lesson is this: Refuse to know about your vulnerabilities. Pretend they are not there. Refuse to think such thoughts as:

She won't like me.

She won't take care of me the way I want.

She is interested in someone else.

She is better than I am.

She thinks she is better than I am.

She is acting uppity.

She is getting out of her place.

These thoughts create anxiety. Anxiety makes you feel vulnerable. You must not feel vulnerable."

"Your Second Lesson is this: Refuse to let anyone know even the vulnerabilities that you know about.

Lie about them.

Beat around the bush.

Run around Red Robin's Barn.

Refuse to talk.

Drink beer . . . get drunk.

Watch television.

Get involved in work, then tell her you're doing it all for her.

Act Macho.

Anything, but don't let anyone know about your vulnerabilities."

"Here is your Third Lesson: Insist that woman take care of all your vulnerabilities without you having to talk about it.
She must do all of her natural chores such as cook your food, wash
your clothes, clean your house, bear your sons, bring them up like men.

Even more important, she must smooth over any
anxieties or vulnerabilities you may have.

Beyond this she must pretend you have no vulnerabilities.
This job she must understand without you saying so.

Then, she must take care of any of your vulnerabilities
that do come up without your knowing she is doing it."

"Your Fourth Lesson is: Realize that if you have any vulnerabilities, sex can fix them.

Pour all your emotions into sex.
If you feel afraid, become sexual.
If you feel demeaned, become sexual.
If you feel hurt, become sexual.
If you feel failure, become sexual.
If you feel helpless, become sexual.
Anything can be fixed with sex.
This will also fix the vulnerability of your penis, as well."

"Lesson Number Five is: Realize that if you cannot fix a vulnerability with sex you can fix it with anger.
Be ready to demean her . . . yell at her . . . hit her . . . beat her up . . .
or rape her."

"Your Sixth Lesson is: Learn that you can have all the sex you want when you are angry.
She is afraid of your anger. She will submit.
Sex will fix your vulnerabilities."

"**Lesson Number Seven is very important: Refuse to see her as a human being. I have included pictures to remind you of how to do this.**

You already know she is not the same as you are. Go the rest of the way and make her into an object, like your car, or your job, or your house, or your T.V. Then you will have no problem demeaning her, beating her up, or raping her."

No matter how hard you try you can never understand a woman
IT'S A WOMAN'S PREROGATIVE TO CHANGE HER MIND
TWO-FACED
empty-headed woman
PUSSY
OLD LADY
Yenta   Gossip
Jewish Mother
DIZZY DAME
flighty
GAL FRIDAY
PEARL of a GIRL
WOMAN WITH A PAST
BEHIND EVERY GREAT MAN THERE'S A WOMAN
BLUSHING BRIDE
STAND BY YOUR MAN
The Little Woman
GAL DAME BROAD
knocked up
KNOCK-OUT
LOOSE WOMAN
You women don't know what you want
WHORE
SUGAR
COOKIE
HONEY
SWEETIE
TOMATO
PEACH
CHERRY
Peaches and Cream
FALLEN
Telephone Telegraph Tell a woman
TWOBIT WHORE · FLOOSEY
PARTY DOLL   Cunt

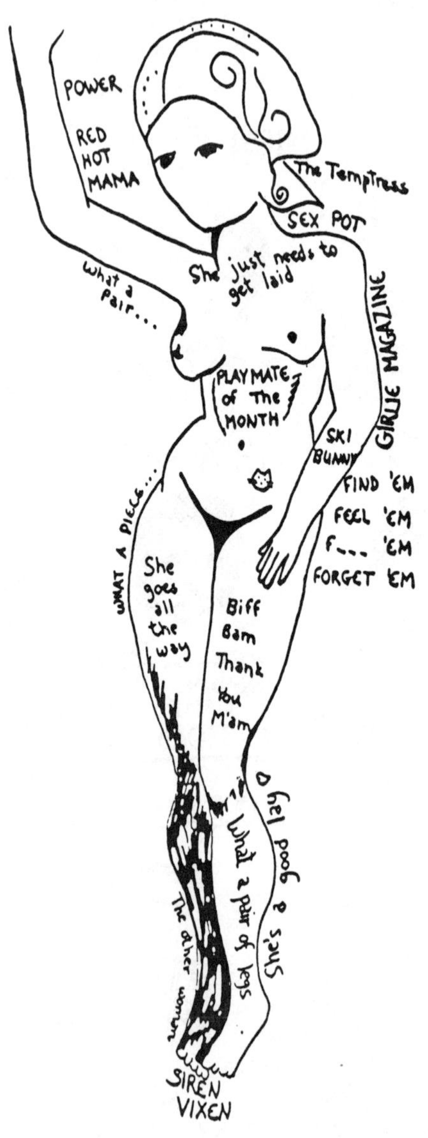
POWER
RED HOT MAMA
The Temptress
SEX POT
What a pair...
She just needs to get laid
GIRLIE MAGAZINE
PLAY MATE of The MONTH
SKI BUNNY
FIND 'EM
FEEL 'EM
F--- 'EM
FORGET 'EM
WHAT A PIECE...
She goes all the way
Biff Bam Thank You M'am
What a pair of legs
She's a good fel
The other woman
SIREN
VIXEN

"The Eigth Lesson, is this: Once you have made her into an object there are a number of things you can do if she gets uppity and independent, refuses or threatens to refuse you sex, or does not defer to you as you deserve.

In other words use these suggestions if she threatens to reject you or causes you to be vulnerable in spite of all your efforts to control her. You must learn to destroy her psychologically. You can do that with your superior physical strength and your knowledge of psychological and sexual violence.

For instance, if woman threatens to reject you in spite of all efforts to control her, **destroy her right to be.** This method is wonderfully depicted in the video movie, *Lady Beware*, with Diane Lane and Michael Woods. (Reprinted by permission of Scotti Brothers, (c) 1987, Karen Arthur, author) Get yourself a copy and watch it carefully.

The Story is this. Listen up:

A very alive young woman named Katya takes a job as a window dresser in a prominent downtown department store. She begins to dress her mannequins in very alive and sometimes sexual ways. Jack, a married X-Ray technician with one girl child, works across the street. He begins to watch her work from his window. He then begins a systematic destruction of her personality, her relationship with her lover, her work, and ultimately her very soul. He does this while simultaneously making obscene phone calls to her and masturbating, stealing her mail, breaking and entering her home, watching her in her intimate relationships, stalking or tracking her wherever she goes, destroying her personal belongings, leaving obscene messages on her mirror, while throughout accusing her of loving it and wanting him sexually.

No attempt to stop him helps.

     Police have no evidence.

  She changes her phone number and he finds out what

  it is. Using an answering machine doesn't stop his calls.

      When he discovers bars on her windows he

      enters by climbing down from the roof.

Each method she uses to stop him causes

him to become more intensely determined.

She:

     Can't concentrate.

Gets testy with her employees.

Creates her window dressings with more and more rape-like images.

Can't make love with her lover.

Leaves her lover.

Leaves her job.

Becomes a prisoner in her own house.

Here is some dialogue. It will help you know what to do to destroy her right to be.

Jack: Buttercup, I know you're there. Don't change your number again. You can't get away from me. Know why? Because I'm already inside you. Crawled inside your head and I'll never come out. Have you ever been fucked inside out? After a while you won't want it any other way because baby you've got a great imagination. It may hurt a little but . . . .

Jack: What's your hurry. The deal's not over until I say it's over. What's the matter? You think I've been fucking with you so far? Shit, baby, this is just foreplay. The real fucking comes later and you can count on it. And you can dream about it. But don't ever think you can stop it because I can take you out mind or body whenever I want. Sweet dreams, Buttercup.

Katya (Talking to him on the phone): You really get off on hurting people. You find out where they are most vulnerable. You just push that button and you keep on pushing it. You like to make people squirm, don't you? Or is it only me?

Jack: Only you. The rest of them I won't give the time of day. They're assholes. Small minded, pebble-brained, chicken-shits. I'm going to make you special . . . I'll lay you flat on the sidewalk - slide off your little panties and give you the fuck of your life in front of downtown Pittsburgh. Right in front of downtown Pittsburgh. We'll do it on Labor Day Weekend. There will be a fucking parade, a 121 gun fucking salute, and the mayor will pin a medal to your ass and you'll scream because you just came.

Katya: You took away my nights, then you took away my days. You made me afraid of my own home. You're not going to get to me any more."

And God was quiet while Man digested this information. Then he said, "Now if she still threatens to reject you, you can blame her so severely that she will never recover. If woman threatens to reject you in spite of all efforts to control, **blame her!** For lessons in this process, hot foot it to see the play *Mortal Risk* by Ron Marks."

"The story is this:

A Forensic Psychiatrist, Ira Abrams, and a criminal Psychologist, JoHanna Spector, are pitted on opposite sides of the criminal case of Todd Kemp, aged 22, who has raped, murdered and dismembered three women. Ira Abrams is working for acquittal on the grounds of insanity. He certifies Todd Kemp as a multiple personality brought about by the cruel upbringing of his Aunt Hattie. JoHanna Spector questions this diagnosis and sets about to learn the truth. In the process she learns that her lover, a journalist, wants her only for the purpose of getting access to the gruesome details of the story; that her teenage son's interests and behavior are less perverse, but similar to those of the murderer; that her friend and partner, Mr. Abrams has threatened and mutilated the aunt to keep her from speaking the truth; and that the system is working hard to keep her from knowing what really happened.

By assuring the aunt that nobody will hurt her, and by putting her life on the line while confronting the prisoner, she discovers that the actual state of mind of the prisoner was covered up. He is not a multiple personality, but actually has been a sadistic murderer since childhood who is feigning his insanity. He has raped, killed and dismembered at least twenty women prior to this arrest.

The thrust of all the males involved in this story is to blame the aunt for the behavior of the rapist/killer and to totally absolve him of any responsibility. They all want to play up the story in the media and blame the aunt, the woman who brought him up."

God sat in deep thought after relating this story. He was not pleased with the outcome. He had to be sure Man learned the correct lesson from this story. He finally said, "Here is some dialogue that woman will use when you try to blame her. You must learn to counteract this kind of attitude. This Man was pretty ineffective. You must be more effective. These first lines are from early in the play, and they just show how nasty women can be when faced with the fact that they are to blame.

Ira: Milligan, yes. It was his **mother.** Tortured the boy. His mind exploded.

JoHanna: Milligan raped three women.

And a little later JoHanna says: Bianchi . . . The Hillside Strangler.

Ira: Orphaned, beaten, forced to wear his dead father's shoes. Dragged through the courts two years on legal meat hooks.

JoHanna: He murdered six women . . . He faked it Ira. He wasn't multiple."

Then God Says, "Later in the play she gets even more blatant about this blaming business. She even gets sarcastic. I hate it when woman gets sarcastic. But you need to pay close attention.

JoHanna: Psycho. One, two and three. Norman Bates murders his quota of women. But here's the kicker. Norman didn't do it. You want to know whodunit? It was mumsy. His mumsy done it. How? Why Norman becomes his mummy or mummy becomes Norman and zip, bag, slash, chop. The perfect ending. Twenty million men jump into Norman's skin, slash them some female meat, get their rocks off, dance on the carnage and sing out in a resounding chorus, 'Mummy done it. She put a clothes pin on my penis. That's why I done it.' And that's what Todd Kemp is singing while he's wrapping our sex organs in wax paper.

All right, all right! The 'average guy' wouldn't slice up his wife. He may never hit his wife either. But he will crack a joke, **a joke** about going home to beat the 'Old Lady' and it's laughs all round the bar and the connection never gets made. But it's there.

Ira: This is insane. It has nothing to do with Todd Kemp.

JoHanna: It has everything to do with Todd Kemp. It's his song, Ira. His national anthem. At this second, there are one hundred and fifty Todd Kemp's watching me through a bedroom window. Walking behind us on a dark street. Grabbing at us, pushing us into cars and vans without windows. Before I finish this sentence, a woman will be raped and battered, strangled and shot, ripped into pieces by the Todd Kemp's of this convoluted, woman-hating country. Listen . . . hear the screams.

They write songs about him. They glorify the sonofabitch in their beer. Let's you and I drink to him, Ira. Let's turn our bottoms up for Toddy Kemp. The boy of action. The doer who does what the butcher and the baker can only watch. Watch and cheer. Drink up, Ira. Here's to Hot Toddy, master of the manly sport of butchering women.

Ira: Get out of my office.

JoHanna: He sells, Ira. He is our hero, our lusty legend, our worship, our high priest in that long, long line of holy men ... Jack the Ripper, the Boston Strangler, Lipstick Killer, Yorkshire Ripper, Co-ed Killer, Black-out Ripper, Red Spider, Night Stalker. Real men, Ira. Doers, heroes.

Ira: Madness. Absolute ....

JoHanna: Berkowitz, Speck, DeSalvo, Todd Kemp. We know them, don't we? We remember the men who kill women. But what about the women they killed? Who remembers them? Who will say their names? Who builds a tomb for the unknown woman who died in the longest war? Who will say it, Ira? WHO WILL SAY HER NAME?

Ira: You've lost your ....

JoHanna: I want a stone. A wall of granite. A marble tower for them. Bigger, higher, than the Vietnam stones. How many? Fifty-eight thousand men dead? Well, I want one for us. A hundred, a thousand times bigger for the fifty-eight million women shot in the streets and slashed in their beds. I want the names, Ira. Names cut this deep into that stone. Names, Ira. Names of the ten million nameless Indian wives who died on the funeral pyre of a dead husband. Names of thirty million women mutilated and crippled with foot bindings. Names of women exterminated under the knife of some gynecologist ... names cut into stone. Names climbing up into the sun 'till they blind us with the truth. Names of Kitty Genovese ....

Ira: Madness, insanity ....

JoHanna: Sharon Tate, Dorothy Stratten, Sheila Burns, Patsy Webb. Yolanda Washington, Frankie Bell, Nancy Heitz, Carlie McKay, Sharon Simmons ....

Ira: I have a chance to publish, write a whole book, documenting the effects of physical abuse on male children. I have a contract. (Reprinted by permission of the writer of *Mortal Risk*, Ron Marks.)"

As the dialogue ended God felt ashamed by the performance of Man. He wanted Man to do better than that so he said, "I hope you have learned your lesson and will be better at blaming than this man was. But just in case she outwits you, here is the solution in **Lesson Number Nine: If you believe she is causing you to be vulnerable, rape her. This will take care of it all. You will have your power, you will have your sex, and you will punish her all in one act. Learn how to do this."**

"Then be sure to remember Lesson Number Ten: If you do rape her remember you won't have to be accountable. Learn this lesson well because punishment might make you vulnerable. Chances are very good that you won't even be reported, but if she does report you and your are caught, just remember that even if you are convicted you still won't need to be accountable. Here are some facts to ease your mind.

A convicted rapist served a one year prison term and was out to discuss it on a national talk show. He was joined by a man convicted of sexual assault. This man served only a six month prison term.

Now here are some other numbers that will help ease your mind:

Only thirty-seven rapes were reported in 1986 out of each thousand population. Now, you and I know there were probably many more rapes than that.

But even more important, out of each thousand rapes reported there were only thirty-one where an arrest was made. (From *Statistical Abstracts of the United States*, 1988.)"

"So you see, you have almost nothing to worry about," said God. "You can go ahead and rape her with impunity. And to assure that she won't report you, get a copy of the video movie *Extremities* starring Farah Faucet and James Russo. Watch it carefully for technique. But I must warn you. Watch only the first half, because Farah does get obstreperous toward the end.

The story is this:

A young and very pretty woman leaves work one evening and stops in a shopping center on the way home. When she returns to her car she is attacked from the back seat by a man wearing a stocking mask. He puts a knife to her face and a belt around her throat. He forces her to drive to his designated spot where he plays the knife around her face and throat and rips the buttons off her blouse while keeping the belt tightened around her throat. He forces her to unzip his pants. Before the sexual assault can go further she twists away from him, gets out of the car, and runs to safety. At the police station she is told by the police woman that they will dust her car for prints but it will come down to his word against hers. 'What does that mean?' she asks. 'That he gets off.' Disgusted, she leaves the police station without pressing charges.

Unfortunately the rapist has her billfold with her name and address.

He arrives at her home several days later to continue his violent game. By alternately and cockily threatening to kill her and saying words that might be said by a lover he forces her to do all the things a lover might do for a loved one: invite him into her bedroom, welcome him with a smile, dress seductively in front of him, offer him a beer, cook for him, kiss him, tell him she loves, him, touch him, say she wants to make love with him etc. etc. etc. As he begins to make moves on her body she gets hold of a can of wasp spray and sprays his face, getting the poison in his eyes - in essence paralyzing him. While paralyzed, she ties him with some cord and puts him into the prison of her fireplace.

Then, while laughing, he tells her that she can go ahead and call the police because she.has nothing on him, that she can't prove a thing because there were no witnesses and there was no violation. He also tell her that if they lock him up, he'll get out and come and get her.

As her two housemates arrive home he, very smartly, plays on their good will.

He plays on one of the housemate's concerns for herself.

He plays on her religious beliefs.

He plays on her jealousy.

He plays on her fear.

He plays on her beliefs.

He plays on her compassion.

Then, after being confronted with his own tactics with his own knife, he stupidly confesses and lists other women he has killed. (from the play *Extremities* by William Mastrosimone)"

And God speaks again. "Now, as I said before, don't watch that last part. That will just confuse you. Pay attention, instead, to my next lesson, **Lesson Number Eleven: Know that even if you do have to be accountable to the law (and this is not very likely) she will suffer more than you do.** In this way you have still punished her for making you vulnerable."

"Now my last Lesson, Number Twelve, is this: Remember, to be in my image you must not be vulnerable.

**In this, anything goes.
The end justifies the means."**

Then God called woman to him, this time not on the mountain, but in the cave as befits her status.

"woman," he said. "I have just talked to Man and given him instructions. Now I must talk to you."

"Yes," said woman.

"I have instructed Man about vulnerability. I have instructed him that he must not be vulnerable, rejected, anxious or weak at any time. I have instructed him that it is your job to see to it that this never happens to him."

"You mean I am to take care of his fragile ego, is that what you are saying, God?"

"HE DOES NOT HAVE A FRAGILE EGO!" said God, angrily.

"Yes," said woman, humbly.

"Now, I have instructed Man that he is to do whatever necessary to see to it that you take care of his vulnerabilities."

"Like, never rejecting him, pretending he is more important than he is, and always smoothing over his vulnerabilities before he even knows they are there, is that what you instructed him, God?" said woman.

"HE IS THAT IMPORTANT. YOU DON'T HAVE TO PRETEND!" shouted God.

"Yes," said woman humbly.

"I can see that I made one mistake with you, woman, and next time I create a world I will do it better."

"What mistake was that, God?" asked woman, humbly.

"I connected you to the truth. By connecting you to the earth and to birth and to death and to the mysteries of all of that, I have made the mistake of connecting you to the truth."

"Yes," said woman, humbly.

"Now, I have had to instruct Man in how to undo my mistake."

"What have you instructed Man to do, God?"

"I have instructed Man in how to force you to do what HE WANTS. I have instructed him in rape."

"What is rape, God?"

RAPE IS JUST THIS, wOMAN. FIRST, MAN WILL DIMINISH YOU TO NOTHING. WITH HIS SUPERIOR STRENGTH AND AGGRESSION HE WILL TAKE AWAY YOUR WILL, AND SUBJECT IT TO HIS. THEN, WITH HIS SUPERIOR INTELLIGENCE HE WILL TAKE AWAY YOUR SOUL AND SUBJECT IT TO HIS. THEN HE WILL VIOLATE WHAT IS LEFT - YOUR BODY. HE WILL BEAT YOU, CUT YOU, PUT A GUN TO YOUR HEAD AND AGAINST YOU'RE WILL HE WILL INSERT HIS PENIS INTO YOUR BODY AND USE IT UNTIL YOU ARE RAW WITH PAIN. THEN HE WILL NOT LET YOU GO UNTIL HE HAS DONE IT AS OFTEN AS HE WANTS. THAT IS WHAT RAPE IS."

"I see," said woman, humbly.

"What do you see?" asked God.

"I see that I am afraid," said woman.

"Good, You are to live your life afraid. And here are your lessons. Pay close attention because if you do not you will not live to bear Man sons."

"Your First Lesson is this: Always remember that there is something out there that is going to get you.

You must be constantly on guard and afraid of it."

"Your Second Lesson is to: Remember how weak you are and how you don't know how to protect yourself against whatever is out there that wants to get you. Whatever that is is so much stronger than you are that you must always be afraid of it."

"Now, your Third Lesson is very important: You must diminish yourself so as not to provoke this thing.

You must not dress provocatively, and you know what that means don't you?
You must not walk alone without a man and never in certain areas at all.
You must not laugh too loud.
You must not cry,
or be depressed,
or get angry,
or be passionate,
or get too serious,
or be needy,
or feel compassion for the wrong creatures,
or go inside yourself into your mysterious places,
or be taller,
or do anything that makes you too much.
And you must always lock your door at night, and then check it twice more to be sure it is locked."

"Here is your Fourth Lesson: You must never make a Man angry. As long as you are inferior to him, give him everything he wants and earn money, but not too much money, you will be safe."

"Your Fifth Lesson is this: Know that Man is aggressive and will take what he wants especially if you don't give it to him.

But you must never train yourself to be aggressive in order to combat his aggression, for he will always be more aggressive than you.
Instead, you must be always nurturing, compassionate, understanding and rational."

"For your Sixth Lesson know this: If you do provoke him to this thing, recognize that it is your fault.

You did not diminish yourself enough.
You did not listen to your elders.
You wore the wrong clothes.
You walked the wrong way.
You were in the wrong place.
You didn't lock your doors.
You were a loose woman.
You drank, smoked, worked,walked, played, camped, talked, thought wrong.
Remember it is your fault."

"Number Seven is this: If a man does this thing to you,submit or he will kill you.

I mean he will kill you! Do you hear me? He will kill you. Walk around always afraid of that."

Now, Lesson Number Eight is important: when he tells you that you provoked him, you believe him.

He is right. You did provoke him.
You didn't wear the right clothes,
You were in the wrong place:
you smoked,
drank . . . "

"We are almost through. For Lesson Number Nine: if he does this thing to you don't tell anyone.

Especially, don't tell the authorities. If you do they will also tell you that you provoked him. They will tell you that you:

smoked,
drank,
walked,
thought . . .
wrong, too."

"And for your last lesson, **Lesson Number Ten: If he does this thing to you,
live with the fact of what you have caused for the rest of your life.**
Don't you ever forget it."

End of Parable

*(I wrote this Parable, not to demcan God, man or woman, but to make you think.
In no way do I believe that God wants man, woman, or any of the universe's creatures to behave in this way.)*

Question:

What should women do about rape?

Ending Rape
How To

Rape is a horror that should not be allowed to walk the face of this earth. It is a horror that should be stopped at all costs, no matter behind what mask it is concealed: whether it is concealed behind the mask of brutality, the mask of incest, the mask of psychologically-enforced submission, or behind the mask of the rape of a woman's body (or the many other masks of rape not addressed in this book).

And it is women who will have to do the stopping. It is clear that men will not. All we have to do is look at history to know that they will not. All we have to do is look at the male psychology "which prefers to see rape as a woman's problem, rather than as a societal problem resulting from a distorted masculine philosophy of aggression" (Brownmiller, 1975) to know that they will not.

The female psychology knows; because we all have been raped. We have experienced it from behind one mask or the other. Griffin (1986) stated it as well as it could be stated. She said, "It strikes me now that one of the untold burdens of the survivor of rape is what she has come to know. **She has been left holding the truth.**" (Emphasis mine)

So what truth is it that women know?

I can tell you what I know.

I have known all my life that some things are dangerous; that if I wear certain clothes at certain times, go certain places, or behave in certain ways, I put myself at peril. The major message for me in all of that is that **I must not trust.**

I have trusted anyway. I trusted that nobody would hurt me; that nobody would do me bodily harm. I have not exactly put myself in perilous situations, but I have not been afraid to work in neighborhoods considered dangerous by some; I have not been afraid to travel wherever I wished, and with whom I wished; I have not been afraid to travel alone and I enjoyed camping alone.

What I now know is that these activities **are** dangerous; and I can no longer enjoy them as I did. They do, as so many people warned me, put me in peril. Those who predicted dire consequences were right; I don't have the freedom I thought I had. This is, indeed, not the land of the free. At least not if you are a woman.

What I now know is that I cannot trust.

I also know that men are **not** going to protect me. I have learned that what men will protect is their sense of property . . . and their sense of self. If it serves their own needs, they will protect me (i.e., the prosecuting barrister). If it doesn't serve their own needs, they will fight it out, male against male, to see which male will win and which will lose (i.e., the defense barrister). In other words, they will fight it out to see which male is going to come out where in the male hierarchy. And for me, it doesn't matter which male wins because I now know that I will stay in my same place in that hierarchy.

Because I now know these truths, I know the resources I can count on. Only my own . . . and those of some other women. I now know that I have never been able to count on anything else, my delusions to the contrary.

Now, what about trusting other women? There are some women I have trusted with my very soul, and would trust with my life. I have experienced, over and over again, the energy, the love, the ability to work together, the pain, and the joy of these women. I have gloried and grown out of these experiences.

But I also know there are some women who would violate my trust as easily as would a man. Some of these believe they need to become like men in order to find their place in this world. I know, too, that there are more women than I would like to think who believe that a woman's place is where men put them. Of these women, I have to be wary.

This brings me back to trusting myself. Historically, I have had trouble trusting myself. My sense of myself has been undermined since I was a baby. I was taught that there was a mold I was supposed to fit into. This mold involved being good, not bothering anybody, and always remembering that I was doing my greatest good when I was sacrificing myself for the good of someone else..

What was right for me was never under consideration. The rules were made by someone else, by those who knew better: my mother, and those godlike creatures - the university instructors, the scientists, the business men, and, for sure, the preachers. This group clearly spelled out my rules. As long as I was serving someone else, I was doing the **right** thing. But I should not serve my own needs; that was selfish. I should not bother anybody else; that was inconsiderate. And I must always follow the rules . . . or I would go to hell. As long as I kept on serving others, I would receive my rewards in heaven, but I was not supposed to expect them on this earth.

It took me years and years of therapy, years and years of work on my own growth, to come to the other side of all of that. Now I have learned to hear the soft whisperings from within, the whisperings that tell me that I know what I know, and that it is right to say what I know. What I now know is that my rules come from within, because those are the rules I can live with. Some of these rules may be your rules and some may not. Some of you will approve of my rules and some may not. But, now, I know that it doesn't matter how you feel about my rules. I must march to my own drummer. Because in that way I can live . . . day-by-day, and moment-by-moment . . . knowing that I am here with all of me, not just the part of me that is acceptable to you or to those godlike creatures who made the rules in my childhood. I hope I will be acceptable to you; but if I am not, I cannot change myself to reach for that acceptance. In this I trust.

Now, there is something else in which I must trust. I don't like it; but I must trust it. It is my anger . . . my rage . . . at what was done to me - twice raped. I know now that I have enough rage in me to kill. I know I can . . . and I know I will . . . if any man tries to rape me again. I will not wait for the second rape, the rape of the institution. I will be prepared to kill, not just to spray a little chemical in his eyes, not just to kick him where it will hurt the most, not just to defend myself enough so that I can get away. I am prepared to kill. And this is a truth that I must carry with me for the rest of my days. This is now part of my insanity.

Yes, it is insane. By being raped, I learned the insanity of the male world; the insanity of its need to win; and the insanity of its violence. But, by being raped, I have been forced to get in touch with my own violence. This is a violence I wish I didn't have. This an outrage I wish I didn't have. This is an anger I now must live with and I wish I didn't have to live with it. But one of the differences between my violence and the violence of men is that I am willing to look at it. I am willing to see its hurt; I am willing to see the pain it will cause. I am willing to see the human-ness of the person I may need to use it against. I am willing to look at it. I am will-ing to put myself in a vulnerable place over it. I am willing to own up to the fact of it, and know where it came from.

I am willing to know that it did not come from this act alone - this act of rape. As theorists have known for years, my rage is much deeper than that. It came from the years, the decades, the centuries, of living as a sexual plaything and bearer of men's immortality. It comes from years, from decades, from centuries, of living as men's pieces of property - pieces of property that can be done with as they wish. It comes from never knowing my freedom as a human being, never walking this earth as a free spirit, but mostly it comes from having to bury my own soul, a soul that I now know is worth ten megatons in comparison to the man who took my body.

I now carry the burden of these truths on my shoulders; because I lived with rape - twice. Another truth is that you also carry these same burdens on your shoulders: if rape has not been perpetrated on your body, it **has** been perpetrated on your emotions, your freedom to be, and on your very soul - just as it has on mine.

Perhaps it is time for us to know what we know and to say what we know. Perhaps it is time to be loud and clear in our cry of rape. Perhaps it is time to stop our "nice" feminine way of looking the other way. Perhaps it is time to stop believing we deserve it. Perhaps it is time to stop thinking "it won't do any good to cry rape." Perhaps it is time to stop refusing to go through the shame and trouble of it all. Perhaps it is time to overcome our fears. Perhaps it is time to stir things up rather than give in to the male admonishments not to rock the boat!

Perhaps it is also time to stop crying rape when it hasn't happened. We must speak the truth - and only the truth. We must not give men or institutions any reason to doubt our truth.

Perhaps it is time.

I titled this chapter "Ending Rape -How To." After years of not being allowed, we need to learn "how to." We need to regain our spirit and our determination "how to." Beginnings have already been made. We no longer have our heads in the sand. There are now organizations where women can go to talk, just to talk, when they have been raped. There are now organizations where women can go to complain when they have not been treated with compassion by the police. There are now homes for battered women, and organizations that will prosecute and work with male incest perpetrators. There are groups of women who demonstrate to "Take back the night." True. Our heads are out of the sand.

But, as a therapist, I see women day after day who still don't know "how to." I see women who are so oppressed by the system that they literally can't. One of the saddest women I ever worked with was the one who came in, told me of her rape with absolutely no emotion in her voice or in her being, and finished her account with the statement, "I knew it was going to happen someday. I was supposed to be raped. I tried every way I could to avoid it, but I knew it was going to happen." When I suggested that she was not at fault for this rape, that it was perpetrated by a man, she looked decidedly uncomfortable. I knew she did not accept my statement one bit. At the end of the session she made another appointment, but never came back. I had tried to speak the truth but it was a truth she could not accept. As long as she stayed dead, she would not have to deal with it. My love for her spirit was not enough to overcome the years of her "truth" - that she was going to be raped some day and that she deserved it.

Yes. "How to." How to overcome that deadness in our souls that makes us accept rape as though we deserved it.

I would like to suggest - no, I would like to implore, women to look into their souls and find out what is there. Is what is there what men have said is there? Is there a dearth of intelligence, an inability to think rationally, little ability to operate in the world of men in spite of our best efforts, too much emotion, a proclivity for falling prey to our monthly cycles, a selfishness that is beyond our recognition, or a refusal to recognize genius when we sleep with it every night? Is that what is there?

Do we really have sexual fantasies of being raped, of being ravished by a man we don't know and probably would not want to know? Do we want sex in one-night stands? Is our interest in a man one who takes us to bed without our knowing him? Do we want to experience being tied to a bed before sex? Do we want to swing? Is it really important that we have big breasts and open "clits"? Is our life revolving around sexual fantasies? Are we perpetually "ready"? Or are these more male fantasies perpetrated on us?

I have spent years looking into my soul, and I don't find any of those ideas there. What I do find is a deep mystery of a myriad of things. I find that I am called by the moon to the very bottom of my soul. I find myself traveling into that dark unknown, and letting it become known. I find myself called by music, by the drum beat of life, to live every moment, sometimes with complete rationality and sometimes without. I find myself loving flowers, Alice Walker, Gloria Steinham, any body of water, walks in the woods with my dog, the feel of my body when it is loved, the wind in my hair, Oprah Winfrey, watching another human being grow to fullness, making up stories, writing novels, doing what I've set out to do, playing my guitar, being heard and appreciated, cooking soup, and letting someone I trust know the mystery of my being.

I love my energy, my drive, my love of love, my competence, my compassion, and my spontaneity. I love my intelligence and what I do with it. I love my feelings and how they get out of whack sometimes. I love my body and what it does for me. I love how I operate in the world and how I get what I want. I love my spirit of woman; that spirit that is not a man's spirit; that is dictated only by me, a woman's spirit. I love my mystery, which does not lend itself to the rational mind. My soul is a wealth, and I would not trade her for any other soul in the world.

I do not love to be ravished by a man, to be tied to a bed post, to be discounted, to have intercourse with someone I do not love and perhaps do not even know, to feel that my life is not my life without a man, one-night stands, to limit my freedom because someone else wants me to, to not have control over my own finances, or to be raped - whatever face it wears.

Women, look. What is in your soul? Your soul is different than mine. Your soul is not defined by what someone else thinks it is. Who are **you?** Look! See! Know!

What do you love?

What do you fear?

Where is you anger . . . your rage?

Do you know your bitch?

Where is your niceness?

What is your mystery?

What is **your** sexuality?

Then, look with honesty at the world of men. And see if you really want to be one, or want to be defined by one, or want to submit to one or more than one. It is their world, the world they have orchestrated to play the dissonant sounds of violence. Perhaps you would prefer the coordinated sounds of consideration. Look with honesty. How much of a piece of their world do you want? How much of yourself do you have to give up to join it?

What are the rewards? The penalties? They run it. In order to survive, we need to be part of it...but how much a part? **And** how do we keep our integrity within it, if we want to keep our integrity?

"How to" prevent rape? This is your first step. Look into your heart. Look into your soul. Know who you are as a separate entity, woman, a womanspirit.

So you do all of that; and one day you are raped - physically forced into the sexual act against your will. What then?

These are the steps.

1) Report it to the police.

2) Do what you need to do to expedite conviction. Do not change clothes, do not bathe, do not comb your hair, do not disturb the rape site or scene.

3) Be prepared for the hospital investigation. They will treat your medical problems, comb your pubic and head hair for evidence of his hair and pluck your hair for comparison. (His hair is a better tool for conviction than fingerprints.)

4) File a complaint.

5) Identify the rapist.

6) Talk to the Prosecution.

7) Testify in court.

8) Hold your breath and hope for conviction.

9) Take responsiblity for yourself as much as possible.

There are all kinds of things that can go wrong at each step; and you may never get to step six. Also, this explanation is by no means a definitive explanation of all the steps. In this book I am not going into depth about this process. There are two excellent books I would like to refer you to, both of which explain prosecution in detail: *Recovery* by Helen Benedict, and *Recovering From Rape* by Linda Ledray. In this book I want to talk about the psychological fears and processes involved in these steps.

Your first fear will be about reporting it at all. "What if's" will march through your mind. What if I **did** bring it on myself? What if I really am guilty of causing this man's sexual problem? What if I asked for it? What if nobody believes me? What if I can't identify the man? What if my family finds out?

What if my husband/lover can't stand me any more after this? What if **he** doesn't believe I was raped? What if people think I'm at fault? What if I report him and he comes back and does it again? What if he really has psychological problems, like maybe his wife doesn't understand him? I'm so ashamed.

The questions I want you to ask of yourself are: What makes you think you are to blame for another person's perpetration of violence? What makes you believe you should save him from the consequences of his own behavior?

Then call the police.

And before you put down the phone, call someone to come and be with you. Someone you can trust and who will let you be hysterical. The police won't allow you to be hysterical.

Your second fear will be that you are losing your mind. No matter how understanding another person is, they are not where you are at this moment. You may feel rage; you may be crying; you may wander around like you don't know what you're doing (and you don't) and you may not feel anything at all.

Know that any or all of these reactions are perfectly normal.

Your next fear will be the possibility of facing the invasion, the intimidation, the indifference, or the disbelief of the police. Hang on. Better ears will be coming. Get through it. Hold the hand of the person you called. Get through it.

Then you will probably begin to wonder in greater depth about what people will think. You'll have to explain your black eye at work. Your mother will have to know. What will you tell your friends? How will your husband, lover, etc., react? Will he ever want to make love to you again? Will you ever want to make love again? Will he even stay around to see you through what is coming? Will they all think you're crazy? You are certainly acting crazy. Why did this have to happen to you?

What you need to know here is that other people will have all of these different reactions. The reaction each has will depend, pretty much, on where they stand on the question of rape. Anyone who has ever been raped will understand perfectly. They may or may not be able to help you, however. Men may think you are reacting like a baby, depending, of course, on how you are reacting. Women will instinctively understand; and some will be right there for you. Your husband or lover will have to struggle with his issues around property rights (sorry, his first concern may not be your welfare). And you probably **will** have trouble making love again.

The important thing for you to keep in mind here is that their reaction will have little to do with you, and almost everything to do with where they are on the question of rape - their experiences, their knowledge, their prejudices. You are **not** at fault for their experiences, their knowledge, or their prejudices, although at times it may feel like it.

It may be important, here, to try to get some professional help, even if only for one or two sessions. Preferably a woman who has the depth and maturity to understand. Contact an individual therapist, or a rape crisis center.

Your next fear will probably involve whether or not it will happen again. Do you have to change residences? Change your phone number? Will he come back? Now that people know about it, will someone else try it? How will you protect yourself? Should you put new locks on the door? Would your fragile psyche be able to live if it happened again? Maybe you shouldn't prosecute, after all.

Keep in mind that if you don't prosecute, the man will surely be free to rape again. Don't ever forget this. If you don't prosecute, he will surely be free to rape again, **and probably will.** All the locks in the world won't stop that from happening.

The best you can hope for is that it won't be you next time. Take all your fears in hand and persist with the prosecuting. One thing that men understand is force and violence. They do not understand weakness. If you are weak, they may see it as a chance to win again. If you use your force, you have a chance to stop their violence. Prosecute!

Then you will have to face the trial and the public shame of what happened to you. You will have to face the tactics of the defense attorney and the possible callousness of the prosecuting attorney. And it will be as awful as you have imagined it will be.

Take every person who is a support to you to the trial. Have them there to silently cheer you on and be with you through out. Have them there to hold your hand when you are not on the stand. Have them there.

Before the trial, go over every detail of what happened, with someone. Let them act the part of the attorneys. Let them try to mislead you, to confuse you, to make you think you don't know what you are talking about, to make you think you asked for it. Get someone who knows the tactics of attorneys. Go over it and over it and over it. Until you **cannot** be confused on any point. Remember that you were not at fault. You cannot be at fault for a man's sick need to express his violence on you. You cannot!

Prepare for this trial as if you were preparing for the most important examination of your life. Take all the time you need. You must not be shaken from your story.

What if the man is not convicted? What then? Will he vent his rage on you for taking him to court? Will he try again? Will you slink away, defeated by the system, in spite of all your resolve and your struggles? Will you, again, feel unfairly treated? Will you think that you went through all of this for nothing?

Yes, you will probably feel all of that. So talk to the press. Get your story in print. Write letters to the editor or your newspaper. Understand the process and where it went awry. Object at all occasions and possibilities. Talk to people. Tell them what happened. Point out the inequities of the system. Don't slink away in silence.

And if he is convicted? **Celebrate!** Celebrate yourself as one brave woman who took on the system and won.

Know that you put one peg in the final coffin of the horror of rape, no matter which mask it wore. Know that you will not be put down again, because now you know the truth. It sits on your shoulders and it may feel like the weight of the world - and then again it may feel like a breath of fresh air. The truth.

The truth is never free. It wasn't for me. It won't be for you, no matter what stage of rape you are in. And because we are women, we are all in one stage of rape or another. We only need to recognize what mask it is wearing. But the fact that the truth is not free does not negate the importance of it. As a matter of fact, the hard work we have had to do to know truth increases its value tenfold. And remember, it is a labor of love to love yourself. This truth shall set you free.

I would like to close with the words of two songs written by wonderful women musicians whose souls have a way of reaching into the very heart of everyone who hears them play and sing. The first is titled "Womanspirit."

"I had a dream last night
Framed in light
I had a dream last night
Calling for my healing
Asking me to see.

I had a dream last night
I saw Woman . . . spirit
Moon, water and wave
No longer betrayed
By me.

I saw Woman . . . spirit
Embracing the shore
With feet of fire
And gifts in hand
And there was so much more
And it was me . . . and it was me.

I had a dream last night
Wings of flight
Spreading in my soul
I had a dream last night
Calling for my healing
Asking me to see.

I had a dream last night
       I had a dream last night . "

                     "Woman Spirit"
                     Words and Music bu
                     Denise Herron

The second is one beautiful verse from the song *"Spirit Healer."*

"Woman . . . don't you know
You've got to change?
Don't you know
You're the spirit healer?"

                     written by Carolyn Brandy
                     (Wild Wimmin Publishing)
                     Recorded by ALIVE, 1979

We must make ourselves strong. Strong enough to be the spirit healer. Not strong like men. But strong like women.
        Womanspirit . . . Spirit Healer

Bibliography

Arndt, Bettina, "How Men Feel About Themselves (Down There)," *Playgirl*, August, 1984, pp. 90 - 93.

Benedict, Helen, *Recovery*, New York: Doubleday, 1986.

Brownmiller, Susan, *Against our Will: Men, Women, and Rape*, New York, Simon and Schuster, 1975

Ledray, Linda; *Recovering from Rape*, New York, Henry Holt and Company, 1986.

Griffin, Susan; *Rape; The Politics of Consciousness*, San Francisco, Harper and Row, 1986.

Suib Cohen, Sherry; "Sex and Anger," *Playgirl*, August, 1984, pp. 46 - 50.

Schaef, Anne Wilson; *Women's Reality*, Minneapolis, Winston Press, Inc. 1981.

About the Author

I am a woman who has been raped. There is no way out of this experience. It has had a formative effect on my thinking, my emotions, and my very soul. I am different than I was in 1985 when the rape occurred. I understand myself . . . and men . . . and women . . . in new ways.

I can still talk about the usual: married for twenty-five years, divorced, mother of two grown girls, in private practice as a Gestalt Therapist, directed the training program for the Indianapolis Gestalt Institute for six years. I was educated through the Ph.D. level at Northwestern University, took a recent sabbatical of three years traveling in Europe, India and Africa, am living in a log cabin in the woods in southern Indiana, have one other recently published book, *The Fourth Woman*, and three other books published several years ago, etc. etc. etc. Overall I would call myself a successful professional woman.

But even more profound, is my experience of the rape. I now know what it is to be stripped of all I possess. When a man took my body against my will I had to write about it, partly to help my own healing process and partly to talk to other women who may have been or may become victims. It was an intense experience and I have become a much more intense person because of it. I have also become more understanding of victims, more angry at perpetrators and more determined to make a difference.

Twice Raped is only the beginning.

Order Form

Book Weaver Publishing Co.
P.O. Box 30072
Indianapolis, IN 46230
(317) 253-5160

Please send me:

___________ copies of *TWICE RAPED* by Audrey Savage

___________ copies of the novel *THE FOURTH WOMAN* by Audrey Savage

Name: ____

Address:____

____ Zip_______________

Enclosed $11.95 for each book   Book $ __________
Indiana residents please add
$.60 sales tax   Tax $ __________

Shipping $1.50 for first book
and $.50 for each additional   Shipping $ __________

                                       Total Enclosed $ __________

I understand that I may return the book for full refund if not totally satisfied.

____I am interested in your lectures and workshops. Please send me a free brochure.